tetherless

The Port Allegiance Chronicles

BOOK ONE

tetherless

THE GRASS ISN'T ALWAYS GREENER...

C.K. O'DONNELL

ISBN: 978-1-7345063-3-4 (Paperback)
ISBN: 978-1-7345063-1-0 (Hardcover)
ISBN: 978-1-7345063-2-7 (eBook)

Library of Congress Control Number: 2022913072

Published in the United States of America by Redline Press

Interior illustration by Eri Griffin, Edinburgh, Scotland
Cover design by MiblArt (Please Support Ukraine)
Interior design by Rebecca LeGates
Edited by Lisa R. Messinger

To Pat,
my best friend,
my biggest supporter

"Shit-Eating Grin"

When we first met,
something was askew about you,
like you seemed too good to be true.

And as time passed,
down dropped your mask,
and what you feared most,
you exposed:

Your
splintered soul,
your dark, empty hole,
a lifetime devoid of empathy.
You manipulate, you triangulate
with a thirst to replenish your supply.

"You're the problem," you projected,
petty and disaffected,
your own lens
cracked.

Your shit-eating grin,
never again—
goodbye,
Ty!

—Abbie Spencer

CHAPTER ONE

ANOTHER ROUND OF GUNSHOTS—another desperate person trying to climb the thirty-foot-high wall across the street from Abbie Spencer's bedroom. In the darkness, she climbed out of bed and peered through the cracked windowpane.

A spotlight shone on the hapless victim, their body tangled up in the razor wire at the top. Blood filtered through the back of their denim jacket, and below, on the hood of Abbie's beat-up white Subaru, lay their boot. Just another casualty vying to pillage the rich in Port Allegiance, the exclusive city beyond the wall. Some were lucky enough to climb over undetected, but most were dumb enough to believe they'd get out alive.

She sighed. If blood splattered on her car one more time, she'd start parking in the alleyway.

A hair past 5:00 a.m. The coffeepot wouldn't percolate until seven. The saying "It's five o'clock somewhere" also applied to morning coffee. The only difference was that the evening fix induced the bed spins, while the morning fix induced sanity. As if the pot had summoned her, she tapped the BREW NOW button on her new/old wristwatch she'd found at the thrift store.

While waiting at her desk, she booted up her laptop, her thoughts firing off the poem she had written last night. A security verification dialog box popped up, and she held her retina to the camera at the top of the screen.

Log Life, her journal app, was still open. She typed:

Sunday, December 16

Dear Journal,

Hangovers and poetry, like a country music song saddled in angst. It's trippy, mourning a relationship that never was. Even so, I can't live like this anymore. Don't worry, I'm not suicidal. But if I don't break up with Ty tonight, my fear is that he'll forever relegate me to a life of chaos. I'm seriously reeling from the ultimatum he dumped on me last night: "It's either me or your uncle Jesse." Screw you, Ty Hawkins! One year tethered to this sociopath, and I'm done. Only I can fix me, right? Okay, enough of my psychobabble... Gotta get coffee, hangover from hell withstanding. (I've sworn off the hooch—I promise this time.)

Love,
Abbie

Dressed in tattered blue jeans and a gray hoodie, she pulled her black stocking cap over her long sable hair, then stood before the full-length mirror, hardly recognizing her reflection. Way too much booze and junk food hung on her tiny frame like an ill-fitted suit. Disgusted with how she'd allowed her health to tank, she ambled into the kitchen, half her brain blocking out the god-awful stench of a decomposing rodent trapped inside a wall somewhere, and the other half anxious about finding the right words for the impending breakup. He wasn't going to take it well, that was for sure.

Before pouring her coffee, out of mindless habit, she opened the drawer below the coffeepot and retrieved her birth control packet. She stared at it. No point in taking them anymore, so she chucked it into the trash can—a good sign Ty would soon be out of her life.

A floorboard in the hallway creaked.

She flinched, the pain anchoring deeper in her temple. It was too early for human interaction, at least until the caffeine started coursing through her veins.

Dad… A lit unfiltered Camel cigarette sat in the corner of his lips. His three-packs-a-day habit showed in his sallow skin. And he reeked of stale alcohol. Disgusted, she glared at him. He had promised the family he'd quit drinking. Like Mom hadn't noticed?

Abbie's face reddened at his deceit, but she wouldn't confront him again. Besides, he'd deny it—even with the evidence wafting up her nose. Honestly, she'd respect him more if he'd say, "Yeah, I'm drinking—and if you don't approve, go fuck yourself." At least then he'd be telling the truth, and it would ease her feeling of him gaslighting her all the time.

His expensive brown loafers caught her attention. "Where'd you klep those from?"

"Where do you think?" he said wryly. "I bought them, smart aleck."

He must've stolen the money from the gas station where he worked. But now he was blathering on and on, not leaving her a single second to respond. She dropped her eyelids and felt herself sinking into the floor. *Please, make it stop...*

"Mornin', girl." Mom's voice snapped her out of the fugue. "Other than the drama outside, how'd you sleep?" A restless night had matted her red hair into a bird's nest in the back, and like Abbie, she had freckles scattered about her cheeks and forehead.

"Slept fine." A lie. The police sirens had kept her up most of the night...not to mention the rodents scratching in the walls and ceiling. She poured the coffee, thick and black, and took a sip, the flavor rolling her eyes back into her head.

"Hey," Mom said, "your uncle Jesse pulled the Christmas decorations down from the attic for me. You wanna help decorate the tree later?" She smoothed back a few wisps of hair clinging to her daughter's cheek.

Christmases hadn't been the same since they'd moved to Eureka, California, six years ago from Sandpoint, Idaho. Eight hundred twenty miles south from happiness. Decorating sounded like a lousy idea, so she declined. Feeling like Scrooge, she took Mom's hand. "How are you feeling today?"

"She thinks she's sick all the time," Dad cut in. "Nothing a little fresh air won't cure."

Abbie lashed out. "What do you mean, 'she thinks'?"

"Well, what do *you* make of it? Some days, she's depressed as hell and hides in our bedroom, and the next day, she's fine."

The asshole always acted up when the attention veered away from him. And poor Mom... Her body tightened. Dad had never hit her, but his words inflicted a worse pain. She flanked the sink and washed the dishes, not wanting Abbie to see her hurting.

Abbie stroked her back. "Here, let me clean up." She ran the mug under the water, then adjusted the faucet. "There's no hot water."

Mom sighed. "Guess the tank went out again."

"Tell Jesse to fix it," Dad said. "He does *everything* right. And no, thank you, I don't want any coffee this morning, dear." He grabbed a Mountain Dew from the fridge and stormed into the living room.

Abbie whispered, "Why can't Dad fix the tank? If he wasn't such a drunk, he'd be a little more productive."

Mom withered again. This was neither the time nor place to bad-mouth Dad; her mom lived with enough stress without Abbie jabbing the wound.

"God, I'm sorry." Abbie regretted running her mouth. "Enough about him. Tell me how you're feeling."

"Please don't apologize. Well, Dr. Xavier wanted me to try this new antidepressant, but I'm not sure. You know how I hate pills…"

Nothing unnatural ever entered Mom's body. The stubborn woman would rather suffer a blinding migraine than take a painkiller.

"He did give me a vitamin B_{12} shot yesterday to see if it'll help. And waking up this morning, I did notice a change."

Dad shouted from the living room, "He's too old to be practicing medicine anymore! Your mom needs to get off her keister and get some exercise! That'll fix her."

"Prick," Abbie said under her breath.

Mom gave her a disapproving look and headed for the back porch. "Come on, I have a bucket of vegetable scraps for Liza."

More unwelcome bloviating from Dad: "I smell bacon and pork chops," he taunted.

The hell he'd butcher her beloved pig! Abbie snatched the five-gallon bucket by the handle and stormed out the back door. Alone and unnerved by the East Bay Serial Killer's recent abductions, she stood in the mud and glared at the house. *1850 Myrtle Avenue—such a dump.* Wind banged the shutters against the dilapidated craftsman-style house with its rotting shiplap siding and chickens running amok. The property, however, did boast the most magical old-growth redwood tree in town. It was three hundred feet tall and fifteen feet in diameter, and the entire family guarded it with their lives. But it was Liza who truly guarded it; she lived in the chain-link fence pigpen surrounding the tree. Best fertilizer ever.

The three-hundred-pound black-and-white hog squealed with delight upon seeing her favorite human. The goofy thing managed to buck her back legs over the top of her wiry head.

What a character! Abbie entered the pen and scratched Liza's back, but Liza wasn't having it. All she wanted were the scraps in Abbie's bucket. Abbie chuckled. Who needed human friends? Liza had been the most loyal best friend a girl could ask for.

A sound emanated from the chicken coop. Uncle Jesse was shoveling soiled sawdust through the door into a wheelbarrow. His salt-and-pepper hair had recessed to the top of his head, and because he was such a good sport, Abbie often teased that his forehead had turned into a fivehead. He wore his remaining hair in a long braid hanging down his back. It looked spindly, but who was judging?

As she slogged through the mud toward him, Sideshow Bob greeted her. He was her favorite chicken, whom they'd believed was a hen but turned out to be a rooster. Roosters usually acted aggressively with hens, but once they'd discovered his mellow disposition, they let him hang with the ladies in "the boudoir"—Uncle Jesse's name for the chicken coop.

"Mornin', Uncle Jesse," she said, peeking through the coop door, happy to see him.

"Lookie here, if it ain't my favoritest niece!" He kissed her cheek.

She chuckled. "I'm your *only* niece."

"You're still my favoritest," he insisted, combing his goatee with his fingers.

Liza had joined them and rooted her cold, wet snout into Abbie's hand, looking for more scraps. "You've had enough, you greedy thing," Abbie said firmly, but without any conviction. Liza continued rooting.

"That hog of yours sure sits on her throne," Uncle Jesse said.

True. Liza had been queen of Myrtle Avenue since he had found her years earlier, near starving, when he caught her rummaging through the trash behind his auto shop. Abbie had nursed her back to health, and after several years, she had won first place in 4-H at the fair. That wasn't much of a feat, though, considering Liza's only competition had the personality of a bucket of slop.

"You workin' today?" Uncle Jesse asked.

"Not 'til tomorrow afternoon."

"How 'bout loadin' up my truck with camping gear, and we'll spend today and tomorrow morning hunting? Then on the way home, we'll hit the dumpster."

The freezer *was* nearly empty—but her breakup date with Ty… Still, Uncle Jesse's offer was tempting. He had taught her to shoot the Winchester .30-30 Grandpa Spencer had given her. He also taught her how to field dress and wrap the kill. Whenever they hit the Clyde's Market dumpster, she'd stand guard while he jumped in and packed out the perfectly good food, only a few days expired. Most of it they kept for themselves, and the rest they fed to the chickens and Liza.

After thinking hard about his hunting proposal, she explained she'd already made plans to spend the evening in bed reading—a lie, of course. She thanked him for the offer and promised they would hunt some other time. As she turned to leave, he stopped her.

"Just spotted your dad in the living room window… Kindness, darlin'."

"I've already dealt with the POS this morning. He slithered into the kitchen smelling like a snake pickled in ethanol."

Uncle Jesse dropped his head in a moment of pensive silence. "You think you got it figured out, but you don't. So, stop judging the broken."

She rolled her eyes. "You don't know what you're talking about. He's your brother, and you love him, I get it. But he's *not* my dad. Biologically, yes, but that's where the connection stops."

"Maybe if you weren't stagnating, you wouldn't hold so much anger. You've been eighteen for three months now, Abbie, but you have yet to apply for a job in Port Allegiance. Working at Pacific One Fishery is a dead-end job. Do you wanna stand at a conveyor belt hour after hour, day after day, lopping off fish heads? And what about friends? You haven't had any for years."

The old hurt flooded in as the elementary school bullies chanted in her head: *Abbie Flabby, puddin' and pie, sat on a boy and made him cry…* That was the year Abbie died inside and demanded people call her Meg, the name of the protagonist from the classic Disney cartoon *A Wrinkle in Time*. Come ninth grade, though, she'd resurrected Abbie; she wasn't a child anymore.

Stifling the tears, she wished he hadn't made the jab about her lack of friends. Her mind wandered back to when she and her family had moved to California. They had stopped in Lake Tahoe, where she'd met the boy with sad brown eyes—her first and only true friend. His name was Dylan. Dylan Rhodes…? Yes, the last name sounded right. Although they had only known each other for three days, the memory of them becoming lost in the snowy forest together sent a shiver down her spine.

Uncle Jesse continued, "It would be good for you and your dad to have a little distance. I understand leaving your mom would be hard, but I hate watching your spirit bein' sucked out of you. If you get a live-in job in Port Allegiance, you'll make a ton more than minimum wage, plus you'll be right over the wall. And—"

"I know, I know," she said gently, far too familiar with this monologue. "As it turns out, day after tomorrow, I have another appointment at the West One Recruiting Office. And I'm *not* canceling last minute this time."

"Cha-ching, cha-ching!" he exclaimed with a grin. "Your dreams of college are about to come true."

Abbie stood at her bedroom window, squinting into the foggy night, waiting for Ty's headlights to filter through. Maybe he had gotten into a fatal truck accident. *One could hope...*

Shit—she didn't mean that...or maybe she did. The long minutes waiting for him to arrive had grown into a cluster of unrelenting dark thoughts, all meshing into a ball of tangled rubber bands.

For the past year, her and Ty's pattern had been predictable, repeating itself ad nauseam. She'd climb into his truck, and he'd give her a long-stemmed red rose and apologize for his rotten behavior until she caved. How could she stay angry? He always had her best interests at heart... *Not.*

His black Silverado materialized out of the mist and stopped in front of her house.

Now or never... Avoiding her family, she snuck to the front door, put on her black stocking cap, and slipped into the brisk night air right over to Ty's truck. The fog glazed her arms and face, and she cursed herself for forgetting a jacket. But once this unpleasantness was over with, she'd be back in her cozy bed, reading the new mystery novel she'd bought at the thrift store. That peaceful notion summoned the breakup speech. *We're not good for each other anymore... I think you'd be happier with someone more compatible with you...*

His black-tinted windows reflected the blazing streetlamp, an annoying glare in her eyes. As she climbed into the passenger seat, a plume of cigarette smoke and the blare of thrash metal assaulted her senses, piercing her brain like a red-hot poker, a painful reminder of the year she had wasted on him. She coughed and fanned her face.

"I have a surprise for you, baby," Ty said with his usual shit-eating grin.

The whole "baby" thing disgusted her now. It should have been a tender, devotional expression shared between two people who adored each other, but no adoration remained in her since his mask had dropped.

Ty flicked on the cab light. Between them rested the requisite long-stemmed red rose…and a bottle of Captain Morgan rum.

This is the surprise? What an unimpressive gesture. Except for the Captain… She might need a swig after all.

Through the smoke-filled cab, she analyzed his mood—good, bad…? Always a guessing game. A dozen roses and an entire case of Captain wouldn't placate her after the ultimatum he'd dropped—not to mention him stealing her ATM card last week and withdrawing three hundred bucks to buy drugs. Tonight, he'd promised to return the cash. After that, they were *finito*, done with. Thank God he was taking her to Denny's, where she'd be safe from his retribution…and there was sure to be retribution.

Tipping his Old Milwaukee, Ty guzzled, wiping the foam from his mouth with his jacket sleeve. His new buzz cut emphasized his pit bull jaw and bushy blond eyebrows. She hated the tuft of hair growing on his chin, but not as much as the grenade tattoo on his neck. The stupid thing looked like a pineapple.

He took a drag of his cigarette and exhaled more toxic smoke into the cab. "How 'bout hittin' Roxie's after we chow?"

The bouncer at Roxie's, Ty's drug buddy, knew she was underage, but he let her in anyway. Abbie stared at her house and wished she were inside. "You know I hate loud music."

"You've never given it a chance," he scoffed. "You're always judging, always criticizing. Nothing is ever good enough for you…"

Him and his weaponized phrases. She had documented enough of them to publish a book titled *1000 Ways to Traumatize your Girlfriend*:

Maybe if you lost weight, you wouldn't act so prickly.

You are in serious need of mental help.

You're too sensitive.

I never said that.

…Fuck you, Ty.

His eyes seared a hole through the side of her head, and he cleared his throat. "Not a thank you for the rose and liquor? They ain't cheap, baby."

Yeah…that you bought with my money. Taking a deep breath, she faced him—but before she could reply, her eyes shifted to a bruise peeking out from his jacket collar.

Catching her stare, he tugged at his collar, lowering it. "Me and the old man got into it again. He'll be pissin' blood for a spell, but I got the best of 'im this time." He lifted his shirt. Bruises and scrapes covered his ribs and abdomen.

"Ouch," she mustered flatly.

Digging into his pocket, he pulled out a pill bottle. "Want one? Helps with the pain."

He enjoyed messing with her head that way—tugging at her heartstrings. Manipulating, rather.

She shook her head. "I'm fine." Anything but fine, she cracked open the Captain and took several huge swigs, the liquor scorching her stomach. Then she set the rose on the dash and waited for that loving tingle to filter through her body. As the breakup speech cycled through her head on repeat, Ty's blathering lips barely registered her silence. Something about how his old man had called him a loser because he had no job. For once, Scoop Hawkins hadn't lied.

What the hell—? Out of nowhere, a raging energy consumed Ty. He slammed the gear into drive, and in seconds, the truck was blazing clockwise along the thirty-foot-high stone wall at seventy miles an hour. Dodging parked cars and oncoming traffic, he left skid marks and blasting horns in his wake.

And then she realized: that was no aspirin he'd swallowed. Clenching the dashboard, she glared at him, wild-eyed. This would not end well. "Stop the truck and let me out!" She begged him to slow down, but he hit the pedal harder.

"You haven't listened to a damn word I said, have you?" He adjusted the rearview mirror, then clipped an oncoming truck's mirror, leaving his own dangling. And ahead, moving in closer, a line of stopped cars waited to enter the busy intersection. Closing in, faster, faster… Screaming, she threw her arms up over her face.

In one swift move, Ty cranked the steering wheel, and her head slammed against the side window. She dropped her arms and exhaled hard. Only luck had spared them.

Open the door and jump! Seizing the door handle, she calculated her chances of survival at this speed. Not good.

He took a hard left at the Tokeland Pot Dispensary—no restaurant tonight. His plan made her shudder as he expected sex. "A guy has needs," he'd say. And he preferred the abandoned Sequoia Zoo, his former employer, the place where he'd fed the lions before the doors had closed months earlier. For him, taking her there induced the sense of danger he craved, but for Abbie, the concrete floor in the lion's den didn't exactly get a girl in the mood.

An escape plan… *Think, dammit!* The perfect idea struck her. Once they arrived, as certain as the sun rises, Ty would piss away his beers behind his truck. Then she'd grab the billy club from behind his seat, knock him unconscious, and bust out his headlights. She'd then steal the lantern from the floor, run to the nearest house, and call Uncle Jesse and beg him to save her…*again.*

Her fingernails dug into the seat cover as Ty slammed on the brakes in the center of the zoo's pitch-black parking lot. He killed the ignition. When he headed to the back of his truck, Abbie chugged more Captain. Stupid, but necessary. Out of her mind, she quickly reached behind the seat for the billy club.

Ty flicked on the cab light and eyeballed her. "Oh good, you're grabbing the blanket. You're in for a ride, baby."

Shit! Her plan was a no-go, and probably a mistake anyway. If she accidentally killed him, she couldn't live with herself. But that moment was her chance to prove her strength and conviction, to show him she wasn't an appendage, a brainless accessory attached to him like the spellbound girl he expected.

Grabbing the lantern and taking a lighter to it, Ty then grabbed her arm and pulled her toward the lion's den—because God forbid they soil his precious seat covers if they did it in the truck.

With the Captain in tow, Abbie took another big gulp, the amber liquid dribbling down her chin. "Stop, Ty. I'm not doing this. You need to take me home."

He snickered, and as he held the lantern up to her, a menacing shadow swept over his face, like a back-alley creature waiting to devour her. "Yeah, right. You're real funny."

"And you're out of your mind. We're done. I want out. I'm applying for a job in Port Allegiance. A fresh start. Without you." It wasn't her planned speech, and she'd never been so brazen. She waited for his face to redden, the angry blotches dotting his skin.

"*Excuse* me?" he said, stopping cold.

As Abbie jerked free of his clutches, he grasped the weight of her words. Fuming, he contorted his mouth into a sick semblance of a grin. "So, little Abbie Spencer wants to rub elbows with the rich, huh? You and your worthless ideas to earn money for college. Never gonna happen, baby," he ranted as he circled her, eyeing her up and down. "And why would someone hire a girl like you? Look at you. You're pathetic."

She glared at him as she considered bashing the bottle across his face. Instead, she took another swig and laughed. "Coming from a guy who still lives at home with Daddy. From someone so insecure, he stalks his girlfriend's every move, accuses her of cheating when she hasn't, steals her money. The list goes on and on. You want more? Do you? Who's pathetic now, Ty?"

Rage sparked in his eyes. His upper lip curled under, furrowing his nose.

He wouldn't dare. He'd never hit her.

With a quick right hook to her ear, he knocked her to the ground, the blanket flying from her arms, the bottle of Captain shattering and soaking her long hair. Blinding pain shot through her head, and she fought to stay conscious.

Ty's footsteps scuffled closer, and she tightened her body, preparing for a brutal kick. Instead, he did the unforgivable: he snatched her grandpa's stocking cap from her head and stomped it into a murky puddle of water. He'd violated the only possession she'd ever cared about. Curling into a ball, she whimpered.

He sauntered over to his truck. The engine roared to life, revving. That's how he'd do her in: he'd run her down.

Directly ahead of her, the headlights lit up the desolated parking lot. Frantically, she searched for a hiding place. At the periphery, she spotted her escape: an opening in the fence. As she stumbled to her feet, her mind dissolved into a drunken haze. She ran toward the opening, but three openings now crisscrossed over each other because of her blurry vision, and her body careened off course before she face-planted onto the concrete.

When Ty revved the engine again, the muffler backfired. He screamed out the window, "You better run, bitch!"

As the Captain was crushing her with the weight of a boulder, she rolled away, smashing her hip bones into the concrete, and didn't stop until she ran up against a steel post. *The escape hole! Where'd it disappear to?* She had no sense of up from down or left from right.

The headlights seemed to taunt her as they drifted backward menacingly. Like living entities, they willed themselves back the distance needed to gain speed and run her down. She scooted behind the post and waited. Then the Silverado burst into action, burning rubber, the screeching hanging in limbo until the concrete set the truck free. In a flash, the lights rocketed toward her. She clenched her jaw and waited for impact.

Ty spun a doughnut and stopped beside her, a cloud of smoke radiating from the tires. He climbed out and immediately pulled his knife, the shiny blade gleaming in the headlights. On his knees, he held it to her jugular. "I could gut you right here, right now. I'd throw your body in the ocean, and nobody would be the wiser. You'd be another missing ho from Eureka. Because I'm such a nice guy, I'll spare you. But watch your back. And if you say a word to anyone about tonight, I'll gut your fucking uncle—and your mom, too."

Then he got back in the truck and tore off, leaving her trembling in his dust. The blurry red taillights glowed like the devil's eyes as they dissolved into nothing.

Abbie fell over sideways, panting. She waited…and waited some more. When it became apparent Ty wasn't returning, she struggled to her knees. What now?

The blanket. She felt around for it, running a hand over the rough concrete until she touched the soft fabric. Then she rolled herself into a burrito, shivering. As time passed, the only sounds were those of distant sirens and the scurrying of rats, or maybe something bigger. As the black cloak of night swallowed her, she imagined her family safely in bed sleeping, unaware she had ever left the house.

Eternity awaited—that was how long before daybreak. Would she end up another victim of the East Bay Serial Killer? Just another corpse found in the city dump, or a bloated body washing ashore in Humboldt Bay?

A breeze washed over her, carrying the scent of eucalyptus. She imagined herself afloat on the Van Duzen River and reaching a fork. Which way to paddle? One branch of the river might flow into the shark-infested Pacific, while the other branch might lead to a warm and peaceful beach somewhere. She couldn't risk the sharks, so she fought the current and swam to shore before passing out drunk.

CHAPTER TWO

Half an hour past sunrise, Uncle Jesse sat in the hospital waiting room as Abbie waited in a private room for Dr. Xavier, the booze from last night creeping up her throat. So much for her sobriety pledge.

She cursed Uncle Jesse for bringing her there. He said Dr. Xavier needed to check her eardrum to make sure Ty hadn't perforated it. It did throb something fierce, and she wished the incessant ringing would stop. She wrinkled her nose. Didn't take a brain surgeon to find the source of the pungent odor. Across from where she sat, multicolored blotches and drip marks stained the wall. Abbie figured the patient before her had lost their stomach contents, like she was about to do.

What was she thinking, abusing herself like that? She thought back to the day she and Ty had met at Clyde's Market. After self-checking her groceries and coming up short, Ty, waiting behind her with a case of beer, had stepped forward, added his beer to her bill, and paid for everything together. He had been so charming, so sweet. Not exactly her type, though… In the parking lot, after some persuasion (pressure was more like it) on his part, she agreed to go on a date with him. He had to be a decent guy; after all, his dad, Scoop Hawkins, was the new cop in town and bowling champion of Oxnard, where they had moved from.

Looking back at their first date and moving forward, it was clear that drinking had been the glue holding their relationship together—and if she was honest with herself about the past year, it was the only way she had tolerated him. Initially, his love-bombing made her feel special, the way he attended to her needs. Like a child predator, he found her at her lowest, spotted her weaknesses, then moved in to lay claim, to control and manipulate. And she had allowed it. Had she ended the relationship before it began, he would've continued his drugged-up path alone, and possibly—hopefully—he would've died from an overdose, saving her from this nightmare.

She flinched when Dr. Xavier, a man in his seventies, entered the room, his smile jolly and sincere. His hair was white and perfectly slicked back, his skin wrinkled, but in a rugged cowboy sort of way. He knew too much about her: annual pelvic exams, birth control, the nasty STD Ty had given her a few months back—so damn embarrassing. *I didn't cheat, I swear. Yeah, right.* A pang of shame flushed her face. And to top it off, Dr. Xavier now knew Ty had hit her.

He looked up at her and his pale-blue eyes twinkled like a crystalline sky. "Hello, Abbie. Says here you took a blow to your left ear."

Too embarrassed to answer, she nodded.

"Would you like to talk about it?"

He'd always been an empathetic listener, but this morning, she yearned to get home and climb into bed. "There's nothing to talk about. Ty and I are done. Finished."

Doubt she'd keep her promise showed on his face. But she'd prove him wrong, or prove herself right—whatever.

He sat on the round Naugahyde seat and rolled himself toward her. "Just know I'm here for you." With that, he lifted the otoscope to her ear and peeked inside. After fiddling around for a few seconds, he pulled it out. "Your eardrum's inflamed, Abbie, but it's not perforated. You got lucky, this time."

"There won't be a next time," she said, tapping her foot aggressively.

He sighed, and they engaged in a stare-down. When she couldn't handle it anymore, she looked away.

Randomly, he said, "I made a house call last night to check on your mother, but your dad said she was fine, that she had hit the sack early. You tell me—how's she doing? I'm concerned."

A conversation worth having. "Living with my dad would make anyone depressed. She sleeps a lot, barely eats anything. I hope the B_{12} shot you gave her works."

"We'll see. Encourage healthy eating habits, and most of all, get her outside when it's sunny. Her vitamin D levels are low, too."

Healthy eating habits? As helpful as Dr. Xavier was, he didn't live in her family's reality; he didn't know most of their food came from a dumpster. But she did agree to help Mom get out of the house more often. She stood to leave.

"Hold on," he said. "By law, the hospital called the police here to take your assault report."

Damn Uncle Jesse. Her back stiffened, her sweat turning to ice. Due to city budget cuts, Ty's dad was now one of two cops in Eureka, and she'd rather slit her own throat than have to speak with him about this.

"Don't worry," Dr. Xavier said, trying to ease her discomfort. "I requested Officer Fennimore. He's one of the good guys. Is it okay if I let him in now?"

She nodded and relaxed a little. "But I want my uncle here when he questions me."

"You got it." He took her hand. "I hope this is the wake-up call you needed."

Thanks, Dr. Persistent.

After Uncle Jesse picked up some pain medication at Clyde's Market, he drove them home, his veiled disappointment in Abbie hurting worse than Ty's punch to her ear. Guilt, what a shitty feeling. She'd never jeopardize her uncle's trust again. He was decent and good, and he certainly didn't deserve the hell she had put him through over the past year.

Speaking with Officer Fennimore hadn't been as painful as she'd feared. He had called the judge and asked him to grant an emergency restraining order against Ty, which the judge approved. Fennimore said Ty was in a world of trouble. Not only had he assaulted Abbie last night, he had also plowed over an elderly woman as she was crossing the street in a hit-and-run. She hadn't died, but he had broken both her hips. Given her advanced age, Abbie wondered if she'd ever walk again. There was a witness who vowed to testify, to ensure justice. Ty was an animal, a waste of oxygen.

Channel nine crackled on the CB radio. Abbie cranked the volume, and they listened. Just the usual drug bust recital. Ty's dad, Scoop Hawkins, was part of a raid on Humboldt Hill, and according to Ty, Scoop usually kept some of the drugs for himself. Apparently, the fringe benefits outweighed his crappy pay. Abbie cringed thinking of how she had once consorted with the Hawkins clan.

Uncle Jesse broke the silence. "You're gonna tell your folks what happened last night. They deserve to know. Ty's gone too far this time. Your dad needs to be on the lookout for him. Gotta be able to protect you and your mom when I'm not around."

"You mean you, me, and Mom need to protect ourselves," Abbie said sarcastically. "Ty wouldn't hurt a hair on Dad's head. Haven't you noticed Ty morphing into his replacement son?"

"I've noticed," he said, his lips tightening. "Ty knows not to mess with me. I'll kick that sorry punk's ass. As for you and your mom's safety, after I get you in the house, I'm heading to the hardware store and investing in better locks and securing the windows. But something needs to change beyond that. You need to get the hell out of Dodge, Abbie."

She wholeheartedly agreed with him. They'd be safe, especially when Uncle Jesse was home, and she was keeping her appointment at the West One Recruiting Office tomorrow. Time to grow a pair and not cancel again. A new life, a new beginning.

When the dispatcher on the CB radio mentioned Officer Fennimore, Abbie and Uncle Jesse leaned in closer.

"Suspect, Ty Hawkins, apprehended and arrested," Fennimore said. "Headed to county jail now."

"Copy that," said dispatch.

Uncle Jesse slapped his knee. "Holy shit. Fennimore did it—he busted the bastard! I bet he found him at that drug dealer's address you gave him."

Abbie dropped her head back, the pressure in her chest magically disappearing. She chuckled. It was like the heavens had unfolded their arms, setting everything right with the world. "Until Ty's day in court, we're safe."

"Glad you're gonna be okay, darlin'."

Her mouth curled into a sheepish smile. Uncle Jesse was exactly what she needed. There was a certainty about him, a peace.

He pulled up to the curb in front of their house. "Ready to go inside and tell your story?"

"Not really. Dad's gonna give me a ration of shit. Mom's gonna freak out, ask me why I look so dreadful."

"She loves you. It's what she does."

"And it's what Dad does, too." Abbie exited the truck, her hip bones aching from rolling on the concrete last night. She held Uncle Jesse's arm, and they slothed up to the front door, where he used his key to get in. Sure enough, Mom and Dad were up and watching the morning news.

Mom jumped to her feet. "I thought you two were still in bed!" She looked Abbie over, her eyes widening. "What happened to you? You look dreadful!"

Half annoyed, half amused that she'd been so on the mark, Abbie eased herself onto the sofa, Uncle Jesse sitting next to her. He took her hand.

"She's gonna be okay," he said. "Go ahead, tell your folks what happened last night."

"Good grief," Dad said, rolling his eyes. "Did she get mugged again, giving food to those loser street dwellers?"

Coming from the biggest loser of all. Priceless.

"Brodie, please," Mom said, pacifying him in a tone that made Abbie's stomach churn worse. She sat beside Abbie and examined her more closely. "Please, honey, go ahead and tell us what happened to you."

"I broke up with Ty last night. He didn't take it well; he went ballistic."

"What do you mean, 'ballistic'?" Dad asked as he turned off the television.

"He hit me, then said some really disturbing things."

Mom's nostrils flared. "Oh my God, he hit you?! Where? Are you okay?"

"I'm fine," she said, adjusting her butt, trying to get more comfortable. "He clocked me in the left ear. Dr. Xavier said he didn't perforate the eardrum. I hope this damn ringing doesn't last long."

"You press charges?" Dad asked, like she better not have.

"I did," she said, eager to break his miserable little heart. "And apparently, after he abandoned me in the zoo's parking lot last night, he ran over an elderly woman, broke her hips, and drove away. Officer Fennimore just busted him and threw him in jail."

Uncle Jesse said to his brother, "That little prick is as mean and scrappy as a rooster in a cockfight. If the judge allows Scoop to bail him out, and he comes here looking for Abbie, I'll fucking bury him."

"We'll do it together," Abbie said, squeezing his hand. "Thanks for the support. Now, not to be a party pooper or anything, but I need caffeine, and badly." She shuffled to the kitchen, Mom following.

Mom was about to say something, but Abbie cut her off. "No more Ty, okay?"

Nodding, Mom sat at the table, her lips sucked inward.

Feeling like she was under a microscope, Abbie savored an entire banana, then washed it down with coffee. The combo, her proven cure for a hangover, had become her morning habit. She'd downed nearly a fifth of rum last night, which was more than a little concerning.

Abbie hoped someday she and Mom could discuss why they had both picked such worthless men. But how could they have an honest conversation about it when her mom hadn't taken the time to reflect on her own life? It was like she merely existed, never challenging the status quo.

"Ty's the best boyfriend you've ever had," Dad shouted from the living room. "What did you say to him that pissed him off?"

"Don't listen to him," Mom whispered. "He doesn't know what he's talking about. He's not well."

Like a grenade whose pin had been pulled, Abbie stomped into the living room and exploded in Dad's face. "I bet you wouldn't believe me if I told you Ty threatened to gut me, Uncle Jesse, and Mom, and then toss our bodies in the ocean!"

Mom gasped from the kitchen.

"Yeah, right," Dad said. "I *don't* believe you."

He always took Ty's side. They'd sit in the wood-heated shed and drink beer and brag about their hunting exploits into the early-morning hours.

Breathing heavily, Abbie lumbered back into the kitchen and focused on a photo hanging on the wall. It was of Dad and Uncle Jesse playing Frisbee at city beach in Sandpoint. Had Dad not moved them to California to escape his guilt over the death of her little brother, Sammie, Abbie wondered if their relationship might have been less volatile.

As she grew lost in the photo, Mom considered her and whispered, "I know he's flawed, and his words cut deep. I don't know how to make this better for you."

Abbie sighed. *You could start by telling him to shut the fuck up.* "I love you, Mom, but I'm exhausted. Don't wake me up for lunch or dinner." With that, she shuffled to the wall phone next to the fridge, dialed her boss, and told him she was taking a few personal days. He wasn't happy about it, but she didn't care.

CHAPTER THREE

Tuesday, December 18

Dear Journal,

WTF has become of my life? I awoke from a dream where I was Rip Van Winkle, a character from a fairy tale who accepted a drink of liquor from a group of little people (all with Dad's face), then awoke twenty years later as an old person. I won't allow him to dictate my moods. It would sure be nice if Mom would stand up for me and defend me when he launches his verbal assaults. I tell myself she's abused, too, but it doesn't make it any less painful. Someday I hope she actualizes her own dreams, instead of having mine spur her on. I love her dearly, though. I always will. It's time I look out for myself. My appointment at the West One Recruiting Office is at 8:00 a.m.— plenty of time to pull my shit together.

Love,
Abbie

IN HER BEDROOM, she knelt before her teal-blue hope chest with black metal accents she had inherited after Grandma and Grandpa Spencer had died from a COVID variant. Had they caught the virus eight months later, they would've lived, as by then, CDC scientists had eradicated all variants of the virus. So unfair. With a tear forming in her eye, she lifted the chest's lid, dug under the quilts, and found the tattered hatbox buried at the bottom, which she and Mom had filled with keepsakes right before Dad dragged the family away from Sandpoint. She set it on the floor, her heart drumming. The day had come: the day she needed to open it. Her hands shook as she lifted the lid.

On top of the pile of photographs lay a faded picture of her little brother, Sammie, who had drowned the month before she and her family had moved to Eureka. It was unfair that humans rented but a minuscule time slot on earth.

Gently setting the photo aside, she continued sorting through the memories. Under a stack of her kindergarten crayon drawings, she found the sealed manila envelope and stared at it. *You won't own me again, Ty Hawkins.*

Working a finger under the envelope's glued flap, she slid it to the other side, careful not to tear it. She removed her birth certificate and social security card and studied them. If the documents cleared security at the West One Recruiting Office, the authorities would grant her the limited Bronze Access Card and permission to apply for a job within the city of Port Allegiance. If, by chance or by a miracle, she got a real job, then Pacific One Fishery, where she had been working for the past three years, would forever be a part of her past.

After slipping the documents back into the envelope and zipping it into her purse, she peeked out the window. Of course, Ty wasn't stalking her. Officer Fennimore had arrested him, and he was behind bars. She was safe…for now.

No time for a shower, and she hadn't done her laundry for a week, so she dug through the pile of dirty clothes on the floor and dressed in her least stained jeans and a green plaid shirt. It was time to leave for the most important day of her life.

Silence permeated the house as she made her way to the kitchen. Dad and Uncle Jesse had already left for work, and Mom was asleep. With everything Abbie had been through with Ty, she had thoughtlessly forgotten to ask her mom how she was feeling yesterday. Tonight, they'd play cards and talk.

As she poured coffee into her travel mug, a needle-nosed rat scurried across the countertop and dragged off a crust of burnt toast. Before she could swat it away, the rodent dove into a hole in the plaster wall. Securing a live-in job in Port Allegiance couldn't come soon enough.

In the foyer, she pulled her black stocking cap over her head. When she grabbed the doorknob to leave, she froze. A long-lost sensation flooded her senses: freedom. An expanse of open road lay before her, paving the way to a better life.

And then the door blasted open, driving the knob through the wall.

Ty!

She gasped in horror, and in her haste to back away, she tripped over her own feet and fell to the floor. The look in his eyes terrified her, a remnant spark from Sunday night—a drug-fueled rage that consumed his entire being, a burning desire to set the world on fire.

Who was going to save her this time? Mom's herbal sleeping pills had likely conked her out.

"Abbie Flabby, glad you're home," he sneered menacingly. "Thanks for inviting me in."

As he grinned and moved closer, she tore down the hall to her bedroom, but as she swung the door closed, he barged through with his shoulder.

Her Winchester .30-30! She grabbed it from under her bed and leveled it at his face, the barrel of the rifle wobbling. "Who let you out of jail?"

"It's called bail, baby."

"Bail?" she said loud enough for Mom to hear. "You don't want to do this, Ty. Just leave. I don't want to shoot you, but I will if you don't leave me alone."

"Restraining order?" he snickered and sized her up, ignoring the threat. "*Seriously?* You can't stop me from seeing my baby girl."

Gauging by the smell of liquor wafting from him, this would get ugly—and fast. Time suspended as she stared into his vacant blue eyes. She couldn't look away—and if she did, even for a second, he'd pounce.

"Please, Ty, I don't want trouble," she begged. "Don't you think you've punished me enough?"

"I think you're a filthy whore. Tap that thing? No, thanks. No guy will ever want you."

As he stepped closer, a shadow flickered in the hallway. Uncle Jesse—holding a baseball bat. He tiptoed into the room, and as he jockeyed into batting stance, a floorboard beneath him squeaked.

Ty spun around and lunged, and Uncle Jesse, snarling, swung the bat directly into his shin. The bone gave a sickening crunch. Wailing, Ty crashed to the floor like a toppling tower.

"You're fucking dead, old man!" he screamed through gritted teeth, his blotched red face looking like it was going to burst. He struggled to get to his feet, but his calf and foot dangled limply below the break. As blood seeped into his jeans, his eyes slowly rolled back, and he fainted, head clunking heavily on the floor.

Uncle Jesse dropped the bat and shook his head. "What a pantywaist. I'll grab the duct tape." With an air of satisfaction, he strolled out, a man not in a hurry.

How could Uncle Jesse be so calm? Abbie choked down the boulder in her throat as she imagined Ty waking up. What if he used his arms to drag himself to her and grapple her to the floor? Shaking away the image, she crouched sideways, and as she retrieved the bat, his eyelids fluttered.

"Hurry! He's waking up!" she hollered.

Uncle Jesse sprinted back, rolled Ty onto his side, and bound his wrists. "You're safe, darlin'. He ain't goin' nowhere. Good thing I forgot my shop keys on the kitchen table." He checked his watch. "It's seven forty. You best not miss your appointment. I'll call 911."

Abbie ran through the rain to her Subaru, parked across the street alongside the stone wall. She slammed the car into drive and forged northwest on Myrtle toward Humboldt Bay, right off the Pacific Ocean.

Dozens of homeless people patrolled the litter-strewn street, their shopping carts heaped with soaking wet treasures. And on one corner of Park Street stood Tony Wilkens, the fifty-nine-year-old vet who had gone bonkers after returning home from Afghanistan. Poor guy had watched as the Taliban opened fire on his platoon and scrambled his best friend's brain. Tony lived in Bum Jungle, a burned-down city block scattered with tents directly across the alley from her house. If she wasn't running late, she would have stopped and paid him a visit. As she zoomed past him, he waved a spray-painted sign:

THE EAST BAY SERIAL KILLER
IS COMING FOR YOU.
WHO'S NEXT?

Trying to put the cancerous mess called Eureka out of her mind, she listened to Keith Urban, her favorite country singer, and sang along, an image of the Bronze Access Card dangling like a carrot in front of her speeding vehicle. A new life outside Eureka…no longer looking like a lobotomy victim from mindlessly standing at a conveyor belt for hours on end. Not reeking of fish would be a nice bonus, too.

Her boss at Pacific One had offered her the swing shift manager position (no conveyor belt), but it didn't pay much more than she currently earned, and the sixteen-hour shifts sounded brutal. The thought of it triggered the urge for a drink of the hard stuff. Reflexively, she glanced at the glove compartment, where she kept miniature bottles of various liquors. Showing up drunk to the recruiting office was a sure way to ruin any chance she had. Time to bury her impulsive, reckless behavior.

Merging left onto Allegiance Boulevard, she soon approached the north Port of Entry, a row of military-style tollbooths. Above, observation towers boasted numerous armed guards. The steel-cold image didn't jibe with the magical arched gateway she had fantasized about in her dreams. Over the years of living in Eureka, she had searched for an aerial view of Port Allegiance, but KnightScape, the only legal search engine in the country, had blurred out everything within the wall.

Up ahead, outside the wall, a sign read, WEST ONE RECRUITING OFFICE, NEXT RIGHT. She soon turned into the parking lot and parked in lucky space thirteen, the car's grill mere inches from the wall, which was a feat of engineering. Each stone interlocked with the next, reminiscent of the walls of a citadel called Saksaywaman in Cusco, Peru, which she had discovered in an issue of *National Geographic*.

It was now 7:42 a.m.—record time. Previous trial runs had taken three minutes, and the walk had taken thirty.

Earlier, hope had filled her, but now that she was here, each beat of her heart made the whole situation feel increasingly dire. The voice of Ty, that 150-pound dumbbell, called to her from her bedroom floor. *"Look at you,"* he mocked. *"Who'd hire a girl like you? You're pathetic."*

Abbie glanced at the glove compartment again, the temptation filling her mouth with saliva. *One little bottle won't hurt, right?*

No! Don't do it! Instead, she dug through her purse, found the Sour Patch Kids, and popped a few in her mouth.

Sucking on the tart, sugary candy, she rested her head on the steering wheel and banged it hard enough to stop the unnerving thoughts. "Damn you, Ty Hawkins. I can do this. Hell, yes, I can!"

Now stop thinking and hustle!

Catching her breath after a power sprint, she entered the windowless concrete employment office, which smelled of body odor and bleach. The flickering fluorescent lights and roving ceiling cameras added to her nausea.

Ten feet ahead stood a row of guards wearing the Port Allegiance uniform. An officer approached her with a leashed Labrador retriever. The dog sniffed her black hiking boots, then stood on his hind legs and sniffed the rest of her—like she might be hiding a weapon in her ear.

"I'm clean," she said, wishing she could give the dog a quick pat on the head, but knowing better. "I have an appointment to apply for an access card, but I'm not sure where to go, and to top it off, I'm gonna be late."

He sized her up, then pointed to his right and strutted away to torment another scared applicant.

Duh—had she bothered to turn her head, she would've seen the screening area, where the applicants were removing their shoes and placing their belongings in a tray on the conveyor belt as if TSA at the airport were screening them.

7:56. *Dammit!* Six grubby people waited in line ahead of her. Zero chance of the recruiting office granting them an access card, obviously. Then the realization hit: she blended in perfectly.

When she was finally at the front of the line, she placed her shoes, purse, and jacket in the tray. On the other side of the walk-through metal detector, an armed officer—a surly woman with a clearly crappy attitude—motioned her in, and after Abbie passed through, the woman ran a wave scanner over her body.

No cavity search, please, oh, please. Her legs grew flaccid, and a wave of weakness nearly dropped her to the floor. "Ma'am, please, I'm going to miss my appointment."

"Maybe you should have allowed more time. Now get moving. You're already checked in. Take a seat, and your officer will call your name."

Right on cue, the loudspeaker blared: "Abilene Spencer, desk four."

Where's desk four? Scanning the room, she spotted a row of ten desks, each marked by a pole with a red light and a number on top. She sprinted to her officer, who wore a gold button-up shirt, his sleeve covered in a mass of merit badges. She sat quickly, practically tipping the chair over.

"Driver's license and documentation please," he said evenly.

"Of course." She dug through her purse and handed them to him.

"Date of birth?"

"October 8, 2022."

First, he inspected her driver's license photo and compared it to her face. Then he ran the birth certificate and social security card through the scanner.

After a few seconds, the computer said in a monotone male voice, "Documentation verification fail," and instantaneously, a warning siren on the pole next to her wailed to life, its light flashing red. As she cowered in her seat, a guard moved in and stood behind her—and she could have sworn the ceiling camera swiveled around and zoomed in on her face.

When the officer silenced the alarm, she said, "I…I don't understand. What's going on?"

Why doesn't he answer?

Squinting into his monitor, he finally said, "Why doesn't the name on your application match your documentation?"

As she sat there stunned, her thoughts congealed.

"You wrote 'Abbie Spencer' on the application, but your documents read, 'Abilene Faye Spencer.'"

How could she have been so careless? Inhaling, she focused on speaking clearly. "My mistake, sir. My birth name is Abilene Faye Spencer, but I've always gone by Abbie. It's my nickname. I guess I should've written my legal name on the application form." She forced a guilty grin.

The officer leaned back and studied her, clearly questioning whether she was lying. Then he dismissed the guard behind her. With a few clicks on the monitor, he said, "Good thing I'm in a charitable mood today. Now, time for the contagious disease test. Slide your left hand into the white box and keep it flat and still. You'll feel a slight prick."

A slight prick? Needles terrified her. One more trauma after Sunday night and this morning with Ty, and she was liable to have a stroke.

He cleared his throat. "Ms. Spencer, your hand," he ordered.

"Is this gonna hurt?"

"It depends. Insert, please."

Depends on what? Sliding her hand into the white box, she noticed small lettering on the lower left: MULTI-GUARD 2000. When a sphincter-like apparatus gripped her wrist, she resisted the urge to wrench her hand back.

Ouch! Might as well have been a harpoon impaling her index finger.

After a few seconds, the computer said, "Step two granted."

"Now I am going to ask you five questions," said the officer. "Yes or no answers only." He tapped his monitor. "Is today Tuesday, December 18, 2040?"

"Yes." *Jesus, a lie detector test?* She had nothing to hide, but feared failing anyway; she had wound her nerves tighter than a cuckoo clock.

"Have you ever been convicted of a crime?"

"No."

"Have you ever been dismissed from any job you have held?"

"No."

"Do you promise to take the oath of secrecy never to disclose to the outside world what you have witnessed or heard within the walls?"

"Yes."

"Have you answered the questions truthfully?"

"Yes."

"Step three granted," said the computer.

When the officer tapped the monitor and the sphincter released her hand, she pulled it out and inspected her aching finger. The white box had placed a Band-Aid on it.

"Congratulations, it's your lucky day." The officer grabbed his giant red stamp and marked the back of her hand APPROVED.

Stunned, elation replaced the ache, and her body tingled.

He pointed to a red X on the floor. "Stand there for photo documentation. Do not smile or show your teeth. No hats allowed."

What the hell? A photo? Disappointed it would forever show her lack of preparedness, she removed her stocking cap and stood before a white screen with a height chart, looking like Ty's vomited leftovers. Holding her breath, she peered into the camera. With a flash of light, Port Allegiance officially inducted her into their database.

The officer handed her a laminated Bronze Access Card. It shimmered in the light from above, wondrously warming her hand.

"Since you have never entered the city, here's a quick rundown on how it works. You will load toll money onto your card using the ATM over there." He pointed. "It takes cash or credit cards. If your vehicle is older than three years, you must leave it in our park-and-ride and catch the bus into the city." He slid the bus schedule toward her. "Before entering the bus, a port guard enforcer will ask you to open your mouth and will administer a secondary contagious disease scan. If you pass, you must swipe your card along the register next to the door, then place your hand flat on its screen. If the two credentials don't match up, it will not be pretty. The register will alert the enforcer, and he or she will transport you to detainment for evaluation. When you leave the city, you must swipe again. Laws apply to the southern Port of Entry as well. Do you understand?"

"Yes, sir. Thank you." She pulled her cap back over her head.

He slid a sheet of paper across the desk with a username and password, along with the rules and regulations for using the job search computer. "Remember, you may only apply for one job at a time. When you find one you are interested in, click on the link. A video interview screen will pop up, and you will meet your employer. Look directly into the camera and answer their questions to the best of your ability. We don't allow hats during the interview. There's an open computer to your right. Good luck, Ms. Spencer."

Video interview? Talk about putting someone on the spot.

"Thank you," she said again and walked away, not sure if she wanted to laugh or cry.

First, she loaded her Bronze Access Card with toll fare, paying with bills. (As if she owned a damn credit card!) Then she headed toward the computers, ten of them, separated by partitions. She sat at the one assigned to her and squirmed in her seat. When she removed her cap, her hair stuck to her scalp. Begrudgingly, she logged in.

In the center of the bright-blue screen, a username and password dialog box popped up. She dutifully typed in, *abilene.Spencer.390.* Password: *021191.*

Employers had posted seventeen new jobs. She read the descriptions and dropped a handful into the comparison cart. One job stood out: a kitchen porter/servant—and it paid five times the money she earned at Pacific One Fishery! Although she had no experience with cooking professionally, if her current boss had forgiven her for taking the personal days, he would give an excellent reference, and once the homeowners met her, she hoped they'd like her enough to choose her to be a part of their family.

She applied lip balm and tucked her hair behind her ears. When she clicked APPLY FOR JOB, a red light illuminated at the top of the monitor, and the face of an ethereal woman with platinum hair filled the screen. Within seconds, Abbie discovered the woman wasn't human but an interview replicate, which became obvious from the odd twitching of her head—a glitch in the system.

"Good morning, Abilene Spencer," the replicate said, her voice like a silky path to salvation.

Creepy. What was she supposed to do? Answer back? She paused briefly. "Good morning?" she replied, feeling awkward.

"Thank you for applying for the position. During the interview, please address me as Mrs. De Young. You will be working for me, and as such, you must observe proper etiquette at all times. Do you understand?"

Abbie wasn't stupid, and the patronizing tone coming from this nonhuman annoyed her. "Yes, Mrs. De Young, I understand."

"Splendid. Let's begin with the workings of your brain. Relax, and I will take you on a journey."

So damn weird. "Okay…"

"Imagine yourself strolling through a neighborhood, and you come upon a purse lying on the sidewalk. You open the wallet in search of identification, but what you see first are several five-hundred-dollar bills peeking out. What do you do?"

Easy answer. "I'd ignore the money and find the rightful owner."

The replicate twitched again, then cocked her head and looked sad. "But your family is starving, and there's no money to buy groceries."

A trick question. In all honesty, in said scenario, she'd keep five hundred and then turn the purse over to the police. But honesty was not the ticket here. "Stealing is never okay."

"Stealing is never okay," the replicate repeated back. "Now you're on a farm. What are you: The sheep or the wolf?"

More trickery. She considered the question carefully. The sheep would be a fenced-in prisoner, and by contrast, the wolf would reign free over her territory. But if she said "a wolf," which would be truthful, Mrs. De Young might deem her unfit to live within the confining walls of Port Allegiance. She grew dizzy wondering how to respond. Nerves spiking, she blurted out, "I'd rather be a hog. Shit. Didn't mean to say a hog… Oh man, I cursed! I'm so sorry."

"Now, Abilene, cursing is forbidden."

The fuck? A nonhuman had shamed her. "It won't happen again, Mrs. De Young."

"Very well, Abilene. Let's move on to your hobbies."

Dumpster diving, thrift store shopping, collecting aluminum cans. Ever try it? "Well, um, I read a lot. Mostly about science, geography, travel. I'd love to travel someday. I love classic country music—Keith Urban, Blake Shelton, the Dixie Chicks. My grandparents got me hooked on them. But the problem with listening to your favorite childhood songs repeatedly as an adult is that the songs lose their original nuance, and absorb negative stuff from the present—you know what I mean?"

"I don't answer questions, Abilene," the replicate said curtly. "I see your weakness. In your words, what is it?"

Rambling on about crap replicates don't give a shit about, apparently. She nibbled her bottom lip. *Come on, you gotta fight for this job. The human Mrs. De Young surely isn't as creepy as this creature.* Lifting her stocking cap to the camera, she answered, "My weakness is this cap. It once belonged to my grandpa. I wear it to feel safe. What I want you to know most is that I'm honest and I'm hardworking, and if you hire me, you won't be sorry."

"Your interview is over."

On the desktop, embedded in the Plexiglas, a red light flashed, and next to it, a menu materialized.

Update Resume
About
Log Out

"What a clusterfuck," she mumbled as she logged out, then noticed the replicate was still peering at her through the screen, and she wasn't happy.

Disappointed by blowing her opportunity to work in Port Allegiance, at least for now, Abbie sullenly parked her car along the wall across the street from her house. Damn, her finger still ached. She pulled off the Band-Aid to find a droplet of blood and a puncture mark.

She searched the street for Uncle Jesse's truck, but it wasn't parked in its usual spot. He was likely giving a statement down at police headquarters. He'd catch hell for breaking the leg of Scoop's do-no-wrong son. Nobody messed with his kid, period. Scoop was surely at the hospital with Ty now. What lies had he told his dad this time? Probably claimed Uncle Jesse had whacked him unprovoked. Could Ty press charges against him? But he had violated the restraining order. Either way, Ty's defiance of the law guaranteed he'd be spending years behind bars. By this time, surely the doctor had already set the broken bone. She hoped he'd suffered as much pain as he had inflicted upon her.

As she climbed out of her car, her eye caught the tail end of a shape moving into the shed behind her house. A thief? She and Uncle Jesse stored their camping gear inside.

Tiptoeing alongside the house, she grabbed a fallen branch from the old-growth redwood tree. Wasn't much of a weapon, but it would inflict a painful whipping. As she crept closer, there was a clunking sound, then a plume of dust puffed out the door.

"I've got a gun!" Abbie shouted. "And I'm a damn good shot!"

One final clunking sound, and Uncle Jesse peeked out.

"What are you doing?" she said, confused and tossing her makeshift weapon aside. "Where's your truck? And why are you drenched in sweat?"

He avoided eye contact, wiped his brow, and shut the door. "Truck's parked in the alley. Decided to clean up out here, get the gear ready for our next adventure."

Never had he sweat while preparing for camping. And why didn't he ask her if the recruiting office had granted her a Bronze Access Card? Normally it would've been the first thing out of his mouth. Something was off.

"You're a lousy liar. Tell me what's going on," she demanded.

The look on his face told her he wasn't about to budge. "Go inside and visit with your mom. She's having a rough morning."

"Don't use Mom as an excuse," she scolded, planting her hands on her hips.

A low, guttural hissing sound came from above—

Slowly, she drew her eyes to the leaden clouds, where a group of turkey buzzards circled. Her eyes widened. Uncle Jesse's strange demeanor, the buzzards circling overhead, sniffing out blood or carrion…

She pushed passed him and barged inside the shed.

"No, Abbie. Please!"

Her hope chest. On the floor. She gulped. "What the—?"

"Lemme explain." He pushed past her and sat on the chest.

They stared wild-eyed at each other. Silence spoke where words failed. Outside, not a barking dog, not a siren, nothing.

An inhuman squeak emitted from her throat.

"Right after you left," he explained, "Ty woke up and started spouting a bunch of shit. Same tirade he gave you about killing you, your mom, and me. When I went to punch him, he managed to chomp down on my arm." Uncle Jesse rolled up his plaid shirt sleeve, pulled off a bandage, and revealed the blood oozing from a full set of angry teeth marks.

Slapping a hand over her heart, Abbie croaked, "Put the bandage back on. I think I'm gonna be sick."

He obliged and finished his story. "He wouldn't let go, Abbie. The pain—I couldn't take it another second. Autopilot kicked in, and I grabbed the bat and whacked him on the head. I didn't want him dead. I didn't mean to kill him! I just wanted him to unclamp his jaw."

The visual made her wince.

"Then I heard your mom moving around." He dropped his head into his hands. "I panicked. I was terrified. I didn't know what to do." He took a deep breath. "Finally, I pulled my head out of my ass, emptied the contents of your chest onto your bed, and—"

"You put Ty inside," she finished, aghast.

"Yeah," he confessed, confirming the obvious. "When your mom got in the shower, I dragged the chest out here, and that's when you showed up."

She stared at the chest. Ty—the guy she'd spent a year of her life with, the guy she'd once cared about before learning his true nature—lay dead inside. She had wanted this… but it was only talk, right? Had she willed this to happen? Other than when Sammie had died, that degree of darkness had never filled her. Not after Dad yanked them away from Sandpoint to escape his own misery, or during the past year, when Ty had abused her emotionally. There was no way she'd allow her uncle to go to prison for merely defending himself.

"Scoop," she said, the realization hitting her like a backhand to the face. "When he figures out Ty's missing, his bloodhound instincts will send him sniffing out every square inch of Humboldt County. What are we gonna do with the chest?"

He raised a hand to stop her. "There's no 'we,' Abbie. You *are not* involved in this mess. I've already made plans for after nightfall. End of story."

"What plans? Tell me," she insisted.

"Fine. I'm heading up to Sue-meg Park. The state abandoned it years ago. Gonna check to see if the last remaining bluff drops directly into the sea. If it does, then tonight, after it's dark, I'm gonna drive the chest there, then send Ty over the edge. If the tide washes him ashore, the likelihood of Scoop or Fennimore pinning it on me will be slim to none. They'd probably think the serial killer had taken him out."

The hairs at the nape of her neck raised. She wouldn't allow Uncle Jesse to make this journey alone. "You can't hoist the chest into the bed of your truck by yourself. If you throw out your back again, you're screwed. And I know damn well you wouldn't ask for help from anyone—especially from Dad. You'd be risking him getting drunk and running his mouth."

"I dragged the chest here by myself, didn't I?"

He sounded like a petulant child. "Lifting it is a whole different ball game, and you know it."

He thought for a moment, then sighed deeply and surrendered. "I don't like this one bit, but fine. You can help me load the chest, then you'll go inside and forget everything."

Wasn't gonna happen. "You need me to help unload it, too. So what time are we leaving?"

"This is wrong on so many levels," he said, shaking his head, then buried his face in his hands. "My job is to protect you, not make you an accessory to murder."

She walked over to him and wrapped her arms around his slouching body. One thing was for sure: they'd keep this secret locked in a vault for all eternity.

CHAPTER FOUR

It was now midnight, and Abbie sat on her bed, watching tree branches cast eerie shadows on her walls. Dad had finally fallen asleep in his easy chair with the television on, and Mom had been asleep for hours. Having spent the entire day and evening fighting off a slew of clashing thoughts, Abbie couldn't shut off her brain. She envisioned Ty's bodily fluids saturating the bottom of her hope chest. She wished Uncle Jesse had rolled him up in her bedroom rug instead.

His words from yesterday looped in her head: *If Scoop bails him out of jail, and he comes here looking for her, I'll bury him.* Was Ty's death really an accident? Did it matter if it wasn't?

When Uncle Jesse walked in holding a flashlight, she winced.

"Stay here, Abbie, please," he whispered in a final entreaty, his sorrow plain on his face. "I can find a way to do this myself."

"Not on your life." She stepped to him and laid a hand on his cheek. "We're in this together."

He let out a few quick breaths, as if psyching himself up for what lay ahead.

As he guided her through the night fog, the crunching leaves underfoot sent Liza grunting off somewhere in the darkness. Liza had always hated Ty. In fact, he was the only person she had ever rammed with her head. Ty had kicked her in response. In that moment, Abbie should've defended her beloved hog. Kowtow to a guy—never again.

She held the flashlight while Uncle Jesse unlocked the padlock to the shed. As he swung open the door, there it lay, her teal-blue hope chest that had lost all hope. On the brink of a breakdown, she resisted the urge to run back to the house.

"Let's make this fast," Uncle Jesse said, holding the chest's metal side handle. "Grab your side, and we'll drag it into the alley, and don't stop 'til we get to the back of my truck."

Without replying, Abbie took hold, and they power-dragged the chest across the dirt. But with Uncle Jesse bearing most of the load, she couldn't keep up, and the chest sidewinded.

Ahead, in the shadows, was the tailgate of his truck. What if their neighbors overheard the ruckus and peeked out their window to find them maniacally dragging a chest? Scoop would certainly question them, and call them as witnesses at the trial.

At the truck, they released the handles and stared at each other, both gasping for air.

"It's gonna be a heavy son of a bitch," he said grimacing. "You're gonna have to put all your weight into it. On the count of three, lift by the handle, then finagle your leg underneath so you can hoist from the bottom, okay?"

She nodded rapidly.

"Ready?"

She hadn't stopped nodding.

"One, two, *three!*"

Nearly blowing out her bowels, she lifted with all her might, higher and higher. One more inch, and she could slip her leg underneath. But then, *bam*—the taillight busted out.

"It's okay," he said, grunting, his part of the chest rising higher than hers.

"Slow down," she begged, straining.

"Got my hand underneath," he said. "You?"

"It's too heavy—I can't do it!"

"Sure, you can! Fight for it, Abbie!"

Imagining her uncle dying in the gas chamber sent a jolt of adrenaline through her limbs, providing the strength she needed. She slipped her leg beneath, grabbed the bottom, and hoisted so high she tumbled backward—sending the chest crashing to the ground. The impact busted the latch, and Ty's folded-up body spilled out. From his resting place, he leered up at her—one eye, anyway; the swelling had pinched the other one closed, and pus or some other bodily fluid oozed from it. She retched a few times, then scrambled backward, the gravel eating into her hands. In a stupor, she fell onto her back and stared into the night sky.

Uncle Jesse rushed to her and scooped her up. "I'm gettin' you into the house."

"The hell you are!" she exclaimed. "Put me down. We're sticking to the plan."

"Stubborn, just like your mom."

"Thank you."

After hoisting the empty chest into the back of the truck, Uncle Jesse lifted Ty's torso and Abbie his legs, and they slung Ty onto the tailgate. At her uncle's insistence, he alone crammed Ty back into the chest, blood smearing his jacket.

As they drove through Eureka to Highway 101 North, Abbie, lost in a haze, stared out the window at the homeless people wrapped in black garbage bags, the storefront eaves barely protecting them from the falling rain.

"Penny for your thoughts," Uncle Jesse said softly and turned up the heat.

"You know how I love dark, drizzly nights, lying in bed, or on the couch wrapped in a blanket, reading a good book, drinking tea."

"I know," he said with a nod. "I doubt that'll comfort you in the same way again after tonight. I still think it's a mistake, you comin'."

"Leaving you alone to deal with this yourself? I'd never abandon you."

The scene from earlier when Ty spilled out of the chest made her gag.

Then, flashing lights lit up the interior of the cab, and a few bleeps from a siren accosted them. "You gotta be kidding me." Uncle Jesse squinted into the rearview mirror. "This better be Officer Fennimore and not Scoop."

She spun her head around. "It *is* Scoop! What're we gonna do?" she asked frantically.

Uncle Jesse pulled up to the curb in front of Roxie's, Ty's favorite bar, home of Eureka's greatest heavy metal cover band, Death Cross, their bass thumping like a terrified heartbeat. Ty's body was currently wearing the band T-shirt that read, BANG YUR HEAD 'TIL YUR DEAD.

The irony was not lost on her. "The fat bastard just stepped out."

Uncle Jesse peered down at his bloody jacket. Without making a scene, he casually unzipped it and slipped his arms through the sleeves. The second after he crammed it under the seat, Scoop tapped on the window with his flashlight.

When Uncle Jesse opened the window, the smell of cigarette smoke and weed from Roxie's flooded the cab. "Evening, Scoop. What's the problem?"

A droplet of snot hung from the tip of his pitted nose. He shined his flashlight inside the truck, waving it around as if looking for something. Domination was his game, like Ty's. "You got a busted-out taillight."

To Abbie's horror, Scoop then shined the flashlight on her hope chest. She slid down in the seat as she imagined him climbing aboard and opening it. She clutched the door handle, her knuckles white.

"Whatcha hauling this chest around for?" Scoop moved in for a closer look.

Abbie sat upright and spun her head around. On the passenger side, the lid of the chest had pinched a piece of fabric from Ty's flannel shirt, and it fluttered in the breeze. If Scoop circled the truck, he'd recognize it as the shirt he'd bought for Ty's twenty-third birthday last month.

"Oh, that," Uncle Jesse said calmly. "Abbie's helping me move some tools from our house to my auto shop. Big job first thing in the morning. Gotta be prepared, ya know."

Scoop leaned inside the cab and sniffed. He pulled out a Breathalyzer from his coat and held it to Uncle Jesse's mouth. "Blow hard."

"Aw, you know damn well I quit the swill years ago, Scoop. But whatever," Uncle Jesse said, losing his patience. He took a deep breath and blew.

Scoop inspected the gauge reader. "Jesse, Jesse, Jesse. You must have had a wee relapse. Point one nine—way over the legal limit."

"That's bullshit!" Uncle Jesse shouted, losing his cool.

Scoop dropped the Breathalyzer into his pocket. From the other pocket, he pulled out an electronic ticket pad and wrote him up for a DUI and the busted-out taillight. "Sign here," he ordered.

Staring straight ahead, Uncle Jesse sat with his lips pursed.

"Sign the damn pad," Abbie urged quietly.

"This is bullshit!" he shouted again, then begrudgingly signed.

"Tell you what," Scoop said with the same shit-eating grin as Ty's, "you have that pretty little niece of yours drop the charges and the restraining order against Ty tomorrow, and I'll hit the delete button on your DUI indiscretion."

"Yes, sir," Abbie piped up. "First thing in the morning."

"Good girl. Now, best hightail it outta here."

She prayed Scoop would be the one hightailing his dishonest ass outta here before Ty's rogue fabric caught his attention.

He strode away, then stopped and headed back to the truck. He asked Abbie, "You seen Ty around?"

The memory of Ty's gooey red eye leered at her. "No, sir. When you see him, tell him he better return the money he stole from my bank account to buy drugs with."

"Best watch your mouth, Abbie. My boy don't steal from little girls." He crammed a wad of tobacco in his bottom lip, then he sauntered to his patrol car like he was the king of Humboldt County.

Twenty-five miles north of Eureka, the Sitka spruce trees along the Redwood Highway towered like shadowy corpses rising from the grave. And now Ty would soon find his grave at sea. A roll of thunder echoed from someplace in the distance. Abbie leaned forward and peered into the black sky, where veins of lightning flashed inside the ominous low-hanging clouds.

"Almost there, darlin'," Uncle Jesse said.

"I can't shake this feeling someone's following us," she replied, paranoia's claws digging in.

"I've been on the lookout," he reassured her. "Hasn't been a car for miles." Turning left into the abandoned park, he drove past the moss-covered registration kiosk, its windows long since busted out. They followed the meandering road through the trees and finally parked at the trailhead. Judging by the undisturbed soil, nobody had used it for weeks, if not months. Nobody dared hike there anymore. With the rising sea levels, landslides had sent most of the park into the sea.

The incoming fog lent an eerie calm to the scene. When Uncle Jesse killed the high beams, the dimmer light illuminated the bluff's edge, maybe twenty feet away. She rolled down her window and listened. The dull, relentless roar of the surf crashing on the rocks below made her shudder.

"Spooky," he said, taking her hand and squeezing gently. They stared straight ahead.

None of this nightmare would've happened had Ty not hit her that night at the zoo. Why did she ever climb into his Silverado? She knew how unstable he had become, how he could snap over the most insignificant things he deemed disrespectful.

With a heavy sigh, she pulled her hand away from Uncle Jesse's. "Let's get this over with."

He nodded. "You drop the tailgate, and I'll get into the bed and push the chest toward you. Easing it to the ground will be a hell of a lot easier than hoisting the son of a bitch."

As it turned out, her uncle was right, as usual. Gravity was their friend.

"On the count of three," he said. "One, two, three, *go*!"

The headlights guiding their way, Uncle Jesse led as they dragged the chest over the soft bed of tree needles and small branches. He stopped within a foot of the bluff's edge, the roaring surf now deafening. Unlatching the chest, he said breathlessly, "From here on out, I'm finishing what I started. Go back to the truck," he ordered.

Abbie ignored him and stubbornly dropped to her butt, eased her legs back, and set her feet on the side of the chest.

Reluctantly, he sat next to her. "One, two, three!" And they catapulted Ty into the abyss.

Air—she needed air. *Breathe, breathe...* She lay on her back, clutching her throat. Peering up into the trees, numb to her core, she said, "Try finding him now, Scoop Hawkins, you worthless piece of shit."

CHAPTER FIVE

Wednesday, December 19

Dear Journal,

I could've sworn the nightmare was real. Ty's cold, dead hand reached out to clamp my ankle, and my body scraped along the dirt until it gave way to an endless free fall toward the sea. As we fell, he worked himself eye to eye with me, his breath smelling like death as it blew into my face. "Together forever, baby," he maliciously whispered into the wind. As we were about to hit the black sea, I jolted awake and sat upright, drenched in sweat. What Uncle Jesse and I had done last night with Ty's body—was it real, or had it been a nightmare? Good God—it was as real as the bile leeching up my throat.

I'll be honest with you. I'm glad Uncle Jesse killed him. Does that make me a bad person? What constitutes morality? Is it enough to be a good person in general? Who decides what's morally acceptable in society anyway? The people in power have broken the system, and since repairing it seems unlikely, isn't it justifiable to take matters into my own hands? Vigilante justice. Why not? It feels like the world is ending anyway.

Love,
Abbie

SHE HIT CTRL+A ON HER KEYBOARD, and as she deleted the journal entry, the doorbell rang. Then it rang again. Why wasn't anyone answering? More importantly, why would anybody disturb them at this early hour? Heavy-footed, she made her way to the door.

Shit. It was none other than Scoop Hawkins and his tyrannical smirk.

"Top o' the day to you, Abbie."

Would he sense her guilt about what they'd done with his son's corpse? With all Scoop's flaws, he was a damn good detective. "What do you want, Scoop? Kinda early for a social visit."

"You hear from Ty yet? He didn't come home last night."

Nonchalantly, she reached for the doorjamb to steady herself. "No, sir. Ask Darrin. That's his bouncer friend down at Roxie's."

"Already spoke to him. Ty woulda let me know if he wasn't gonna come home. Somethin's wrong."

"He'll turn up," she said, feeling half bad for him. "Probably hanging with friends."

His worry turned to anger. "Just a friendly reminder to drop those charges and the restraining order against Ty if you wanna keep your uncle outta jail. You got today, and that's it."

Bastard. Empathy—screw it. She slammed the door and fought from breaking into a crying fit. As she stepped into the kitchen to douse her sorrows in caffeine, the doorbell rang again. She threw her arms up in the air with exasperation. "What the hell is it now?"

But it wasn't Scoop. It was a silent metallic hydrogen drone.

"Abilene Spencer?" it asked in a feathery woman's voice.

"Yes, it's me."

Its mouth, shaped like the cash dispenser on an ATM, opened, and out rolled an envelope. "Use a finger to sign on the signature pad." A white screen popped up.

Abbie took the envelope and signed, and the drone floated away. She opened the envelope and read:

To Ms. Abilene Spencer:

After much consideration, we have selected you for the live-in kitchen porter/servant position. Please read and sign the enclosed contract and disclosure forms and bring them with you on Thursday, December 20, at 9:00 a.m. Use the WOODLAND bus stop. The enclosed map will guide you to Redwood Manor. Use the front gated entrance (pass code included) and follow the signs to the staff entrance. We are looking forward to meeting you.

Signed,
Ms. Barker
Chief of Staff

Job interview yesterday, and a drone-delivered acceptance letter today? Last night's traumatic deed overshadowed what should have been a momentous occasion. Finding herself alone in the house, Abbie figured the best way to purge the dark thoughts from her head was to visit Uncle Jesse at his auto shop and share her good news. But first, she called her current boss and apologized for having to quit her job so abruptly.

Now it was time to pretend Ty was alive and hit the courthouse to comply with Scoop's blackmail demand.

After leaving the courthouse and driving to meet up with Uncle Jesse, Abbie spotted Tony Wilkens, her veteran friend, leaning against the wheel of an abandoned train car at the base of the old railroad crossing. She threw her Subaru into park and jumped out.

A joint hung from his lips, but when he tried to light up, the wind killed the flame. As she shielded the joint with her hands, he inhaled a deep puff, held it, then exhaled.

"This is some good bud, Abbie," he said, a wave of euphoria softening his face. "Wanna hit?"

"No, thanks. I'm good." She hated the stuff; it made her paranoid. Studying his olive-and-tan camo shorts, she said, "Winter's here. I hope you have warmer clothes."

"Winter? Time sure is having its way with me." His eyes closed slowly, and as he withdrew to someplace in his mind, he made a pained face and twitched a few times. Abbie wondered if it was bad weed or shell shock that had stolen his moment of peace. Tucking five bucks into his hand, she told him yet again the war had ended. But she doubted karma would get her back into God's good graces—if there was a God. She doubted that, too. Tony would insist otherwise. She enjoyed their philosophical debates.

Driving south on Myrtle Avenue, Abbie circled the wall clockwise and turned right on Harris Street. She parked in front of Uncle Jesse's auto shop, formerly a brewery, the steam-fired kettles still standing in the back room. She was proud of him for saving the money to rent the building and start his own business. And since he'd become the go-to guy for anything mechanical, business had picked up. He refused to apply for a Bronze Access Card, though; he'd never feel comfortable associating with those snooty Port Allegiance types.

She hadn't seen him since they returned home from the bluff at 2:30 earlier that morning. They'd hugged while standing in the hallway, then parted ways to their bedrooms, both too despondent to drag their feet another inch.

When she stepped out of her Subaru, the sound of his pneumatic torque wrench rapid-fired like a machine gun. After last night's horror show, she questioned how he could focus on work. She zigzagged through a slew of broken-down cars, the scent of auto grease conjuring sweet memories of handing her grandpa Spencer tools while sitting in the engine cavity of his classic '73 Ford pickup. It was probably worth a fortune by now. But Dad had pawned it to pay for their move to California. *What an idiot.*

Bells jingled as she entered the main office. Uncle Jesse's assistant, Kevin, straight out of high school, sat at the computer, wearing greasy overalls and a JESSE'S AUTO baseball cap.

"Hey, Abbie. Haven't seen you in ages. Whatcha been up to?"

She hung her purse on the wall-mounted coatrack she'd made for Uncle Jesse's birthday last year. "Oh, livin' the life, you know?"

He stood, leaned closer to her, and whispered, "What's going on with your uncle? He's in a weird mood."

"Did you ask him?"

"No. He's sending out some pretty dark energy. Thought it best if I kept my distance."

"No idea." She shrugged as she lied.

Something shiny on the desk caught her attention: a pile of rectangular metal objects, similar in shape and size to a credit card, but somewhat smaller. She picked up the top one and studied it. "What is this newfangled doohickey? And why does it say 'Jesse's Auto Repair' on one side?"

"Oh, that. It's called a QDAC. Stands for Quick Data Access Card. Stays in your wallet. Just sync it with the same eye you synced your computer with, and you're good to go. Holds up to ten terabytes. We found a great deal on a hundred of them, and if customers pay their bill in full, they get one."

Abbie shook her head. "Wow. Where have I been? Aren't you small-town boys advanced now?"

"Hell, yeah, we are. Take one."

"Really?" She flipped it around in her hand.

"Your uncle would insist. Lemme get 'im for you. Don't reckon you came here to see me," he joked.

She slipped the memory card into her wallet—like she needed more useless junk. "Thanks, Kevin. It's nice to see you."

Smiling, he ambled to the garage and hollered, "Hey, Jess, you have a visitor!"

"Be right there!" Uncle Jesse called back, his words stifled, as if he'd crammed his face into a muffler. He rolled to the office while still lying on a creeper and peeked in. When their eyes met, he froze. Last night's shared memory transcended any words.

"I need to talk to you," she said.

A quick nod, and he hoisted himself off the ground and stepped into the office. He looked at Kevin and said, "Kev, can we have the office for a minute?"

"No prob. I'll start organizing the new air filters."

"Before you do that," Uncle Jesse said, "please finish greasing Mrs. Bledsoe's bearings. She'll be here any minute."

"On it." Kevin nodded and closed the door behind him.

Uncle Jesse grabbed two bottles of water from his mini fridge and handed one to Abbie. He sat behind the desk and gestured for her to sit in the chair across from him. "You able to sleep?"

She cracked open her bottle and chugged. "No. Slept like shit. Could've slept all day, but Scoop came by. He's worried because Ty didn't come home last night."

"Let the bastard worry," he said.

Abbie nodded. "Exactly how I feel. Just left the courthouse. I dropped the charges against Ty. If Scoop doesn't drop the DUI charges against you, so help me God…"

If Uncle Jesse's looks could kill, Scoop's fate would be the same as Ty's. Time to share the good news. "Guess what? After Scoop left, a drone delivered a letter for me. That job I applied for—I got it! It's at a place called Redwood Manor."

He stared at her for a moment and grinned. "Well, I'll be damned. With the drama I created, I forgot to ask you how it went at the recruiting office. What job did you get?"

"Servant slash kitchen porter. I'll work under the head chef and ensure the kitchen stays clean and orderly, plus do basic food prep, washing, peeling—you name it. Grunt work, mostly, but it's okay, you know how I love to cook. Not knocking Mom, but it'd be cool to learn how to cook professionally."

"Awesome. So, you'll have a bunch of duties. No more standing at a conveyor belt for hours on end mindlessly lopping off fish heads. When do you start?"

"I have to be there tomorrow morning at nine."

"Geez, that soon?"

"I'm not complaining. Already called my boss and quit. He wasn't happy with the short notice."

"Aw, who cares? There's no lack of workers out there to replace you. Glad you're movin' on, darlin'." He began chewing the inside of his cheek, his mind palpably heavy. "We need to address the elephant in the room, though. But damn, this is gonna be tough."

"It doesn't need to be," she said.

"How could it not? What I did, what I allowed you to help me with… The effect it'll have on you… I was dead wrong. I should've made you go back into the house. You shouldn't have to live with the image of Ty spilling out of—"

"Stop," she said. "Yeah, that was the worst part. But I'm relieved he's dead, and I'm not saying it to make you feel better. He would've killed Mom, you, and me—there's no doubt about it. You have no idea the shit he subjected me to the last few months we were together."

Uncle Jesse paused before speaking. "Why did you stay with him? Please help me understand."

This time, she wouldn't clam up like she had when he drove her to the hospital. But even now, with her limited energy, it would be hard to offer him a full psychoanalysis of her motives.

"It's complicated," she said introspectively. "I've worked out the reasons why in my head, and trust me, I won't ever allow another guy to control me again. Can that be a good enough answer for you?"

He shot her a proud smile as he nodded. "Okay, darlin'. Good for you. Blue skies ahead, right?"

"Nothin' but," she agreed. "Hey, you super busy today?"

"A few small jobs. Why?"

"Let's go home and grab our rifles. We'll head up into the mountains and have some target practice therapy, blow off a little steam."

"You're on, darlin'," he said without hesitation.

CHAPTER SIX

Thursday, December 20

Dear Journal,

Today signifies the end of an era, but my mood doesn't match this exciting day, my first day working at Redwood Manor. I see Ty everywhere. Even in my damn coffee cup, swirling around like he's drowning. His hand reaches up and grips the rim of my cup, his gooey, deranged eyes pleading for help. Can Uncle Jesse and I have a normal life after what we did?

Wish I was little again. I miss the elaborate tales Uncle Jesse told in a spot-on Southern accent, about a little girl (me) and a vicious, gun-toting cat named Guillermo (imaginary). We traveled the Wild West by horseback and hunted outlaws. We didn't kill any, only dragged 'em back to the sheriff. The simple black-and-white stories he told usually ended with the good guys saving the day. But things aren't so black and white in real life, and the clarity I used to have about right vs. wrong is foggy in my mind.

And leaving Mom—I know she's happy I got a better job, but her eyes tell me she's gonna be lonely. And I'm scared to be on my own, away from her. Will my new co-workers accept me? Will they be cliquish? Will they treat me like an outcast and bully me, like the kids did in school? Can I fake being social? Sure would be a hell of a lot easier if I could wear my stocking cap. Guess it's time to retire it.

Love,
Abbie

DRESSED IN A SECONDHAND red turtleneck and black pants, Abbie sat before the lighted mirror on her desk. Ty hadn't allowed her to wear mascara, so she piled it on just to spite him. His accusations blared in her head. *Who is he?! Who are you trying to impress?* Ridiculous. No way she wanted another boyfriend. Ever.

Digging through her dresser drawer, she found a pair of knee-high stockings, then sat on her bed and eased them over her stubbly legs. Nobody would notice. She'd already laid out shoes—a pair of black Capezios with a cute strap that wrapped around her ankle—and slipped her feet into them. Then she inspected her outfit, adjusted it, and made sure she looked as acceptable as possible.

"Port Allegiance, here I come," she said with determination.

In the living room, Mom was watching a broadcast journalist give a live report from the town of Galt, California, fifteen miles from the Rancho Seco Nuclear Generating Station.

"What's going on?" Abbie asked.

Mom shook her head. "I always said reopening that nuclear power plant was a terrible idea."

"A toxic waste leak?" Abbie asked, peering at the news ticker.

"They're not sure. A dozen or more people have developed lung cancer in the surrounding area. What could possibly go wrong with the new safeguards?" she said sarcastically.

"Hope they figure it out."

Dad, in his pajamas, sauntered in, scratching his ass. "We all gotta die sometime," he announced unhelpfully.

Abbie bristled. "Could you be any more callous?"

"'Callous' is my middle name." He disappeared into the kitchen, his middle finger swaying in the air.

Bastard.

"Don't let him get to you," Mom said as she stood.

She didn't look like her usual unkempt self. In fact, she looked beautiful, even—a touch of mascara, some lipstick, and she was wearing her best dress, a navy-blue wraparound that hung above the knee. She had a great figure. "Wow, you look terrific," Abbie said. "What's the occasion?"

"Since you're beginning a new life, I thought I'd better, too. I met a lady at the library. She invited me to join her book club. I can't remember the last time I read a book."

Before Sammie died. Mom was fighting to break out of her shell. It was as if she was giving Abbie permission to leave the nest, to find her own way in life. And in response, Mom could take ownership of her life again. Dr. Xavier's B_{12} shot had worked! He deserved a big thank you.

"Proud of you, Mom." Abbie gave her a hug. "I hope someday we can talk about—"

"I hope so, too." Ana nodded into her daughter's neck, then pulled away, tears pooling in her eyes. "Go show Port Allegiance what you're made of, my beautiful, capable daughter. I love you. Now get going before you miss your bus."

Standing outside the Port Allegiance Port of Entry, waiting to enter the white prison transport bus—that's what it looked like, given the barred windows—Abbie shivered, her breath steaming in the gray early-morning air. Calm down, she told herself. She had allowed more than enough time to get to Redwood Manor. At least she was at the front of the line. Hopefully the driver had cranked up the heat.

Pulse racing, she passed through the metal detector, then followed protocol and opened her mouth so the guard could administer the contagious disease scan. He nodded; she had passed. She exhaled deeply when the gate opened. Maneuvering down the bus's center aisle, she held her breath for a moment. God, she hated the stink of public transportation, but Port Allegiance not allowing her to drive in would save her money.

She took the last seat at the back of the bus and looked out the window, avoiding eye contact with the people still searching for seats. Then somebody plopped down next to her—a large man, probably thirtysomething, whose girth spilled over into her seat. Abbie hoped he wouldn't initiate a conversation. As luck had it, he whipped out a newspaper and read. Abbie surreptitiously checked out the headline.

NATIONAL UNEMPLOYMENT TOPS 36%
State Governors to Meet in D.C.

"Good going, President Dung Heap Daniels, right?" the man said, turning to her.

Disparaging nicknames for people one disagreed with weren't moving the country forward. And if he thought she was going to agree with him, it wasn't gonna happen, regardless of their similar political leanings. Uncle Jesse had said never to discuss politics or religion unless you were ready to defend your opinion with your life—literally, in the current political climate. One person's opinion never changed another's, and maybe, just maybe, one's opinion was based on a fallacy. Abbie ignored the man—but the headline was a stark reminder of how truly lucky she was to have a job.

As they passed through the military-style tollbooth into Port Allegiance, the world outside transformed from grayscale to Technicolor. No homeless people with their garbage and waste piled everywhere. Here, charming old-world streetlamps burned with golden halos and captured the dissipating fog in their light. She gazed out at the boutique windows, all decorated for the upcoming Christmas. Only a few people decorated on their block in Eureka. Mom was one of them; she strove to instill the spirit of the season in the entire neighborhood.

The bus passed restaurants and art galleries, full of people spending ridiculous amounts of money on things they didn't need. Was it Abbie's imagination or did the people of Port Allegiance seem like a different species than those in Eureka? Even the weather behaved differently, like the neighboring cities existed on separate planes.

After a few minutes, the bus stopped, and the neon banner at the front read, WOODLAND, her destination. A handful of people stepped off, then the man next to her. She followed, her heart doing cartwheels. What was this new life going to look like? Would she have to socialize with her co-workers? Stupid question. Of course, she'd have to try.

First foot on the pavement, and the aroma of freshly brewed coffee and baked goods welcomed her, gifting her a moment's peace. Directly across the sidewalk, tucked away in a small alcove between Harper Books and Bob's Pet Supply sat Miller's Coffee Shop. She checked the map Ms. Barker had provided in her acceptance letter, and calculated the walk to Redwood Manor would take less than ten minutes. With more than an hour to spare, she thought a hot beverage sounded good. It would make her feel more at home in this strange new city.

Inside, a pretty barista smiled and welcomed her into the dim, cozy place. The soothing sounds of Celtic music played in the background. Eager to sample the good life, Abbie stood under the ORDER HERE sign and asked the barista, "What's your most popular drink?"

The barista rubbed her chin and turned to the menu behind her. "Hmm…I'd say the triple-shot latte."

The eye-popping price induced a gulp. "Nine seventy-five?"

"Plus two dollars for the extra shot."

Why not? thought Abbie with a shrug. It would be her first and last.

As she waited for her drink, she spotted a group of people in their early to mid-twenties, probably university students, their heads buried in their laptops. It was well known that Port Allegiance hosted the most prestigious medical school in the country, and that it was at the forefront of many clinical studies. Only the elite attended, and Abbie was definitely not included.

After a moment, the barista called her name. With her hot drink and suitcase in tow, she found an overstuffed brown leather chair tucked away in a corner niche. She set her purse on the rustic side table next to a copper lamp with a mica shade. As she sipped her latte, she listened to some of the students debate whether viruses could be considered alive. One opposing student, a young woman sparking with ambition, said viruses were incapable of replicating independently, that they must replicate within a host cell, and therefore viruses were not alive. Her male classmate refuted her claim by saying viruses originated in proto-virocells, were cellular in nature, and evolved from a common ancestor, and therefore were indeed alive.

Whatever the truth was, and whether Abbie fully understood it or not, she wanted to join in on the conversation, as the topic sounded interesting. One day she hoped to be a part of such a group, but for now, she had saved a mere pittance for tuition fees. After listening for a while, she took a deep breath. It was time to enter her new world—the world of Redwood Manor.

CHAPTER SEVEN

After turning the corner at Harper Books, Abbie entered a residential neighborhood where old Victorian houses lined the streets. Built in the early nineteen hundreds, she guessed. This surprised her, as she had imagined Port Allegiance to be a modern-day city with modern-day sterile homes. She pulled out the map again.

4355 Waterfront Drive—a block away. With her suitcase wheels wobbling off-kilter, she passed some well-to-dos jogging along the hedge-lined sidewalks, their perfectly groomed designer dogs wearing more expensive clothes than her own. *A gold leash and rhinestone collar—seriously?*

At Redwood Manor, she approached an arched iron gate flanked by heavy stone columns on either side. She found the keypad embedded in the column to the left, then checked the map again

for the pass code. When she typed in *aardvark.71*, the gate slid open.

Strolling along the cobblestone lane, she passed beneath a canopy of ivy-covered oak trees. A bucolic grassy pasture peeked through the trunks, taking her breath away. She inhaled the fresh bay air. A little farther up, around a bend in the distance, stood the Victorian mansion, with its multiple steeply pitched roof gables and tall, narrow windows with diamond-shaped panes. To the mansion's right, about a hundred yards out, was the city wall.

Abbie stood there a moment and imagined living in such a grand house—a new life away from Eureka. Drawing in a few deep breaths, she was ready—readier than ever.

Thirty yards on, she approached a fork in the driveway. In the center, nailed to a post, stood a rustic carved wood sign reading MAIN ENTRANCE, with an arrow pointing left, and SERVICE AND STAFF ENTRANCE, with an arrow pointing right. A cherry-red Volkswagen Beetle with tinted windows and a license plate that said GIRL TOY passed her, heading toward the manor.

Abbie stood before the iron-hinged wooden door, with bronze statues of armed men in uniform on either side. World War II era, she guessed. Counting down from five, she rang the bell.

Soon a man with silver hair, mid- to late fifties, wearing a black suit and bow tie answered. "Abilene Spencer, I presume?"

"Yes, sir. Today's my first day of work."

"Welcome to Redwood Manor's east wing. I'm Rex Clark, the butler. Please come in and follow me to the staff dormitory."

She stepped into a twelve-by-twelve wood-paneled room —a mudroom of sorts, with a boot rack and brass hooks for hanging coats. As she admired the framed photos of different breeds of horses hanging on the walls, the scent of Drakkar Noir cologne filled her nose, like her grandpa used to wear. Rex smelled divine.

"I understand you've come from Eureka," he said as Abbie followed him along the hall's dark, wide-planked wooden floor.

"Yes, sir. I'm happy to be in your clean, beautiful city." She chuckled silently at how he clenched his butt cheeks as he strode along. It reminded her of Uncle Jesse after he had eaten at the Roadkill Buffet and developed a bad case of the shits.

"I don't suppose you'll miss home, then," he said and turned down one of the mazelike corridors.

"I'll miss my family a lot, but it's okay—they're right over the wall."

"A sentimental girl. That's a rare commodity these days."

Sentimental. The word suited her perfectly.

He stopped at a flight of stairs leading down. "Here, let me take your suitcase," he offered, and with that, they descended the creaking, oak-wainscoted stairwell smelling of lemon wood polish. At the bottom, dim sconces illuminated a long hallway with four doors: three to the left, and one on their right, which read RESTROOM. He opened the first one on the left and ushered her in. "Your bedroom, Ms. Spencer."

The small room had a twin bed topped with a fluffy white duvet and crisp white pillows, along with tasteful decor. There was an antique desk; royal-blue-and-gold brocade drapes lined the tall, oversized windows; and next to them was a French door overlooking a cement-rimmed goldfish pond. In the far distance, near the thirty-foot-high stone wall, nestled a group of palm trees.

When she turned to Rex to gush about the view, he was sitting on her bed, smoothing out the duvet. *Weird.* Why sit there when a wing chair sat five feet away?

"You have fifteen minutes to unpack," he said and stood. "When I come back, I will expect your hair to be in a bun, and you dressed in your uniform, which is hanging in the closet. I will then introduce you to the chief of staff, Ms. Barker."

Abbie was still stuck on him sitting on her bed. So inappropriate. "Thank you, sir. I'll be ready."

He left and closed the door behind him.

She meandered around, taking in her new space. On her nightstand rested a black book embossed with the red and gold Port Allegiance symbol. Beside it was a cell phone. She'd ignore these items until someone explained them. The bedroom was extravagant in comparison to her rat-infested room at home. Although only several miles lay between here and there, she felt a galaxy away.

Flinging her suitcase onto the bed, she unpacked her socks and underwear and carefully arranged them in the highboy dresser. That Rex, sitting on her bed? Maybe Ty had screwed up her sensors. Besides, Rex's age probably precluded him from acting on carnal thoughts. She bet he struggled to make it through the night without his prostate pressing on his bladder.

Inside the tiny closet hung four white short-sleeved jumpsuits with black-and-white pinstriped aprons draped over top, and below, a pair of black-and-white Oxford shoes. Puzzled, she dropped to her knees and lifted the tongue of one shoe. How'd they know her size?

She nearly pissed herself when Rex appeared behind her. "What in the—"

"I knocked, Ms. Spencer, but you didn't answer. Why aren't you dressed?"

The creeper hadn't knocked. Shaken, she checked her watch. "You said fifteen minutes. It's been five."

"You're mistaken, my dear. I said five."

She wouldn't argue. But the aroma of Drakkar Noir wouldn't incite warm feelings again.

"Get dressed," he ordered, towering above her. "I'll wait for you at the foot of the stairs. And don't forget your signed contract and disclosure forms."

"Yes, sir." His lack of respect for her privacy bothered her, but it wasn't her place to question him. She dressed hurriedly, then arranged her hair into a bun. Before leaving the room to meet him, she checked to assure the door had a lock. She was relieved to see it did.

Following Rex upstairs and along a window-lined corridor with inlaid peacock marble flooring, she concluded his roadkill butt shuffle wasn't so amusing anymore.

He stopped at an office and leaned into the room. "Ms. Spencer's here."

"Wonderful. Bring her in," a woman said, standing from her desk, where a wall of expansive windows behind her overlooked a courtyard.

Abbie gawked at her six-inch-high feat of an auburn beehive. For a woman likely in her sixties, her body rivaled any fit thirtysomething. On the guest side of the desk stood a girl about Abbie's age with flawless ebony skin and black hair, cropped on the sides, with somewhat longer coils on top. Their matching uniforms looked a lot more stylish on her tall, lean frame than on Abbie's.

"Hello, Abilene. I'm Ms. Barker, but please call me Ms. B."

Abbie nodded, adoring her regal British accent. "Please call me Abbie."

"Of course, dear," she said warmly. "And this lovely girl beside you is Skyla Bishop. She has the bedroom next to yours. I asked her to join us because she will be your mentor for the next few weeks until you acclimate."

Abbie and Skyla both reached in for a handshake. There was something about this girl with big brown eyes. Her underlying expression conflicted with her chipper disposition, as if she was in an internal battle of someone forcing her to act polite, but with a gun held to her head. Abbie sensed she was harboring something deep.

"Glad to get some extra help," Skyla said, motioning for Abbie to sit beside her. "Being one person short puts a burden on the rest of the staff."

"I'm grateful to be here," Abbie responded, taking a seat. "Am I replacing somebody?" She couldn't imagine anyone leaving this gorgeous mansion.

"Yes," Ms. B jumped in. "You're replacing Gia Quinn, who quit suddenly and without notice. Seems she was unable to handle the fast-paced environment, as we have events planned nearly every day of the week. Do you think *you* can handle the pressure?"

"Yes, ma'am," Abbie said, having mastered the art of faking emotional acuity. She was focused so hard on the proper eye-contact-to-looking-away ratio that she hoped Ms. B wouldn't catch how utterly terrified she was. "My former job kept me busy. I prefer it that way. Beats mindlessly twiddling your thumbs all day."

Ms. B smiled, her teeth big and white. "You'll fit in perfectly, then. Your resume said you worked at Pacific One

Fishery in Eureka. I don't imagine you had many fringe benefits working there."

Abbie sat more upright. "No, ma'am. The *only* benefit of living and working in Eureka is the open 10G Wi-Fi spilling over your wall and scrambling our brains."

Ms. B and Skyla laughed, and Abbie felt foolish for inciting laughter; that hadn't been her intention. "If you don't mind me asking, what are the black book and cell phone for next to my bed?"

Skyla collected herself. "The book is the Port Allegiance Manifesto."

"Study it thoroughly," Ms. B added. "It will teach you everything you need to know about the city's rules and regulations, as well as the Redwood Manor rules for proper etiquette when addressing the homeowners and their houseguests. And the cell phone is for you. We use them to communicate among ourselves. You may be asked to run errands off the premises, and this way we can contact you if needed."

An excellent idea, Abbie thought. "I've never had a cell phone. Can I use it to call my family in Eureka and give them the phone number?"

"Of course, dear," Ms. B said. "But only use it for personal calls during break time. And remember, it's against covenant to disclose anything about our society. I've already programmed the phone with the main Redwood Manor phone number, as well as mine and Mr. De Young's."

"The boss's husband," Abbie noted.

Skyla chuckled. "Yes, you can call him Ben."

Ms. B stood. "It was he who watched your video interview—said you were a diamond in the rough. He told me if I didn't hire you, I was a fool."

Taken aback, Abbie squirmed in her seat at the flattery. "Don't know why he'd want me. I completely flubbed the interview."

"He must've seen something honest in you," Skyla observed. "He's an attorney; he has an uncanny knack for spotting sincerity."

Ms. B stood and addressed Abbie. "Come, let's head into the kitchen, and I'll introduce you to the kitchen staff. Then Skyla will show you around the house, after which you can study the Port Allegiance Manifesto. There will be a quiz, but I expect you'll do well. At tomorrow night's soiree, you can show the homeowners how capable you are. Ready?"

"As ready as I'll ever be. I'm pretty nervous."

"Don't be," Skyla said reassuringly. "Most everyone here is awesome."

Most?

A disapproving look crossed Ms. B's face, and Skyla apologized under her breath. Then the three of them walked to the industrial, state-of-the-art kitchen, which the staff had decorated in the spirit of Christmas, which was five days away.

"Listen up," Ms. B said to the three people busily working. "I want to introduce you to Abbie Spencer. She'll be taking over Gia's position. Please stop what you're doing and state your name and job duty, and anything else you want to share with her."

A sixtysomething man with obviously dyed brown hair stepped forward first, wearing a stained white apron that hugged his protruding belly. He took her hand in a hearty handshake. "Finally have some help! Welcome to my domain, Ms. Abbie. I'm Clem, the head chef."

"Trained at Le Cordon Bleu in Paris," Ms. B boasted on his behalf. "He also gave twenty years to the armed forces."

"Very impressive," Abbie said.

A guy in his mid-twenties with an oversized hook nose and short-cropped sandy hair approached. "I'm Carter Waldron, sous-chef."

Clem saluted him. "My sidekick extraordinaire. Going on eighteen months now."

Carter saluted back, their relationship clearly close and lighthearted.

"It's a pleasure to meet you, Carter," Abbie said. "Where are you from?"

"Compton," he said and cringed. "After I got my access card, I lived in Eureka a few years, waiting for an unwitting soul to hire me."

"That would be me," Ms. B said. "Haven't regretted it a single day."

"Brave of you," Abbie said to Carter.

"Brave?" he asked, his eyes a striking shade of green.

"Brave to stay in Eureka, I mean."

He chuckled. "Eureka's a walk in the park compared to Compton."

"Okay, okay, you're a tough guy, we get it," said a pretty, petite girl with chestnut-brown hair gathered into a low bun. She had an upturned nose and full lips, and boobs men probably drooled over. "Hi, Abbie. I'm Kristine Mallory, the brave one's sidekick, and your bedroom neighbor downstairs. I've been here in the kitchen for three years now. It's been an awesome gig, but my passion is the stage," she confided.

She had a snarky tone, and Abbie wasn't impressed with the way she had demeaned Carter. "It's nice to meet you," Abbie said, her words not entirely sincere. "You're an actor?"

"Nah, I prefer working behind the scenes. You'll have to check out the upcoming musical at the local playhouse in two weeks." When she squeezed Abbie's hand and peered at her with spooky black eyes, Abbie instinctively tried to pull away, but Kristine held tight. It was as though she had no irises, only pupils.

"I'd love to," Abbie said unenthusiastically. *NOT.*

"Coolio," Kristine said and loosened her grip. "I'm sure we'll have gobs of girl fun—maybe even a slumber party!"

Girl fun? Girl toy? The red Volkswagen had to be hers. The car payment likely devoured her entire paycheck. There'd be no girl fun between them.

Two guys with shaggy black hair, twentyish, entered the kitchen and stopped, their faces showing discomfort at having walked in on a group meeting. Abbie studied them and noticed they were twins.

"Perfect timing," Ms. B said to them, then addressed Abbie. "Meet Devon and David, housekeepers extraordinaire. They bunk in a cabin with Carter down by our marina."

Abbie approached and offered her hand to the left one first, but he shunned her, his arms stiff against his body. *Odd.* She wouldn't risk another rejection from the other one. "It's very nice to meet you both." With that, they backed out of the room and disappeared around the corner.

"Okay, Abbie's mine for a while," Skyla announced. "Gonna show her around the house."

"Don't get lost," Clem teased.

"See you ladies in the killing fields later," Carter said and pointed an imaginary rifle at Kristine. "You're mine, my fair maiden."

Kristine turned and lifted her backside as if saying, "Kiss my prissy ass."

It wasn't a smidgen cute, as much as Kristine tried. As Skyla pulled Abbie through the kitchen, Abbie asked her what the "killing fields" were.

"Every Thursday, Ms. B organizes a team-building exercise. Later today, we're hitting Journey's Edge Sports Pavilion and having a paintball war, then next week, it's a skeet shooting competition."

Team activities, *ugh*—Abbie's worst school nightmare. She wasn't going to complain, though; she'd say something cooperative. "How fun! I love shooting."

"Gia loved shooting, too," Skyla recalled, her chipper personality darkening. "Everybody wanted her on their team."

There was an interesting story buried in Skyla, and in the twins, too. To Abbie's surprise, she was curious to learn more.

At the far end of the kitchen, Skyla stopped at an eight-by-five-foot giant monitor hanging on the wall. "There are three columns," she explained. "The one on the left is staff schedules, and in the middle are the different events planned during the following months. On the right is where Clem posts the breakfast, lunch, and dinner menus, along with each staff member's duties."

"Wow," Abbie said, reading for a moment. "This place is a well-oiled machine."

Skyla leaned in and said quietly, "Has to be, or Mrs. De Young will come unhinged. Tell ya later how to avoid trouble with her."

Abbie raised her brows and leaned into the monitor, studying the staff schedule column. Monday through Friday, everybody worked from seven to seven, with several generous breaks in between. And on Sundays, the same. "We don't start work 'til noon on Saturdays?"

"That's right. The twins and I don't drink, but everyone else does. So if you wanna get hammered Friday night, you can sleep it off the next morning. Guess it makes up for our shitty hours."

Abbie was grateful to have buried that part of her life. It would be nice to spend weekend mornings having breakfasts at home with Mom and Uncle Jesse. But did Port Allegiance hold her a virtual prisoner until the end of her tenure? Fearing the answer, she asked.

"Of course not," Skyla said. "They don't own us completely. Do you drive your own car, or do you ride the bus?"

"I have a car, but it's too old to enter the city."

"You're a busser, then, like me. I gotta warn you: leaving the city is the easy part, but getting back in can sometimes be challenging. There's usually some idiot trying to sneak onto the bus. When that happens, boarding time can get super long, and trust me, you don't want to be late for work. Ms. B's by the book."

She took Abbie's arm again and directed her to the adjacent wall, where a vintage oak mail sorter hung. Each cubby had an employee name written at the top. Somebody had already added Abbie's name, which made her feel at home.

"You have mail," Skyla said with a grin spanning ear to ear.

Puzzled, Abbie reached into her cubby and opened the envelope. She gasped. *A two-thousand-dollar sign-on bonus?* "I had no idea," she said, holding back tears.

"Ms. B evaluates us every six months," Skyla explained. "And if we do a good job, there's always a raise. She does birthday and Christmas bonuses, too. Don't tell anyone on the outside; otherwise they'll be tearing down the wall."

"This is incredible." Now she didn't have to feel guilty for the latte she'd ordered earlier.

"I had the same reaction when I started. Come on, I'll show you around the house."

Heading down a corridor with a coffered wood ceiling, Skyla opened the wooden ten-foot-tall double doors leading into the ornate great room. Colossal crystal chandeliers hung from the ceiling. Wood-clad windows covered the entire eastern wall, and burgundy velvet drapes framed the windows from ceiling to floor. On the southern end nestled an old-time saloon-style bar, where lit glass shelves highlighted a vast supply of liquor.

"This house is insane," Abbie said. "The homeowners haven't modernized, have they? They've maintained its integrity." She wandered over to a towering Christmas tree, which was glowing with thousands of crimson lights and vintage ornaments. "How many people did it take to decorate this?"

"The whole staff pitched in. Took days, and plenty a night, too. This is where Ms. B and Clem have hosted the staff Christmas Eve party for the past decade."

"You gotta be kidding! The homeowners allow it?"

"Thanks to Ms. B. Clem told me that when the De Youngs moved into this house, Ms. B came as part of the package. She'd been with the previous owners. In the years she's worked here, she's quit her job a few times because of Mrs. De Young's"—Skyla paused a moment to think—"uh, difficult personality. Her husband's cool, though… Anyway, back to Ms. B. Each time she quit, the whole staff up and quit along with her. But Mrs. De Young lured her back with better pay and more control over the staff. That's when Ms. B demanded we get to have our own Christmas Eve party. We deserve it. We work hard, and most of us have no family."

"I love Ms. B more every second." Abbie smiled as she continued admiring the glowing tree ornaments.

"Yeah, she's the mother I wish I had. Let's get moving before we both start bawling."

Down another corridor, Skyla showed Abbie the indoor swimming pool and hot tub overlooking the acres of lawn. Abbie thought her jaw couldn't drop any further, but it did as she gazed at the running track on the second tier above the pool.

"They also have a helipad on the roof. If you had unlimited money, wouldn't you want this, too?"

Abbie paused and mulled it over. "I guess…if life wasn't such a dystopian mess on the other side of the wall. People don't have enough food, and they're not allowed to own their homes, to build equity. It seems like our only purpose is to serve Port Allegiance."

Skyla's shoulders dropped, and her zesty spirit faded. "People have choices, Abbie. Port Allegiance isn't holding anybody captive. People *can* move away if they're unhappy."

Abbie wished Skyla had better insight. "But, Skyla, if a person can't afford a car, or find a decent-paying job, they're stuck."

"Listen," Skyla said sympathetically, "I'm from Garberville, and life's even worse there—but I found a way out. We can't save the world, but we can have fun trying. Come on, there's more to show you."

"Ladies!" a man bellowed from behind them.

Skyla and Abbie jumped, then turned. It was Rex, his hands resting on his hips.

"Ms. Bishop," he said, "I overheard you ladies speaking in the great room. I don't recall gossiping being part of the training. I'm certain Mrs. De Young would be upset if she knew you spoke so poorly of her."

Skyla raised one eyebrow and gave him a glassy stare. "Won't happen again." She took Abbie by the arm. "Come on, I'll show you the rest of the house."

When they brushed past him, he ogled Skyla and grabbed her wrist. "You look very pretty today," he said with a sneer, his grayish-white teeth looking translucent in the sunlight filtering in from the glass roof.

She gave a sideways twist and freed herself, and with that, she and Abbie ducked into the hallway. When it was safe, Abbie stopped and asked her about him.

"He's harmless," Skyla reassured.

The hell he is.

"He thinks he has all sorts of power around here because Mrs. De Young uses him as her personal assistant. I'm convinced he has early-onset dementia—forgetting names, forgetting the oddest things. But for as long as I've been here, he hasn't done anything inappropriate, other than boss people around and make misogynistic comments."

Abbie thought back to when her grandpa on her mom's side had developed Alzheimer's. He had been in his fifties, too. Skyla's diagnosis of Rex made sense, and it explained why he had forgotten how much time he'd given her before retrieving her to meet Ms. B.

As they continued down the marble-floored hallway, Abbie studied the massive oil paintings along the walls. She stopped and stared at one in particular. "Can't be." She moved in closer. "This is a Van Gogh!"

"I know, right? Only housekeeping can touch them when they dust." Skyla stopped at an arched wooden door bearing a small bronze emblem with a raised star in the center. She pointed at it. "This means Mrs. De Young has forbidden the staff to enter without permission first. Even housekeeping."

"What's in there?"

"It's her library. You can tag along the next time I deliver room service to her." She opened the smaller-scale door next to her. Inside was a powder room with blue-and-gold damask velvet wallpaper and gold fixtures.

"Hello, ladies," greeted a man from behind them.

They spun around to find a tall, black-haired man, graying at the temples, standing by an oil painting. He was wearing a fedora and a pinstriped suit as if he'd stepped out of a 1950s gangster movie.

Skyla stood at attention and cleared her throat. "Ben, hello. I'm showing our new hire around the house."

"Abilene Spencer, it's wonderful to meet you," he said genially, and she watched the tail end of his left blue eye veering off to the side before she shifted her eyes away. They met each other halfway and shook hands.

She wasn't sure which eye to look into. "Please call me Abbie, sir. Your home, it's...it's stunning. Thank you for hiring me."

"You're a welcome addition," he said smiling. "It was sad to see your predecessor, Gia, leave, but it seems she moved on to greener pastures. As for you, I noticed the video interview made you nervous, didn't it?"

"You have no idea. My nerves got the best of me. I'm so sorry for cursing."

"Thought nothing of it," he said, brushing away her words with a hand. He studied her face, then a playful smile crossed his lips. "Minus the truck-driver cursing, you're old-school: introspective, unlike the young adults of today. You and I, we have something in common."

"Oh? What's that?"

"The hat I'm wearing—I, too, need it for security." He removed it. "I began balding in my early twenties," he confided. "It's plagued me ever since. Can't wear a toupee because it inflames my psoriasis. So, you see, we all have our insecurities."

Skyla was right: he seemed pretty cool. "Yes, sir, we're all human, aren't we?" she offered.

He nodded and chuckled a little. "We are indeed, Abbie. Say, I was going to talk to you both about this tonight, but since we're here now, let's speak."

"Of course, Ben," Skyla chirped.

His cell phone rang with the ringtone "Blue Ain't Your Color" by Keith Urban. Abbie couldn't believe it. Ben, a man of extraordinary wealth, listened to classic country music!

He reached into his blazer pocket and silenced the call. "I have a favor to ask of you both, and you can say no, of course. No pressure, I promise."

"What is it?" Skyla asked.

"I think you both together could help me a great deal." He turned to Abbie. "New employee vetting proved invaluable. I read in your profile that in high school, as an assignment, you made an Envision Plus audiovisual presentation about the plight of Eureka's homeless. You sent it to the governor as a plea for help. The story made the *Sacramento Times*, and because of you, the state awarded a grant to convert part of the abandoned Bayshore Mall into a homeless shelter. Very impressive."

"Yes, Abbie," Skyla said, her eyes beaming. "Very impressive."

"Thank you." Abbie wasn't sure how to respond to this surprising compliment.

Ben continued, "Given Skyla's fine computer skills and your expertise with Envision Plus, would you both be interested in creating a presentation for Mrs. De Young's and my upcoming benefit gala at the De Young Theater for the Arts? It's toward the end of this month, and the proceeds will go directly to our Live a Life Foundation. As Skyla knows, it's a nonprofit that helps kids in Humboldt County with food and clothing. I realize it's not part of your contract, so I'll pay extra if you say yes."

Abbie and Skyla swiveled their heads to each other, and by the look on Skyla's face, her answer was definitely yes, as was Abbie's.

"Wonderful," he said. "Meet me in my office at five this coming Saturday evening, and I'll brief you on what I'm looking for."

CHAPTER EIGHT

THAT DAY, AFTER SKYLA had finished orienting her with the house, Abbie brought the leather-bound Port Allegiance Manifesto from her bedroom to the staff break room upstairs. It would've been more comfortable to hole up in her room, but Skyla had mentioned Carter kept a pot of fresh-brewed coffee heating throughout the day. The instant she entered the room, right off the kitchen, the aroma elicited a wave of euphoria. This much-needed downtime would help to recharge her social battery, and for a fleeting moment, Ty had slipped from her psyche. How far had the ocean current carried him out by now? Had he sunk, or was he floating?

Giving the room a once-over, there was a brown sectional couch, and on the coffee table in front of it were board games: Scrabble, Pictionary, Monopoly, a deck of cards— her favorites. Against the adjacent wall stood a fridge and the coffee bar. Outside the window, sculpted three-foot-high box hedges lined the cobblestone road that meandered to the tennis court. Off to the left was a glorious tangerine tree, its branches sagging with the weight of its fruit. Back home, the homeless would've plucked it clean, then chopped it down for firewood.

She set her steaming mug of coffee on the table, then took up the manifesto, tracing a finger along the red-and-gold embossed Port Allegiance symbol. There was something unsettling about it—like it emitted swastika vibes. Flipping past the title page to the copyright page, she noted the Compliance Society had first published the manifesto in June of 2026, and this current version six months ago. Next page:

Description of Hierarchy

1) **Platinum Access Card** *holders: business owners and homeowners*
   a. Unlimited freedom within Port Allegiance
2) **Gold Access Card** *holders: importers of goods and services*
   a. Provisional freedom laid out in individual business handbooks
3) **Silver Access Card** *holders: domestic servants or workers within city limits (**WITH** ONE OR MORE SKILL SETS)*
   a. Uniforms required at all times, domestically and in public
   b. Eye contact forbidden with Platinum Access Card holders
   c. Sexual relationships between any groups is prohibited and punishable by jail and revocation of access card for life
   d. Additional jobs within Port Allegiance permitted with approval from the Compliance Society

*4) **Bronze Access Card** holders: domestic servants or workers within city limits (**WITHOUT** SKILL SET)*
   a. Uniforms required at all times, domestically and in public
   b. Eye contact forbidden with Platinum Access Card holders
   c. Sexual relationships between any groups is prohibited and punishable by jail and revocation of access card for life

"'Without skill set,'" she murmured. *The indignity of it.* 3c and 4c seemed extreme, but hey, you couldn't have intermixing between breeds. Disgusted, she slapped the manifesto closed. Then it dawned on her. She had already broken the rules when she peered into Ben's eyes.

"You brain-dead yet?" Skyla said as she entered the room with a case of seltzer and headed to the fridge.

Abbie chuckled uneasily. "Most def."

"You can thank Mrs. De Young. She authored the dumb book. It gets thicker and more ridiculous each year." She filled the fridge, then sat on the far side of the sectional and brought her knees to her chest, hugging them like she was anchoring herself for a "get to know you better" conversation.

"You ever have a run-in with her?" Abbie asked, reaching for her mug and taking a sip.

"A few, mostly when I first started. Nothing serious, though. I learned real quick that if you feed her ego, she won't swallow you whole, only in little nibbles."

Abbie drew back.

"I'm exaggerating, obviously," Skyla clarified. "Just be on guard," she warned.

"Thanks. I appreciate the heads-up. Is there any peace around here?"

"Sure. The house calms down around ten p.m. That's when she passes out drunk in her library, leaving Rex to put her to bed."

"How sad," Abbie said with sincerity as her pipe dream job aired its third foreshadowing of what lay ahead: an alcoholic boss, Kristine Mallory, and Rex. Dementia or not, he gave her the creeps.

"Don't feel bad for her. It's completely self-induced."

Abbie nodded, angry about the years Dad had pissed away.

"Tell me about yourself," Skyla said, genuinely interested.

Nobody outside of home had ever asked, nor cared. Intuition said Skyla was a girl she could trust. But opening up and being vulnerable so early wasn't something she was ready for.

"My life's boring, really." She changed the subject before Skyla could call nonsense. "But hey, what's the deal with the twins in housekeeping? I mean—"

"No, it's okay," Skyla said with a sweet smile. "They're nonverbal—a very sad story with a fairy-tale ending. They'd been living on the streets, spent several years applying for jobs in Port Allegiance, but no employer wanted them, until Ms. B watched their video interview, which an interpreter read off Devon's notes."

"What an awesome lady."

"Totally. But Mrs. De Young *was not* happy about it. Because they don't fit her perfection narrative, they keep a low profile, terrified of giving her a reason to fire them. Anyway, enough tea talk."

Abbie agreed. She wanted to know Skyla better. As she awkwardly asked her about her hobbies, Carter strutted in like the big kahuna on campus, a guy joshing around and enjoying his life.

"She sings at the Anchor Lounge here in Port Allegiance," he said, gesturing to Skyla.

"I can speak for myself, Mr. Sous-Chef," Skyla retorted, then winked, the ribbing good-natured. She swiveled her head to Abbie. "I sing every other Tuesday and Wednesday night. Ms. B works it around my schedule."

"You can come with us next week and hear her for yourself," Carter said to Abbie as he headed to the cabinet next to the fridge, pulled out a bag of corn chips, and popped them open.

"We're allowed a social life after our shifts?" Abbie asked, surprised.

"Yep," he said, crunching a mouthful of chips. "You can explore the city, too."

The notion stunned her. KnightScape had blurred the entire aerial view, but now she could find out if her fantasy matched reality.

Carter held out the chips to her.

"No, thanks. My hunger pangs died when I read the meaning of my bronze status." She air-quoted, "'Domestic servant *without* skill set.'"

"Oh, that," he said. "Don't feel too bad. I was bronze for six months 'til I got my commercial fishing license and supplied the house with fresh seafood. You'd think cooking is a valued skill, but it isn't, according to the gods." He turned to Skyla. "Skyla's a silver, too, because she belts out the songs as beautifully as Queen Rihanna."

Skyla buffed her fingernails on her apron, then turned to Abbie. "Ask Ben if he'll vouch for you. He knows how proficient you are at Envision Plus. I'll bet it was an oversight.

You have a valuable commodity to offer. I bet he'd give you a few hours a week, like he did for Gia. He works from home, so you wouldn't need to travel. It'd be perfect."

"Yeah, it would. What are the benefits of upgrading?" Abbie asked.

Carter answered, "Besides the fact that the Compliance Society allows additional jobs, the weekly salaries are way higher."

Skyla added, "Kind of an inside secret. I didn't know this until Ben overheard me singing and suggested I go for the silver. I petitioned the Compliance Society, and he vouched for me. He'll do the same for you, I'm sure of it."

Jesus—a way higher salary? Like Uncle Jesse had said, *Cha-ching, cha-ching!*

Ms. B peeked in. "Jump in the van, comrades. Time to hit Journey's Edge. And, Abbie, you'll have plenty of time to study later."

Abbie needed time to let her dark thoughts about Ty fade a bit, so she sat in the back seat of the Mercedes-Benz shuttle bus, hoping this frivolous field trip would pass quickly. Under different circumstances, playing paintball would have excited her, but living in this foreign city, grouped with people she barely knew, provoked a sense of unease. It made her wish Uncle Jesse was beside her. He loved paintball. This was their favorite family game back home.

Journey's Edge Sports Pavilion was located on the Samoa peninsula, directly across from Humboldt Bay, and only a ten-minute ride from Redwood Manor. Clem was driving,

Ms. B riding shotgun. Skyla and Carter, several rows ahead of Abbie, were carrying on, laughing and poking at each other like kids. When she finagled him into a playful head-lock and gave him a noogie, he cried uncle. Abbie chuckled. If this was what friendship looked like, she wanted a slice.

"It's nice to see you laugh again," Carter said to Skyla, who then dropped her head on his shoulder without responding.

Abbie wondered what had prompted Skyla to stop laughing. Glancing up into the rearview mirror above Clem and Ms. B, she caught sight of Kristine scowling at Skyla and Carter. Chills rushed over Abbie's skin. There was no escaping the feeling something was terribly wrong with that girl—something wicked lived in her.

And the twins, directly in front of her, hadn't moved their rigid heads since the bus left the Redwood Manor carriage house. After they'd crossed the bridge to Samoa, one of them turned around and got on his knees. His toothy grin made her smile. When he handed her a stick of chewing gum, she thanked him for the sweet gesture. With a finger, he drew a heart in the air—his way of forming a connection with her.

Maybe this frivolous field trip wasn't going to be so bad after all.

A crisp blue sky crowned the open-domed arena, the size of a football field, that boasted a swamp with a swinging bridge, hundreds of stacked tires, fake boulders, and a pine forest. Paintball marks blotched the camouflaged obstacles, and in the far corner rose a massive medieval-style castle, so rich in detail it was as though the eleventh century had summoned them. Uncle Jesse would lop off his spindly braid to play here.

She was on a team with Skyla and Carter, while Kristine and the twins were on the other. Whichever team won, Ms. B and Clem, enjoying a cocktail in the arena bar, would grant them paid time off. Not only that, but whichever team lost would have to complete the other team's duties for a day. Either way, by the looks of the arena, it was going to be a lot of fun.

Thanks to Abbie's adept shooting skills, she'd have a competitive advantage. The thought of shooting the twins made her uncomfortable, but all was fair in love and war, as Uncle Jesse had taught her, since he won nearly every paintball game. But today, Abbie envisioned victory—and she'd spend the paid time off with Mom. Maybe they'd pack a picnic and hit the beach. The vitamin D would do them both good.

In a private gathering room, her team (named the Hydras) dressed in impact-sensor camo jumpsuits with built-in sweat-absorbing hoodies. The other team (the Ophidians), currently in a room at the other side of the arena, would wear the same garb. Abbie's team would wear gray bandannas around their necks, and the opposing team would wear black ones, so they could tell each other apart.

Abbie, Skyla, and Carter huddled around the digital arena map embedded in the wall, and Skyla spent a few minutes showing Abbie the best places to snipe their victims. The only rule: no physical touch of any other player was allowed. The first team to collect twenty points (confirmed paintball shots to the enemy) would win.

"And remember," Skyla told Abbie, "the battle lasts only forty-five minutes. If neither team hits the goal score, nobody wins, even if they score higher."

Carter added, "And the second we leave this room, we have an oath to protect each other whenever possible. Never allow your personal need to kill cost us the victory. Now let's gear up!"

On the wall next to the locker cabinets hung a dozen or so helmets with clear visors. Looped over the top of each one was a camo belt with three sleeves, cradling pods of ammo and bottled water. And inside the front pouches: smoke grenades and extra cartridges to power their rifles. Abbie Velcroed a belt around her waist, and when she slipped on her helmet, a score roster lit up inside the visor.

HYDRAS: 0 POINTS

OPHIDIANS: 0 POINTS

TIME REMAINING: 00:45:00

Tiny lifelike avatars represented her teammates, their locations visible anywhere within the arena. Their opponents were invisible to them.

After a light warm-up, Carter initiated a chant. "Redwood Manor, unrepentant like thee, fight 'til our deaths for his majesty to see!" They repeated it twice more and then high-fived one another.

The absurdity of it. But Abbie wasn't complaining; acting the part outside her torturous ruminating about Ty's death was a welcomed change.

When the gong bellowed over the intercom, the Hydras, amped up on high hopes, charged out of the room, Abbie lagging behind. The second they hit the killing fields, the clock started counting down. As they scattered throughout the arena, Abbie ran to center left field, where she took cover behind a giant boulder.

Still as the forest, still as the cougar before she pounces. Uncle Jesse's mantra, a reminder to never let down your guard.

A flash of a black bandanna darted past her, but whoever it was disappeared behind stacked tires. Kristine, Devon, and David were similar in height, the twins maybe five pounds heavier, so without seeing their faces, deciphering who was who would prove difficult.

"Behind you, Abbie! Run!" Carter hollered into her earpiece. As she blasted off like a runaway train, an arsenal of fluorescent-green lasers and paintballs whizzed past her, missing her by inches. A quick glance behind she recognized *Kristine,* her gun now trailing Carter and rapid-firing at him, blasting the backs of his legs.

As Kristine swiveled her rifle back toward her, Abbie took a long, burning slide in the dirt, all the while firing blind over her shoulder. Panting, she rolled behind a giant bale of hay. *Holy fuck!* Kristine's hunting prowess impressed her.

A flashing red light inside her visor read:

HYDRAS: 1

OPHIDIANS: 3

TIME REMAINING: 00:43:08

Yes! Kristine took a hit!

On the left side of her visor, Carter's avatar was running toward Skyla, likely to protect her from Kristine, who had disappeared somewhere in that direction.

One of the twins (who could tell which one?) caught her peripheral vision. He was looking over his shoulder at her as he ran across the moat's swinging bridge to get inside the castle. A grin stretched across his face, like he was egging her on to chase after him—maybe his way of furthering their friendship? Then, gunfire—

"The bitch shot me!" Skyla snarled, gasping for breath.

HYDRAS: 1

OPHIDIANS: 5

TIME REMAINING: 00:42:44

"The bitch"? Abbie chuckled. She hunkered down, her eyes darting in all directions. *Clear.* As she stalked after the twin, a blast reverberated through the obstacles, and she took two stinging paintballs to her lower back.

The shooter—the other twin. He playfully stuck out his tongue at her, then dove behind a fence. God, she was an asshole for presuming they weren't as adept as her! Now, who to chase after? The castle looked like more fun.

HYDRAS: 1

OPHIDIANS: 7

TIME REMAINING: 00:42:27

The bridge over the moat seemed too far away to cross, but she spotted a closer entrance at the base of the watchtower. Avoiding open spaces, she maneuvered through the obstacles, landing at the muddy incline leading into the murky water. *How deep is it? Couldn't be too deep, right? Stupid idea, not taking the bridge.* But Skyla had mentioned their suits were waterproof, so why not? Gingerly, she lowered her foot and turned it parallel with the slope. The second it touched down, it slid, causing her to spread into the splits. Feeling the burn, she swung her uphill leg around, sliding the rest of the way down on her butt.

Peering across the water to the other side, twelve feet, maybe, she admitted this had been a stupid idea. She stood and stepped into the water, which was shallow at first, but then became deeper. By the time she was at the halfway point, she found herself waist-deep and cursing herself.

Something in her periphery caught her attention—the water had developed an odd triangular wake, like something was just under the surface and propelling toward her. Up popped two reptilian eyes, then a scaly spine, and a tail swaying from side to side.

She froze. *An alligator?? Couldn't be real. Surely someone would've mentioned it...*

Its mouth sprung open, and, of course, it was fake, which was obvious from the silver bolts holding its jaw together. Pretty cool, though. Amused, she continued across, the water growing shallower.

A blast sounded in the distance, then Skyla laughed into Abbie's earpiece. "Got her good!"

HYDRAS: 5

OPHIDIANS: 7

TIME REMAINING: 00:31:03

Shit! Abbie had wasted too much time.

"Excellent job," Carter said.

"Thanks," Skyla replied. "Taking off after her again."

The twin. Abbie had better hustle, or she'd lose him. But as she took the first few steps up the muddy bank, her feet slipped, and she slid back down.

From above, the sound of tromping feet was moving in closer—and it wasn't either of her teammates. She slipped and fell along the bank, blindly shooting an arsenal of rounds

101

at forty-five degrees upward until she depleted her hopper. Frantically, she pawed her way up, making it to the top, her fingers caked in mud. She turned to find Carter chasing after the twin.

"Got yer back, Abbie," he called, sacrificing himself as a diversion to draw attention away from her. Two blasts to the twin's shoulder, and Carter chased him into the pines, where they both disappeared.

Hydras: 8

Ophidians: 7

Time Remaining: 00:29:26

More launching paintballs echoed throughout the arena.

Hydras: 8

Ophidians: 8

Time Remaining: 00:29:21

"That hurt like a mofo!" Skyla yelped, her voice amusingly high-pitched.

"Try taking a hit to the gonads," Carter responded, and the girls laughed.

In case she was still vulnerable, Abbie dropped to the ground and army-crawled to the arched stone entryway leading into the watchtower. God, this was fun! Inside the fifteen-foot cylindrical space was a spiral staircase leading to the top, and to its left, the portal leading into the main castle.

Her back against the wall, she hurriedly refilled her hopper with paintballs, then guzzled the entire bottle of water. As she peeked around the archway into a large room with a bubbling cauldron in the center, her eyes widened. The twin, his back to her, was skulking past a suit of armor and heading toward a different room, clearly searching for her. From her belt pouch, she removed a small gray smoke grenade. She'd never used one, but Carter had instructed her that once she pulled the pin, she'd have five seconds until detonation.

You're going down, my friend. A quick pull, and she raised her rifle and launched multiple paintballs into his back, then tossed the grenade his way.

HYDRAS: 13

OPHIDIANS: 8

TIME REMAINING: 00:25:09

"Good job, team!" Skyla exclaimed. "Only seven more for the win."

Eager to discover more of the castle, and expecting the twin to be on her ass soon, Abbie bolted through the only archway leading out. Traveling along the long, narrow hallway lined with an assortment of ancient swords on the walls, she peered over her shoulder. In the distance, the twin had entered the hall. She jetted into a rectangular room at the end. Gargoyle heads birthed from the walls, torches burning between them, lighting up their half-human, half-animal faces. *Cool as hell.*

Tromping feet behind her—no time to look back. He'd caught up with her. But how? A shortcut? As she took off, a green laser shot past her, sparkling over the walls. She tensed her whole body as stinging paintballs pummeled her shoulder blades. *Shit, that hurt!* Trying to ditch him, she tore around the corner, zigzagging through dank rooms. *Call for backup? Nah.*

HYDRAS: 13
OPHIDIANS: 11
TIME REMAINING: 00:16:41

There was nowhere left to run but outside, through the open archway in front of her. She caught her breath in what was a courtyard, of sorts, the castle towering around her and closing her in. This was no ordinary courtyard, though. Before her was a seven-foot wall of stacked railroad ties, with an entry point in the center. Above it, a wooden sign: ENTER HERE, DO NOT FEAR, FOR YOUR FREEDOM IS NEAR.

She spun her head around. The twin's dark silhouette was moving in closer. How'd he track her down? Trampling over gravel, she entered a foyer built of railroad ties, with a slat roof overhead and torches lighting the four-foot passageways to her left and right. The stench of creosote burned her sinuses. *Which way to turn?*

She traversed left, then right fifteen feet, then left ten, then right—*what the hell, it's a maze?* So many decisions!

A flashback: the zoo parking lot. Ty tormenting her with his truck, his knife at her throat, his threats…then Scoop pulling over Uncle Jesse, Ty's corpse in the bed of the truck. She was there all over again, Ty's shirt fluttering in the breeze, waiting for Scoop to recognize it.

Dizziness forced her to stop and ground herself. The more she tried to quash the avalanche of clashing thoughts, the further she detached from her body.

The dim sound of pounding feet on gravel. She stumbled along with tunnel vision, her heart racing out of control. Ahead, in the railroad ties, a dozen or more child-sized openings draped in burlap. A good place to hide—to ease her feeling of impending doom.

Ducking down, she peeked inside the first one: a small, dungeon-like space. In the far corner on a rickety table, a single fake candle burned, illuminating the iron walls and ceiling. Not a safe place to hide. At the second opening from the end, she peered back. *Clear.* She entered the lightless room, and backed into the ties beside the opening, her body trembling irrationally out of control.

At least she was safe. But what was this space? There was a sense of vastness, as if the surrounding walls were as far away as infinity.

Her visor flashed red:

HYDRAS: 18

OPHIDIANS: 11

TIME REMAINING: 00:01:04

"Got 'im!" Skyla shouted, gloating. "You guys okay?"

Footsteps approached and stopped directly outside the opening.

Carter: "Yeah, refilling my hopper. Abbie?"

In the lighted slit beneath the burlap, a piece of gravel rolled in.

Faster than she could scream for help, the twin's arm reached around, clamped her jumpsuit at the leg, and jerked her to the ground. As paintballs pummeled her ribs, she curled into a ball, wailing. Then, like a vulture absconding with its prey dangling from his claws, the twin took off, victory assured.

WTF! He had broken the only rule when he'd viciously laid his hand on her. But more importantly, how had he known her exact location?

HYDRAS: 18

OPHIDIANS: 20

TIME REMAINING: 00:00:00

At half past seven that evening, still suffering residual effects of the attack, Abbie entered her bedroom, having aced the manifesto quiz. She slipped out of her uniform and put on her favorite pajamas, baby-shit-brown long johns which sagged in the butt. Ty had said she resembled a lumpy Idaho potato in them—that they rendered her "unfuckworthy." As if *he* had ever tried to look attractive. Well, maybe in their early days.

Why did she have to go there again?

If she didn't get some fresh air immediately, she'd burst out of her potato skin. As she reached for the knob of the glass-paned French door, she spotted Skyla stretched out on a lounge chair beside the cement-rimmed goldfish pond. She was wearing a multicolored Aztec-print bathrobe with bat sleeves. Perched on the rim of the pond was an old coffee tin with something burning inside. The smoke whirled into the dark, starry sky. Skyla had her hands wrapped around a mug of something steamy. Her head was laid back, her eyes closed.

Abbie didn't like the idea of interrupting her relaxing moment, but the twin cheating at paintball had been bothering her all day, and she'd wanted to talk about it with Skyla earlier but they hadn't had a moment alone.

Hesitantly, Abbie opened the door, and earthy smoke wormed its way into her room. "Hey, neighbor."

Skyla swiveled her head. "Hey there! You pass your test?"

"Easy-peasy." Stepping outside, Abbie plopped down in the lounge chair next to her. "If vowing to obey every covenant warrants a passing grade, then they must think we're pretty damn stupid."

"I know, it's bullshit." Skyla tipped her mug and took a sip. "Ms. B and Clem think so, too. It's unnerving, pledging allegiance to a book that doesn't align with your values. Gotta play the game, though, right?"

Abbie nodded. That's exactly how she'd start viewing it: *a game.* "Thanks again for saving me in that freaky maze."

"I should've prepared you—it slipped my mind. I'm so sorry."

"Don't apologize. How could you possibly know what a mess I am?"

Skyla gave a sympathetic smile. "Hardly. But I suspected something was up when we met. You're good at hiding it."

Heat flushed Abbie's face, her body tensing. Other than Mom and Uncle Jesse, nobody had ever tapped her psyche like that. Something was brewing inside Skyla, too. Because it was early in their relationship, Abbie wasn't sure if asking about it would be appropriate. She did feel like Skyla had potential to be her first female friend, which was promising.

"It's okay," Skyla said softly, "you can talk about it when you're ready. I mean, only if you want to, of course."

Abbie thanked her and took in the sea air, then she recited the story of the twin tracking her down in the maze—how he'd broken the rules by physically grabbing her. How he'd flung her to the ground, then pummeled her with paintballs, clinching the victory for his team. When she'd finished, Skyla was staring at her with her mouth agape.

"Oh, Abbie," she said sympathetically. "I can see now why you were so upset. Must've been terrifying—"

The look on Skyla's face told Abbie there was going to be a "but."

"—but I can't believe either twin would stoop that low."

"I agree. I can't wrap my head around it, either."

"You said it was dark," Skyla said, squinting. "Did you actually see his face?"

Abbie thought back. "The last time I saw it was when he was running over the top of the moat's swinging bridge to get to the castle. He was grinning at me, like he wanted me to chase him, so I did. But it was a trick so his brother could shoot me from behind." She closed her eyes a moment and thought. "The next time I saw his face… Wait. I didn't see it. His back was to me. After I shot him, I threw a smoke grenade his way, and then ran for it. Then when I stopped in the courtyard, I looked back and his silhouette was running toward me, but still didn't see his face."

"Then maybe it wasn't him," Skyla said quietly.

"Well, it wasn't one of us. Neither of you was anywhere near me. It had to be someone from the other team."

Skyla dropped her head a moment. "You said you checked for him before you hid in that room, and it was clear?"

"Yep. And how could he know I had pressed myself against the ties by the entrance?"

"Holy shit," Skyla gasped, slapping a hand over her mouth. "*Kristine.* I'll bet it was her! After she shot me, she snuck into our gathering room and swapped her helmet for one of ours."

That's exactly what happened! "What are we gonna do about it?" asked Abbie expectantly.

Skyla let out a big sigh. "Tomorrow morning, I'll ask Carter if anything roused his suspicion."

There was a clicking sound, like a door closing. Skyla turned and peered at Kristine's French door, the door next her hers.

"Do you think she was eavesdropping?" Abbie whispered, a sick feeling rumbling in her gut.

"Probably." She fanned the smoke so it would scatter. "I can't deal with her right now."

Realizing Skyla wanted to change the subject, Abbie asked, "What's burning in the can?"

"Sage. It was Gia's and my thing." She peered at Abbie as if she were harnessing the knowledge of a folk healer. "I've burned it every night since she left—a ritual to let her know I'm thinking about her, that I haven't lost hope."

"You two were close, huh?"

Skyla nodded. "I don't buy it she up and quit, like Ms. B and Clem believe."

"Why do you say that?" Abbie had a bad feeling.

"Because she gave no sign she wanted to leave. In fact, she'd been working toward law school. We talked about everything, we even had plans to hit the Port Allegiance wharf and watch the fireworks on New Year's Eve." She breathed in the sage. "I don't wanna talk like she's dead, and this makes me sick to say, but I think when she left here that Friday night to volunteer at the Boy's and Girl's Club in Eureka, the East Bay Serial Killer nabbed her."

A shiver shot through Abbie's body. "Did you call the club to see if she showed up?"

"Yeah, I even went there in person. She didn't."

"And her parents? Family?"

"Parents died in a car accident. No other family."

Jesus. What a tragedy. "What about her clothes and belongings? Did she leave anything here?"

"Everything was gone, which is why everyone thinks she quit. I know if it was the serial killer, her clothes would still be here, so maybe I *am* making up shit in my head. I dunno."

"I'm so sorry," Abbie whispered sympathetically, imagining how hard it must be for Skyla to train her as Gia's replacement.

"Thanks," Skyla said, gazing into the sky. "Have you ever been in love? Like, truly in love, where a sense of safety filled you? Like anything was possible?"

"I wish," Abbie said as a shooting star darted behind a cloud. "This might sound strange, but I've been in love with someone I've never met. You know, like hopefully someone is out there in the universe, thinking the same thing about me."

Skyla turned to Abbie. "That type of love will strike you when you least expect it. Just be open and willing to let it in."

Abbie nodded. "How about you? Have you been in love?"

When Skyla didn't respond, Abbie pieced it together and felt a little silly for not realizing it sooner. "You and Gia?"

"Nobody knew, Abbie." Her voice cracked, and she fought back the tears. "If word got out, we'd lose our jobs, our access cards, or worse, get thrown in jail for breaking the rules."

Abbie reached over and took her hand. "How'd you know she was the one?"

Squeezing gently, Skyla wiped her nose on the sleeve of her free arm. "After a year of growing closer and closer and sharing our most intimate thoughts—I don't mean sex or anything, just honest conversations about our pasts and our dreams—it happened organically. One night, right before my singing gig, I felt safe with her watching me change into my stage clothes. As I took off my manor uniform, she witnessed what I was ashamed of, but she didn't run away. She skimmed a finger across the razor marks on my ribs, and then she cried. So ya see, Abbie, she didn't up and quit. She wouldn't have abandoned me."

CHAPTER NINE

Friday, December 21

Dear Journal,

- *Education: John Cabot University, Rome, Italy*
- *Degree: Journalism and Creative Writing*
- *Housing: A cute studio in the Monti district, in the heart of Rome*
- *Job: Barista at a hole-in-the-wall coffee bar*
- *For fun: Studying in the Villa Borghese Gardens overlooking the temple dedicated to the god of healing*
- *Boyfriend: No*
- *Pet: Yes, please—a deserving rescue cat. (Sorry, Liza, you wouldn't fit on the plane.)*

What do you think? For the first time, I'm able to actualize my dreams without the fear of jinxing them. Typing it in felt incredible, gave me hope for my future. And as for Skyla, all she has is hope, too. Her story last night about her love affair with Gia won't stop running through my thoughts. To love somebody so much that you stop doing the one thing that gives you comfort: cutting yourself. Having Skyla explain that physical pain is easier to tolerate than emotional pain was something that hit me hard. I totally got it. My scars have faded, but the memories of being bullied will always haunt me. I love you, Uncle Jesse. Thank you for helping me stop, for accepting me, teenage angst and all.

THERE WAS A KNOCK AT HER BEDROOM DOOR, so she hurriedly typed, *Love, Abbie.*

Seven o'clock. Skyla was right on schedule. She invited her in.

"Good morning," Skyla said, a single red rose tucked behind her ear. She closed the door behind her. "Your first night sleeping in this old musty house. How'd it go?"

"Excellent. It's so quiet here compared to Eureka."

"No kidding." As she strolled around the room, Skyla's mood grew somber. "It's exactly as Gia left it. The bed used to be on that wall," she said, pointing. "But she moved it to where it is now. Said something about it not being good feng shui where it was before." She shuffled to the desk, lost in what had been. "This is where she studied."

"I'm sorry. This must be torture for you."

"Yeah, it's rough. Thanks for listening last night. I didn't intend to overshare, especially on your first day," she said, looking shameful.

"I'm glad you trusted me. I've never had a female friend before."

Skyla's eyes rounded, her chin drawing inward. "Seriously?"

"Kinda weird, I know. You speak to Carter yet?" she asked, to change the subject.

"Not weird, and yeah, I told him your story." She shook her head like she still couldn't believe what Kristine had done. "He was as shocked as I was. Said there was no way either twin would cheat, and the way she had done it so connivingly—"

Kristine pushed through the door without knocking. "Beautiful morning, girlies." She strutted in looking like she had just left a professional hair and makeup studio. She studied Abbie's face too long for comfort, and Abbie held back the urge to knee her in the crotch.

"Wanna borrow my concealer?" Kristine asked snidely.

Skyla huffed. "Could you be any more cringe?"

"Geez, I was trying to be helpful. No need to get all pressed over it." She spun around and snaked upstairs.

"Her nutty behavior is out of control," Skyla said.

"Can't imagine it getting any worse than it is." Kristine was better suited for the stage rather than behind the scenes. Then it dawned on her: Kristine must have a Silver Access Card if she worked with the local theater. The fact she ranked higher than her made Abbie's ego boil.

"Just watch your back," Skyla warned.

"But why is she out to get me?" Abbie sounded mystified.

"I'm betting she sees you as a threat. She's been lusting after the De Youngs' son ever since she first got here, and hasn't been subtle about it. He has a type, and she won't accept that it's not her."

"Son? She's not afraid of Mrs. De Young firing her or landing in jail?"

"Nope," Skyla scoffed. "She knows he wouldn't touch her if his life depended on it, but she won't give it up for some reason. He's hanging with friends down in Pebble Beach but'll be back tomorrow afternoon. Come on, let's get to work. That soiree Ms. B mentioned yesterday is a dinner party for a group of thirty Las Vegas businesspeople. They'll be here at six. We have a shit ton of work to do."

"It'll take eleven hours to prepare for it?"

"You have no idea, my dear. Fasten your seat belt."

At half past four that afternoon, Abbie and Skyla arrived back in the kitchen after arranging dozens upon dozens of colorful fresh flowers in the great room and throughout the mansion. The place looked like a funeral home.

Playing mad scientists, Clem and Carter tossed herbs into a big stainless-steel pot, then took turns tasting their concoction. Abbie's mouth watered as she inhaled the wonderful aroma.

Sweat dripping down his forehead, Clem hollered from across the kitchen, "Skyla, Abbie, grab the cart, get to the meat locker, and bring me thirty Cornish game hens, then get the veggies prepped for my mirepoix. Five, five, five exactly."

Confused, Abbie asked Skyla, "What's that mean?"

Skyla headed toward the meat locker, Abbie following her. "Mirepoix is celery, carrots, and onions, all sauteed in butter. It's the base for most soups. 'Five, five, five' means Clem wants five cups of each, all diced exactly the same size."

"Oh, my mom and I have made that, however you pronounce it. Didn't know it had a fancy name."

"Everything around here has a fancy name. Don't worry, you'll adjust to the lingo in no time." She opened the locker door, and out rushed a plume of mist.

Standing inside, Abbie wrapped her arms around herself and shivered. She followed Skyla as she maneuvered through the hanging beef carcasses until they got to the back, where the Cornish game hens hung by their necks.

"This is creepy as hell," Abbie said. "What if the door closes, trapping someone inside?"

"Never shut it all the way," instructed Skyla.

"That's comforting."

"I love your dry sarcasm. Help me load the cart, would ya?"

Having loaded and delivered the cart to Clem, Skyla grabbed the veggies from the fridge and carried them to a three-inch-thick chopping block next to the sink. "We'll dice together," she said to Abbie. "You can show me your knife skills."

As they diced and chatted about their lives, the kitchen ceiling speakers exploded into an obnoxious techno beat. Abbie looked up to find Clem and Carter bumping hips, each holding two Cornish game hens by their necks. The two sung along as they danced around the kitchen, the hens flopping around obscenely. Who would've thought a sixty-something man would know the words, let alone the dance moves?

Skyla lightly jabbed Abbie in the ribs and joked, "Clem better not quit his day job, huh?"

"He's friggin' awesome," Abbie said with a grin. But she couldn't escape the aching fear there was some invisible force waiting to snatch the fun away from them. She glanced over at the table where Kristine was polishing the silverware and shooting Abbie a side glare.

Enough of this bullshit. Abbie set down the knife and sat beside Kristine, keeping her voice low. "You've had it out for me since I got here yesterday. What have I done to piss you off so badly?"

With nostrils flared, Kristine delicately set down the silver ladle, then whispered in Abbie's ear, "You were born. That's enough to piss anybody off." Then off she sashayed to the dishwasher, leaving Abbie teetering on the edge of lunging at her.

Carter hurried over and sat in Kristine's chair, and tucked a rose behind Abbie's ear, like he'd done for Skyla earlier.

"Thanks," she said, calming down a bit. "Why the hate? I've done nothing to her."

"Ignore her," he said quietly. "She's as toxic as the sea is salty. She's jealous because you and Skyla are bonding. That's probably why she targeted you at Journey's Edge."

Just plain weird. And as for Skyla thinking Kristine was worried Abbie would steal her love interest, her theory was preposterous. Abbie wasn't anybody's type. "Why do they, whoever 'they' are, keep Kristine around?"

A yelling match resounded from Ms. B's office, ending with a door slamming. Everyone stood still as Ms. B stomped into the kitchen, her face red and frazzled.

"What in tarnation was that about?" Clem asked her.

"Mrs. De Young has taken it upon herself to fire the twins and revoke their access cards. Somebody tipped her off to some sort of cheating scheme at Journey's Edge. Both boys have denied it, and I believe them."

"Good God," Clem said. "There's no way they'd cheat—ever."

Abbie, Skyla, and Carter peered at each other, then turned to Kristine. An almost imperceptible micro-smirk lifted her cheek.

This covert sociopath is as evil as they come.

"Well, they're gone now," Ms. B said, fighting back tears. "Two lives destined for the streets. Now we have no one in housekeeping." She peered at each kitchen member. "Which one of you four spread such gossip?"

Nobody spoke up; they stared at her, their faces deadpan. Apparently, Kristine was going to get away with it.

"Fine!" Ms. B shouted, nearing the end of her fuse. "Double duty for everyone until I hire replacements."

At five forty-five that evening, Abbie and Skyla, still seething over Kristine's vicious scheme, stood in the well-stocked pantry, returning the spice jugs to their places—in alphabetical order, of course.

"So, we're gonna let her get away with it?" Abbie asked, hoping the twins had found shelter somewhere.

"I know you're pissed. I am, too." Skyla slid the oregano back into its slot. "But Mrs. De Young isn't anyone to cross. We need to keep quiet if we value our jobs."

"The thought of meeting her later is giving me diarrhea."

Skyla chuckled, thinking Abbie was joking. She wasn't.

"Just avoid eye contact, and she won't hassle you. You'll adjust. Rumor has it she was a decent person before she bought Eureka. I guess her militance grew after she had the wall built—you know, to keep the pandemic from infecting the establishment."

Skyla might as well have punched Abbie in the gut. "Wait, wait, wait... Mrs. De Young *owns* Eureka—and *she* built the wall? So, I now work for the oppressor who has made life hell for the people outside this stone bubble?"

"You didn't know?" Skyla sounded shocked.

"You think I'd work here if I did?"

"It's a job, Abbie." Where spice debris speckled the shelf, Skyla wiped it clean with her hand. "It'll put food in your belly, maybe help you get ahead."

Abbie remembered an investor had purchased Eureka after the pandemic had closed most of the businesses and caused banks to foreclose on the townspeople's mortgages, but as far as she knew, the investor hadn't revealed their name to the public. It didn't matter—this wasn't Abbie's forever job— but hiding her contempt might prove impossible. Like Skyla had said, Abbie would continue to treat it like a game. She thought for a second. "You said Mrs. De Young had the wall built. Not Ben?"

"Nope. The funds came from her father, some mega-rich guy. Ben doesn't have much of a say around here." Skyla broke into Mrs. De Young's accent, as if born with the silver spoon already crammed down her windpipe: "Ben's my little pet, only gets tea and crumpets if he behaves like a good little boy."

Abbie chuckled.

"So, relax, Abbie darling. Nothing to fear. I have your back," she assured, still in character.

When the bell chimed, indicating the guests had arrived, Skyla plucked two fresh aprons from the shelf and said emphatically, "Always, and I mean *always*, wear a fresh one when serving the guests. We can't have a stain, not even a microscopic one. Trust me. Mrs. De Young will spot it."

Abbie removed her soiled apron, then tied the fresh one behind her back. "I feel sick."

"You'll do fine."

"Thanks." She lifted her nose. "Any boogers?"

Skyla chortled. "Relax, you're clean. Now let's get to work."

In the kitchen, Skyla lifted an hors d'oeuvre platter of caviar, buttered toast points, and crème fraîche she and Abbie had prepared earlier. "Grab your platter and follow me, and don't spill the champagne. And remember, we're not permitted to look the guests in the eye, and don't speak to them unless they ask us a question first."

Abbie nodded nervously. Fortunately, her trainer platter held only six champagne glasses; Kristine's held at least a dozen. With grace, Kristine spun her platter effortlessly over her shoulder, the champagne barely moving in the glasses. Abbie figured it might be smart to lag behind her, in case Kristine's foot "accidentally" sent Abbie flat on her face.

In the great room, Abbie took a deep breath and peered around at the guests, who were mingling among themselves. They were mostly men wearing sports jackets and double-pleated, wide-legged pants in a variety of colors. In the far corner, a pianist soulfully played his smooth tunes on the Steinway Model D.

"You're on your own," Skyla whispered, offering a reassuring nod, then took off.

After a few minutes, with Abbie feeling fairly confident in her smiling skills, a blonde woman wearing a gold sequined jumpsuit with a wide, diamond-studded belt sashayed toward her.

"You must be new here," the woman said, and Abbie was acutely aware of her drunken slurring. Another quick eye dart to her mouth. That smile—as fake as her hair extensions. Gauging by the smell of liquor on her breath, she'd already hit the bottle hard.

Abbie stammered, looking down. "Yes…yes, ma'am, I am. Today's my second day."

"Well?"

"Well, what, ma'am?" She didn't mean to sound snarky.

The woman huffed. "Your name. What is it? You *do* have one, right?"

"I apologize. I'm Abbie."

The woman gave her the once-over. "I'm Mrs. De Young. This is *my* house."

"I—I apologize, I should have known. It's a pleasure to finally meet you. You have a lovely home. Would you care for a glass of champagne?" She held out the platter.

"Look at me," Mrs. De Young ordered.

"Yes, ma'am."

An overzealous plastic surgeon had injected way too many fillers into her pillowy face. She was staring at Abbie like she was trying to coax out a memory as to where they had met.

"Where have I seen you before?"

Abbie was certain they didn't hang in the same circles. "No idea, ma'am."

Out of nowhere, Ben nudged his wife's arm. "Darling, Jayden Vaughn has arrived. There's something important he wants to discuss with you."

As Mrs. De Young turned away to attend to her guest, Ben gave Abbie a thumbs-up and took off in a different direction. She appreciated his confidence in her. With a few glasses of champagne remaining, she made her way to a group of men whose glasses looked one sip short of empty. Then her eye caught Kristine at the far end of the room. She and a slick-dressed man in black were engaged in flirtatious grins, his hand riding up the side of her thigh. As Abbie wondered if Kristine sold herself for sexual favors, the guests plucked her platter empty.

That must be how she pays for her new Volkswagen.

On the way back to the kitchen to reload, she noticed a massive oil painting above the buffet table she hadn't noticed before. It was of a woman wearing a leotard and tutu, both arms rounding above her head.

The eyes…the way one side of her mouth curled up a bit…the look of superiority. The vision brought on chills. What was this visceral reaction about? She moved in closer and read the gold plaque at the bottom:

HILDA RHODES
BOLSHOI, MOSCOW, RUSSIA

Rhodes…? Past collided with present, and the strength left her arms. The platter crashed to the floor, shattering the glasses and splattering champagne onto a few of the guests.

What the hell? She was working in the home of Hildabeast, mother to Dylan, the sweet boy with the sad brown eyes! The boy she'd become lost with in the snowy forest of Lake Tahoe during her family's move to California! Mrs. De Young was Hilda Rhodes, the woman who had assaulted Abbie in the hospital for ruining her precious son's life!

As she snapped out of her revelatory memory, the guests were shooting daggers of disdain at her. Ben's mouth was agape, and Rex was snickering on the sidelines.

Flushing crimson, she ran to the powder room next to Hilda's library and locked herself inside. Hunkering over the sink, she doused her face with cold water. Hilda had nearly figured out who she was. Her multiple plastic surgeries explained why Abbie hadn't recognized her. She remembered Dylan as Dylan Rhodes because Hilda had introduced herself using that last name, and Abbie had assumed they shared the same last name. Hilda wasn't stupid, and it was only a matter of time before she pieced it together herself. At the next available opportunity, she'd call her former boss and beg for her old job back. *Dammit! Back to Pacific One Fishery!* She was devastated.

An angry man's words radiated through the iron wall register. Unable to contain her curiosity, she dropped to her knees and eavesdropped.

"…trusted your judgment to choose the team on Terra Isle. You're ultimately responsible, Hilda. Somebody must've seen Gia Quinn leave the facility. What about the security cameras?"

Gia? She leaned in closer.

"I understand your concern, Jayden," Hilda said. "The cameras showed her wearing nursing scrubs when she escaped. We'll find her. And if we can't, and she blabs, who'd believe a scummy tramp like her?"

Jayden yelled "fuck" so loud, it was as if he had pressed his mouth against the register.

"Take a deep breath," Hilda said, placating him. "I have blockades at every exit leading out of Humboldt County, and my men are searching each vehicle. They're watching her known hangouts, too."

Silence.

"Shall we join the others?" Hilda asked in a saccharine voice.

After the door slammed, Abbie gripped the towel bar, her heart flopping against her rib cage. Backing up, she dropped onto the toilet. *Why were they holding Gia against her will? Escaped in nursing scrubs? From a mental hospital, maybe? Terra Isle—an island maybe?* And after witnessing Kristine's insane jealousy firsthand, Abbie wondered if she might be involved.

On the way to her bedroom, she took a back hallway, avoiding the kitchen. No way she could show her face again.

"What happened back there?" Skyla shouted from down the hall.

Abbie glanced back and strode faster. At the stairwell, she skipped every other step on the way down. Behind her closed door, she dove onto her bed and rolled onto her belly. The colliding news of learning she was working in Dylan's house *and* that Hilda had been holding Skyla's girlfriend against her will had Abbie pulling a pillow over her head. She had to tell Skyla what she had overheard, and about what had happened to her and Dylan in Lake Tahoe all those years ago. Skyla deserved to hear the truth, but Abbie's manic thoughts told her to wait until after they settled down a bit. She winced when there was a knock on her door.

"Can I come in?" Skyla asked, her tone sweet and consoling.

"Okay." Abbie rolled over and propped herself up against the headboard, pain pounding behind her eyes.

"What's going on with you?" Skyla sat at the foot of Abbie's bed and stared at her with curiosity. "Why'd you drop your platter?"

"I had another one of my attacks." It wasn't a lie, but an omission of other truths, and it felt terrible. "I'll call my old boss and ask for my job back. I'm sure Ben already told Ms. B to fire my incompetent ass."

"Don't be ridiculous. She told me to find you and bring you back. They aren't petty over accidents, especially with a newbie."

"Oh. Well, that's generous of them." Time for a fishing expedition. Maybe Abbie was wrong to assume it was the same Hildabeast, the object of her childhood nightmares. "Skyla, I'm curious. You said Mr. and Mrs. De Young had a son."

"Yeah, Dylan. Now let's get to the kitchen and reload our platters."

Abbie's stomach dropped, but she followed Skyla back to the kitchen without further discussion.

At eleven o'clock that night, finally alone in the dimmed kitchen, Abbie retired her broom for the evening. She slid down the wall and sat on the floor between the wall phone and the mail sorter, thoughts grinding through her head.

Gia Quinn, the love of Skyla's life. And Dylan's house, for God's sake! Earlier, when Abbie had served dinner, Hilda wouldn't relent in her attempt to figure out where their paths had crossed. Given her hatred for Abbie because she believed she had ruined her son's life, it would be impossible for Abbie to work here.

She asked her wristwatch to pull up her former boss's phone number, then stood and dialed him. On the fifth ring, he picked up.

"It's Abbie Spencer, sir," she said softly. "I know it's late. But this couldn't wait 'til morning."

"Is everything okay?" He sounded concerned. Surprising, given he hadn't been pleased when she quit on such short notice.

"No, it's not, sir. Something's happened, and I can't stay at my new job. Is there any chance I can have my job back?"

"Abbie, I'm sorry, but I filled your position the day you quit. I gave it to a needy mother with young children. You're on your own, I'm afraid."

Lifting her fingertips to her pained forehead, she dropped her head. Misfortune had screwed her over again. "I understand, sir. Thank you for your time." She ended the call and backed into the wall. The only option was to stay and make the best of it, and whatever happened, happened.

Skyla had said Dylan would be home tomorrow afternoon. Enough time for her to concoct a plan. But keeping information from Skyla about Gia gnawed at her. Later tonight, on her computer, Abbie would research Gia on her own. And tomorrow, she'd tell Skyla everything.

The sound of something rolling along the east wing hall, moving closer... She froze, envisioning Hilda rolling in a portable coffin. *Climb in, Abbie, or I'll cram you in myself!*

The overhead lights flicked on. A guy was standing there in the kitchen. Their eyes met.

She scrutinized his facial features. *The dimpled chin and deep-brown eyes. Oh yes, and his wavy brown hair with the cowlick he hated so much.* This tall, broad-shouldered guy was Dylan, so unmistakable she could faint.

"Hello," he said, his voice deep. "You must be new here."

Dumbstruck, she nodded.

He examined her face and paused. "Do we know each other?"

Before she could respond, his eyes widened, and his Adam's apple bobbed as if he'd lodged something in his throat. He coughed a few times and rubbed his whiskered jaw. Then he started toward her, his suitcase falling to the floor. "Is it you?"

Having turned every shade of red on the spectrum, she simply replied, "Yes."

"You're grown up. You're not—" He stopped himself.

"Fat anymore?" she finished for him.

"No, I—I… Seriously, you look great, Meg. Really, you do."

Meg. Of course, that's why Hilda hadn't pieced it together. But this male attention, the way he was looking at her… She grew weak. "Thank you," she said, not comfortable with comments about her looks.

As he walked over to her, he scoped out the kitchen nervously. "Hilda hasn't recognized you?"

"Hilda"? She'd forgotten he didn't call her Mom.

"She recognizes me from somewhere, but she hasn't figured it out. I go by Abbie now. It's my real name. I look fairly different without the zits and braces. And I swear, I had no idea this was your house when I applied for the job! I just called my former boss to get my old job back, but he's already filled my position. I need the money. I can't go back to Eureka."

He gestured for her to follow him outside, where they could speak privately. They exited the east wing mudroom and sat on the iron bench on the porch, the brass chandelier above casting amber hues on their faces.

Dylan's proximity made the muscles at the back of her neck tighten. Other than Uncle Jesse, she hadn't been this close to a guy since the Ty debacle. Rationally, she believed Dylan was harmless, but nevertheless, she scooted closer to the edge of the bench as if she were taking up too much space.

"This is so awkward," she groaned, curling her fingertips under so he couldn't see she'd gnawed her nails to the quick.

"I feel awkward, too. So, it's Abbie now?"

"Yeah. Meg was my childhood escape-from-reality name."

He gave her a sad smile, his dimples as endearing as they had been back then. "I remember you saying how tough life was for you, how you never wanted to leave your hometown, and that your dad was awful to you and your mom."

She didn't want to relive the past, so she changed the subject. "Speaking of moms, would yours really care if she found out I worked here? It's been six years."

"Loyalty is gold to her," he said, swatting away a moth. "If you didn't fess up earlier when she thought she knew you, then she'd view your omission as an unforgivable betrayal. But even if you did fess up, the friendship we made in Lake Tahoe pissed her off. She bitched about it for weeks. She blamed you. She said if I'd stuck to 'my own kind,' what happened to us wouldn't have happened in the first place."

Abbie bowed her head, his words making her feel dirty, like she needed a disinfecting bath.

"God, I can be such a jerk," he said. "That wasn't my perception of you. It's that…well, I'm in utter shock right now we're sitting together after all these years."

"Yeah, me, too." She thought a moment and then added, "So, you think I should quit?"

Closing his eyes, he sighed. "No. Stay. We'll pretend we don't know each other. But if this gets back to her, she'll make your life hell and revoke your access card, or worse. She's vengeful like that; she's done it before to other employees. Is the risk worth it to you?"

The notion of risk at that point was secondary to the news about Gia. Sure, she and Dylan had built a sort of friendship, but she had no idea about the person he had become. He was a little crass earlier. Could she trust him with what she had overheard? Not yet.

She answered his question with a question. "Is the risk of going back to Eureka and living a dead-end life worth it to me?"

He nodded with understanding. "I can see it is. Well, welcome to Redwood Manor, Abbie."

When the lawn next to them blazed with light from the window of the adjacent room, he jumped to his feet. "I'd love to hear about what you've been up to, but we're tempting fate. Tomorrow's Saturday. You're not scheduled to work until noon. How would you feel about meeting me in Eureka at eight tomorrow morning behind St. Mary's Church? The one by the beach. We have a lot of catching up to do."

She wasn't sure. The Port Allegiance Manifesto had said relationships between Bronzes and Platinums were punishable with jail time and revocation of her access card for life. But this wasn't a relationship; it would be two people reminiscing, trying to reconcile their past. Hesitantly, she agreed to Dylan's proposition, but it felt wrong. It felt *dangerous*.

Still in a daze from Dylan's surprise return a half hour ago, Abbie sat at her desk in front of her laptop. Was this need to get Gia back to Skyla redemption for Abbie's role in pushing Ty off the bluff, and for causing Scoop to wonder where his son had disappeared to? Sure, Scoop was a vile human being, but he didn't deserve to hang in limbo for eternity. Neither did Skyla.

In the KnightScape search bar, she typed, *Gia Quinn*.

Hundreds of women's and girl's faces crowded her screen. Apparently, it wasn't as uncommon a name as Abbie had thought. To reduce the number of hits, she added *Eureka, California* after the name.

Two results, both for the same girl.

She clicked on the first image, and an article popped up: *Gia Quinn Awarded Scholarship to Port Allegiance University*, dated six months ago. Skyla had said Gia was working toward being an attorney. Had she started classes before she'd gone missing?

There was something curious about the photo. Abbie leaned in close to the monitor. Although Gia's hair was sandy blonde and curly, she looked a lot like Abbie herself—could practically have been her doppelganger. Odd that not a single person had mentioned the similarities.

When Abbie clicked on the second image, she landed in the East Bay Serial Killer's missing persons chat room. Creator: Skyla Bishop. *Please, anyone, have you seen this girl? She went missing in Eureka on December 14, 2040.*

The absence of a single response was sobering. It was cruel allowing Skyla to believe the serial killer had abducted her. Should she tell her now it was Hilda? No, she'd do it tomorrow, as she had planned earlier.

The guilt sent her back to KnightScape to do more research. She typed in, *Jayden Vaughn, Las Vegas*. She learned that he owned Vaughn Capital Group. *Assets exceeding 32 billion, and shareholder's funds of 15.2 billion dollars as of last year. AAA rating with the Better Business Bureau. Married to Elena, two sons, Chadwick, and Pierce.* She read on until her eyes ached. But nothing in Jayden Vaughn's history revealed anything criminal. In fact, he and his family were world-renowned for their philanthropic work.

In quotes, she typed, *"Hilda De Young, Vaughn Capital Group."* No search results linked the two together. Then: *Terra Isle.* Nothing.

But Gia Quinn was out there somewhere; Abbie could feel it.

CHAPTER TEN

Days earlier

Gia Quinn regained consciousness with a start, her heart racing. Moving down a white hallway. Room after room of people strapped to gurneys. *Drug-induced psychosis? Insanity? The psych ward?* A deluge of terror shot through her body. She bucked and writhed violently until the gurney straps seared her skin.

"Y'ain't goin' nowhere, dollface," a man said nastily from behind.

When she tried to speak, her words became trapped in her throat. Her thoughts twisted into shapes, then into colors. If only her tongue worked, she could move the shapes and put them into the correct box. A loop of crazy, repetitive thoughts filled her brain.

They passed an empty desk. A hint of classical music.

"Where d'ya want her?" the man shouted.

From a back room, a female with a high-pitched, nasal voice hollered back, "Put her in 122! Be there in a minute."

When the man spun the gurney and drove her head against the wall of the room, he came into view. He was a pasty guy wearing powder-blue scrubs. Scraggly brown hair peeked out from his bouffant hair cap.

The young nurse with short brown hair and eyes as icy as a serpent's pushed a medical cart into the room and stopped beside her gurney. "Apply the tourniquet," she ordered in the same high-pitched, nasal voice.

Tourniquet? Please, no! She thrashed around but what a big mistake. The man, his face deadpan, wrapped his hands in a death grip around her throat. She gagged and sputtered, on the edge of passing out.

"You gonna behave?" he asked, his lips tight and curling in.

She nodded rapidly. As she relaxed, the needle plunged in like an ice pick, and pulled out with a squirt of blood.

A wave of euphoria. *That wasn't so bad.*

The peaceful cotton candy cloud opened, and gravity dropped her onto the floor of a sweltering sauna. Before her stood a menacing figure with a blurred-out face. Where the mouth should have been, flowed several blood demons who circled her, laughing maniacally, nipping at her sweaty flesh with their fangs.

Slowly, her vision faded into nothingness.

What seemed like seconds later, she awoke to a blinding light and a brain-piercing ticking sound. Shielding her eyes, she squinted until they adjusted. She was lying naked and alone on a plastic mattress, and shivered uncontrollably.

No straps pinned her down, but her lungs burned and her coughing came in raspy bursts. What had they injected her with? Her tongue, dry and cracked, ached for water. There, on a nightstand, was a water pitcher, which she grabbed, chugging straight from it. When she'd had her fill, she sat upright and swung her legs over the bed, her belly rumbling. She couldn't shake the nightmare from her head.

Acutely lucid, she noted every detail of the room. To the left, above the bolted steel door with a tray slot, hung a clock, the source of the ticking. *2:36.* To her right, a caged window with a steel wall beyond it. A security camera pointed at the bed.

There was an attached bathroom! She needed to pee badly. Her legs quivered, barely carrying her weight. She scanned the tiny room for a camera. A safe zone. After she relieved herself, she inspected her entire body for signs of trauma. The gurney straps had left open wounds, and along the inside of her right arm, needle tracks had crusted atop the vein. She wasn't an IV drug user! Then she peered into the mirror.

What the—? Somebody had drawn the numbers *0187* on her forehead with a black marker. Frantically, she tried to scrub them off with her fingers, but the ink wouldn't budge. Maybe soap and water would help… Nope. Moving in closer to the mirror, she discovered somebody had tattooed her—a forever branding. But why, and who?

Straining her brain, she tried to remember the moments before the man wheeled her into the loony bin, if indeed that's where they were holding her captive. But her mind was empty—as if her life had begun that day.

CHAPTER ELEVEN

Saturday, December 22

Dear Journal,

I jolted awake this morning, sprang out of bed, and stood trembling in the center of a room. Where was I? In my bedroom in Eureka, or my bedroom in Sandpoint? As I stood there disoriented and drenched in a cold sweat, my eyes darted around the room. I was in neither. I awoke here, in Redwood Manor, in my new bedroom, Gia surging through my head. Is she dead or alive?

And what was I thinking, agreeing to a clandestine reunion today to talk with Dylan behind St. Mary's Church? Last night, when we were alone, he must've thought I was nuts. Goddamned Ty. He ruined me.

Love,
Abbie

WHEN SHE WAS BACK IN EUREKA, Abbie swapped the bus for her Subaru, parked behind the church, and waited for Dylan. It was a comfort driving her own car, to have the luxury of going anywhere she wished. No hassle of security checks, or the bus stopping constantly and wasting precious time.

When she dropped her head and closed her eyes, her mind wandered back six years to Valentine's Day, the day on that frigid mountain in Lake Tahoe, where she and Dylan had become lost in the snowy forest.

Cold. Oh, so cold. We prepared to die.

Six years earlier

As Abbie (Meg) floated on the outer edge of consciousness, something slapped at her face, making her agitated.

"Come on, Meg, you can do it. Wake up," the gnat-like voice buzzed in her ear. She tried to swipe at it, but something heavy pressed down on her body.

The words slowly grew clearer. "Meg, Meg, you have to stay awake," a male voice said.

When she opened her eyes, blackness greeted her. Frantically, she searched for something, anything, that would help pinpoint her location. Her lips twitched, and she uttered some words.

"Come on, Meg, keep talking. You're doing great."

"Who's there?" she asked. "I've gone blind!"

"It's me. Dylan. You're not blind, but you need to stay awake. Do you understand?"

Dylan. The boy she'd met at the Timber Crest Lodge in Lake Tahoe? "Why is it so dark? Where are we? Why does the back of my neck hurt?"

"It's nighttime. I carried you to this hollowed-out tree stump. I found a bunch of tree branches under the snow and covered the hole. We're not too far from where you fell on that jagged rock. I think you need stitches."

Yes, that's right. She remembered chasing after their dogs as they followed a wild hare up a game trail. They'd been lost for hours in subzero weather, the crunching snow not quenching her thirst. Then everything white turned black.

"I don't remember falling," she said, adjusting her body under his weight.

"Am I hurting you?" he asked.

"No, but I'm feeling claustrophobic. What if no one finds us?"

"I'm sure our parents are out there searching. Let's keep talking. Tell me a story. It'll keep your mind occupied."

The hours of frigid darkness dragged on, and so did the stories. They fell asleep in each other's arms.

Ty intruded on Abbie's long-ago memory. The terror of seeing his smashed-in face rolling out of her hope chest would live inside her until her last breath. Even in death, he was still controlling her thoughts, stalking her.

And Dylan. Two days into her dream job, and she discovered she worked in his house, and that Hilda was involved in a nefarious plot to find the girl she had abducted.

Can't make this shit up.

A knock on her car window jolted her back to the present. It was Dylan, wearing a brown leather bomber jacket, his face sparkling from the morning mist. Powering down the window, she scoured the parking lot. "Where's your car?"

"It's a long story." His scent of leather and cloves, mixed with the fresh sea air, drifted off him and filled the car. "Can I jump in?"

"Of course," she replied, and he strolled around front and climbed in.

Then she noticed it: the steel-blue scarf dangling from his pocket—the one her mom had knit during their move from Idaho to California. Abbie had left it at the hospital, where the admins had made them share a room because it was the only one available. She remembered the embarrassment of having to share the bathroom with him.

"Can't believe you kept it," she said, gesturing to the scarf. "I have the matching hat and gloves at home."

"I hoped to see you one day and give it back." He handed it to her. The way he gazed at her intently…

She thanked him and swung the scarf over her neck, the soft fabric easing her discomfort.

"I'm glad you showed up," he said. "Let's hit the beach and talk about what happened in Tahoe. You're the one person who knows what it was like…the cold, the misery."

"I was already there in my head when you knocked." The beach was a good idea. Anything to escape the confines of her car.

At the west end of the church, they tramped through pampas grass, their long, sturdy stalks and pinkish whisk broom tops swaying in the wind. The trail meandered toward the North Bay, the route she and Uncle Jesse took when they fished for lingcod.

Two hundred yards to their left was the wall surrounding Port Allegiance, and behind it, palm trees towered into ethereal blue skies. Abbie stopped and took it all in. "Until I got the job at your place, I'd only dreamed about what was beyond the wall."

"The grass isn't always greener on the other side, Abbie. I dreamed about escaping it."

His insensitive statement took her aback, and she debated whether to call him out. *Zip it*, she told herself. *Get to know him better before judging.*

At the beach, they sidestepped scattered garbage and a few hypodermic needles, and hovering above, mewing seagulls awaited a meal. Dylan peered two hundred yards out to Woodley Island, home of the Port Allegiance Yacht Club. Along the water boundary floated dozens of buoys, guarding against infiltrators. If you crossed a nano-inch over the line, you could consider yourself fish food.

"Let's have a seat," he suggested as he gestured to a nearby log.

They sat in silence for a moment, then Abbie asked, "What happened with your frostbite after I left the hospital?"

He brushed back his hair. Frostbite had eaten the top half of his ear. "Ended up losing my little toe, too."

Her throat grew thick, and she rubbed her forehead. "Jesus. And it's because of me. You tied your sock around my neck to stop it from bleeding."

"That wasn't it. That sock came from my other foot." He hid his ear with his hair. "What happened to us was awful."

"Now and again, I think about your dog, Pete, dying in the bear trap," she said, wiggling her feet around in the sand. "The red bandanna you took from his neck and tied to the tree stump saved us. Pete saved us."

Dylan dropped his head and sighed. "To this day, I haven't forgiven myself for not having him on a leash."

"Don't be so hard on yourself." She stifled the urge to rub his shoulder. "He was pretty determined to chase that wild hare up the game trail. He would've pulled the leash right out of your hand."

"Maybe. What about your dog, Casey?"

"She's dead. A few years back, she started having terrible seizures and eventually lost control of her hind legs. Dad shot her, put her out of her misery."

His eyes popped a little. "That's so sad. She was a cool dog."

"She was. But everything dies, right?"

He stiffened.

"I don't mean to be unfeeling."

"You're not. I've often thought about you and your family over the years. I remember your mom, and uncle, is it Jesse?"

She nodded, impressed he remembered.

"Your family was my support system," he told her. "Hilda skied and partied with her friends the entire time, and Ben didn't fly in 'cause he was too busy with an important case. Didn't see your dad much, either, but your mom was awesome, bringing cookies and hot chocolate up from the cafeteria. I remember wishing she was my mom."

"She liked you, too." Abbie would have time to pay Mom a visit after visiting with Dylan, but the shithole of a house was the last place she wanted to be, so she chose to stay away. For that, she was a complete asshole.

She continued, "But your mom, oh my God, holding my throat to the bed at the hospital, getting in my face and telling me I was a troublemaker. She scared me more than spending three nights in our tree stump did!"

A look of disgust washed over his face. "She was awful… *is* awful. When you worked up the courage to tell your mom what Hilda had done, she denied it. Straight up lied. I couldn't believe it."

"I was grateful you caught her doing it. You told my mom I wasn't lying. You defended me."

"Yeah, well, you remember how *that* went," he said morosely.

The image was as clear as if it had happened yesterday. Hilda had snatched the pitcher off Dylan's nightstand and tossed ice water in her own son's face.

He shook his head. "That was one of her milder outbursts. But what she did to you was despicable. She's a certifiable nutcase."

That was the moment Dylan had earned her trust. She'd tell him everything she had overheard about Hilda abducting Gia. But first, they'd become better acquainted.

"So, tell me, what's your story, Abbie Spencer?"

"Life's been tough," she admitted, picking at her fingernails.

"I'd like to believe I'm a good ear."

"Well, I'd rather not rehash my past or my present, if that's okay."

"How about your future? Is that safe ground?"

"The future I can talk about."

"Good." He smiled and cocked his head. "Where do you see yourself?"

"Oh, going to college in Rome," she replied, the images of the campus from KnightScape Earth exciting her. "Been saving tuition money for a few years now."

"What will you study?"

"Journalism. I want to write for a travel magazine someday. My computer is full of poems and unfinished short stories set in places I've only read about in *National Geographic*. But since I haven't traveled anywhere personally, inspiration is hard to come by, especially when I have so much crap going on in life." *Namely Ty, his body washing up on the beach. And now Gia.*

He studied her again, nodding slowly. "I can see life's been rough for you. But you're on the road to moving up in the world. Sometimes it takes a while. You should do what I do. Find distractions that give you some peace. Every Valentine's Day, I stay at the Timber Crest Lodge in Lake Tahoe and hike to our *moai* that overlooks the lake. The sunsets are phenomenal." The *moai*—the place where his dog, Pete, died—was named after the giant stone heads on Easter Island. "It's where I meditate, ground myself, something that's pretty difficult living in Port Allegiance."

She was trying to be empathetic but bristled at this. How could anybody with the world at their fingertips need grounding? And no advice could fix what ailed her. "I used to meditate, too."

"Why'd you quit?"

"My uncle Jesse's friend, some guru wannabe, Harri Babba, assigned me a mantra when I was thirteen. For me to heal, he said I had to give up something I loved for one month, and in return, I'd become an official member of the

Peaceful Mind Club, and my troubles would drift away and dissolve into a black thundercloud. At the end of the month, my dad announced no such club existed, and while giving up junk food saved me from getting fatter, it wouldn't do shit for my anxiety. He's a real asshole."

"That was pretty mean of him."

Abbie thought so, too. "Then I discovered Sour Patch Kids. They help with my anxiety. Unfortunately, Clyde's Market stopped selling them after I bought the last packet."

"Whatever works." He shrugged with a smile.

She thought for a minute. "How'd you remember where the *moai* was? We were hopelessly lost."

"Ironically, there's an old logging road that goes right to it. It's on the map. Blue Ridge Trail. We couldn't see it with the snow cover and fallen tree debris."

"We were so naive," she observed quietly.

"And foolish," he added.

After a moment of reflection, she asked, "So, what are *you* doing with your life?"

"I'm in year three of my MBA."

She calculated his age. Twenty-one now. "Impressive. Bet you'll be happy when you're done."

"You have no idea. I'm looking forward to moving away. I've caught Hilda's spies following me in my car, watching my every move. She's terrified I'll meet the wrong girl, make the wrong friends. Carter, you know, Clem's assistant, he's my one friend she approves of, and it's only because she's vetted him and deemed him trustworthy."

"And Ben? Is he that creepy, too?"

"Not at all. If anything, I wish he was more involved in my life. But every time he and I get close, Hilda drives a wedge between us."

She gave a brief huff. "She triangulates. I know the word well."

"That's right, a form of manipulation, my therapist says. Ben's too weak to defend us. He's the most ineffectual man on the planet. Other than him being an excellent attorney, I don't know why she married him."

Her head was still stuck on the fact he was seeing a therapist. "Geez, Dylan, I'm sorry about your relationship with your parents."

"It is what it is," he said a bit stoically.

The ambiguous saying Uncle Jesse uses, she thought as she zoned out into the bay. Since childhood, she had never accepted what *is,* and certainly never resigned herself to the status quo, like Mom had.

It was time to tell him about Gia. But the private conversation she had overheard was so unbelievable, she second-guessed herself. Maybe she was wrong. Maybe her creative writer's mind had made up the entire story. Why not? She had overheard it immediately after learning she was working in Hilda's house, trauma enough to unravel anyone. But no, no way had she had imagined it; she heard what she heard, no two ways about it.

"There's something I need to tell you about your mother," she said.

"This oughta be good."

"Actually, it's kinda crazy. Last night, your parents hosted a party for a group of Las Vegas businesspeople, and when I learned I was working in your family's house, I freaked out and locked myself in the powder room next to her library. That's when I overheard a conversation through the wall register between her and a man named Jayden Vaughn."

"Sure," he said, nodding. "He owns Vaughn Capital Group. He and Hilda have been working on a money-making venture for a few years now."

"Listen, Dylan, I'm just gonna say it: Hilda abducted Gia Quinn, and Jayden Vaughn is calling the shots."

He burst out laughing. "Abbie, Hilda's a lot of things, but—"

A fury overcame her. "Hear me out, dammit! And don't you dare mock me!"

That got his attention. "That wasn't my plan," he said apologetically, drawing in his chin. "I'm sorry."

"Well, Ty, my ex, used to laugh at me, and mocked me when I spoke. He used to tell me I was delusional, that what I believed happened never happened. And I won't tolerate disrespect from some silver-spooner from Port Allegiance."

She got up and stomped through the sand back to her car, and Dylan ran after her and grabbed her hand. "I am so sorry. I believe you. I believe what you heard. Please tell me everything."

Her triggered reaction must have been the culmination of everything that had happened since Ty had assaulted her at the zoo. Trauma she hadn't fully dealt with yet. She wasn't going to apologize to Dylan, though.

"Fine." She sighed. "Mr. Vaughn was upset with Hilda because she had allowed Gia to escape from a place called Terra Isle. A security camera caught her leaving wearing nursing scrubs. Hilda said she has people searching Humboldt County for her, and said if Gia blabbed, nobody would believe 'a scummy little tramp from Eureka.' Skyla doesn't believe Gia quit, and neither do I. Do you think Hilda sent her to a private psychiatric hospital?" She caught her breath, feeling like a detective on one of those murder-happy television shows Mom loved so much.

This news stunned Dylan. He took a moment to think. "Gia had become increasingly fragile, so yeah, it's possible. But what would she have to blab about? Obviously, she has dirt on Hilda and Mr. Vaughn. I'm guessing involuntary commitment would silence her, but what does she know? You said Gia escaped from a place called Terra Isle?"

"Yeah."

"I've never heard of it."

"Neither has KnightScape."

"There's no doubt it's suspicious. I'll look into it, I promise."

"I need to go," she said, her energy depleted. "Skyla and I have a busy day. And tonight we're making an audiovisual presentation for your parents' fundraising benefit. So, if you don't mind, I'd like to walk back to my car alone."

He looked beaten. "Abbie, I'm sorry for how I made you feel. I mean it."

"It's fine, Dylan. But from here on out, you're the homeowner's son, and I'm the unskilled help, okay? Hell, by law, the Compliance Society would throw me in jail for looking at you."

Abbie and Skyla arrived at Ben's office in the south wing of Redwood Manor promptly at five o'clock to create the Envision Plus presentation for the De Youngs' upcoming benefit gala. The first thing Abbie noticed was the metallic hydrogen drone silently hovering in the open window. It looked like the one that had delivered the acceptance letter to her house four days ago. On the adjacent wall, in between bookshelves, was a lit glass wall cabinet filled with antique rifles and bayonets. One weapon in particular stood out: a flame-throwing rifle, like the one Dad used to burn their crop after harvest back in Idaho. It was an odd addition to Ben's collection, and Abbie couldn't imagine what he used it for.

Law books and manila folders with papers poking out in all directions surrounded Ben, who sat at his desk. Oblivious to their arrival, he licked the back of an envelope, then took a puff of his cigar, the sea air lifting the smoke to the coffered ceiling.

"Hi, Ben," Skyla said softly.

He jumped and stared at them blankly. Then it hit him. "Skyla! Abbie! Our meeting completely slipped my mind. As you can see, I'm neck-deep in my current defense case."

"Is now a bad time?" Skyla asked.

"No, no, it's a fine time," he said, flustered. Snuffing out his cigar, he gestured for them to sit in the chairs in front of the desk.

"Who are you defending, sir?" Abbie asked, hoping she wasn't speaking out of turn.

"Please, call me Ben. I'm defending the mayor of Port Allegiance." He slapped a law book closed. "A woman from City Hall has accused him of sexual harassment." He stopped and looked at them a moment before adding with a surreptitious smirk, "Just between us, of course, he's guilty as sin, but the Compliance Society has ordered me to defend him."

The Compliance Society being none other than Hilda.

Next to his monitor, sat a small red gift box holding a gold infinity ring with diamonds on the side. It was the same symbol as the tattoo on her ankle Ty had insisted she get, along with his name, forever branding her. On her next day off, she'd visit the tattoo parlor in Eureka and have *TY* turned into *CLARITY*.

"I read about him in the paper," Skyla said to Ben as Abbie snapped out of her musing. "The woman has audio proof, but the mayor's claiming it's fake?"

"That's the gist of it," he said, his lazy eye wandering off. "The guy is a real piece of work." He carried the envelope over to the drone and slipped it into its mouth. "Wendy, deliver this to the mayor at 531 Forest Glen Boulevard in Port Allegiance. Signature required. And while you're at it, spit in his face."

"Yes, Ben. I'm on it," Wendy said in her feathery voice. "Your sense of humor is most amusing." She flew away and the window automatically closed, like a garage door.

"Thank you, I try," he mumbled. On the way back to his desk, he tripped on a pile of books, catching himself before he nose-dived to the floor. At his desk, he gripped his head as if he didn't know where to begin.

Now wasn't the right time for Abbie to ask him about upgrading her to the Silver Access Card. Hard to believe this was Dylan's father. For one, they looked nothing alike, and secondly, what Dylan had said about his father was true. The man was ineffectual, a bit like a bumbling idiot. Poor Dylan—she had sure ripped him a new one at the beach that morning. But it was for the best; no way she'd lose her job over him. She asked Ben if he was okay.

He took in a deep breath, his face softening. "It's been a long time since anybody asked me if I was okay. Thank you, young lady. The truth is I'm not. I'm inundated with cases, and Gia, who served as my part-time legal assistant, is gone. I have yet to find someone to replace her."

"I'm so sorry," Skyla said. "Everyone misses her."

"Why do you think she quit, sir? Sorry, I mean Ben," Abbie asked, casting a fishing line and hoping Skyla wasn't upset by the question.

"Skyla and I have discussed this many times. And we always come back to the East Bay Serial Killer. Patsy, or Ms. B to you, believes she quit because she'd had enough of the pressure, and I'd love to believe that, but Gia's prerequisites for law school were at PBU, right here at her fingertips."

As a tear rolled down Skyla's cheek, he addressed her sympathetically. "I know it's been hard on you, Skyla, but we must forge ahead, right?"

She wiped her face and nodded faintly.

So, Hilda was keeping secrets from Ben, too. It was cruel for Abbie to keep the truth from them. She'd tell Skyla about Gia after a little more sleuthing. With Hilda knocked out drunk every night by ten, Abbie figured she might be able to break into her library and snoop around.

Yeah, right. Stupid, reckless idea.

Ben cleared off his desk and asked them to come around. He opened a folder on his laptop, where he kept the photos and videos he wanted included in the presentation, telling them he had faith they'd create something spectacular. "The presentation needs to be around ten minutes, tops, and the mood somber and depressing, like those commercials where hungry, filthy children are begging for food. Images like that sure tug at people's heartstrings."

Manipulative, yes, but effective.

Hilda materialized at the door and cleared her throat, both hands on her hips. She cocked her head sideways and peered at Ben. "Why do you have 'the help' in your office?"

"Darling! I-I-I've gotten behind on my work," he stammered, his face turning ashen. "Skyla and Abbie have generously accepted my request to help with our upcoming gala." He went on to explain the persuasive presentation Abbie had created for the governor, a plea to help the homeless, and how he hoped she and Skyla could help persuade the residents of Port Allegiance to open their pocketbooks as well.

His argument didn't convince Hildabeast. "Meet me in the library!" she bellowed. "We need to talk."

"Can I finish setting up the ladies first, then join you in a moment?" he asked, fighting for composure.

"Now!" Hilda stormed away.

OMG, Ben was a passive little boy cowering before Mommy. *Pathetic.*

He stood. "I apologize for my wife's outburst. Have I given you both enough information to help you get started?"

"Plenty." Abbie nodded, cringing, and he slunk out with his tail between his legs.

Later that night—11:33, to be exact—Abbie crept upstairs to Hilda's library. She hoped she'd get lucky and find information on Gia. If somebody caught her skulking around, like Rex, for example, she'd say she was thirsty and was heading to the kitchen for water. So much for stopping her risky, reckless behavior.

She squinted as she crept down the wide corridor lined with dimly burning sconces. The house was eerily still except for the annoying buzzing that sounded like a pissed-off bee she still had in her ear, thanks to Ty. As she moved past the priceless oil paintings of dead people, their souls suspended on the walls, they seemed to judge her, subliminally telling her she was an audacious fool. One caught her attention, and she stopped: *The Pauper's Noose* by Frederico Balchaise, 1747, in which a young woman hung dead above the church pulpit, the congregation below her cheering. The image was so disturbing that Abbie quickly scampered past it.

At Hilda's library, unnerved and sweating, she stood before the small bronze emblem with a raised star in the center and stared at it. *Do not enter without permission*, Skyla had instructed. One final glance over her shoulder, and Abbie reached for the knob and quietly opened the door, then shut herself in the darkness.

She patted around the wall for the light switch and found a row of about five of them. When she flipped the one closest to her, indirect lighting illuminated the perimeter of the ceiling. Awestruck, she studied the ornate space with its mahogany panels and moldings. The bookshelves likely held every leather-bound classical tale written throughout the ages. Inhaling the smell of the musty old treasures, she fantasized about climbing the sliding wood ladder that allowed access to the book-lined balcony above.

On the wall across from the desk was a stone fireplace, and above it hung a massive elephant head. Beyond angering her, it brought on waves of sadness. Hunting for food was one thing, but this…

More than a century of history lived within these walls. Respectable people had gathered here, lived their lives, but Hilda had tainted its legacy; she didn't deserve to occupy the space.

Abbie shook herself from her dark thoughts. Time to get busy. But where to start? At the far left of the room stood an out-of-place modern workstation, and next to it, wooden file cabinets. Each drawer front brandished a label holder with the letters *A* through *Z* dropped inside. She made a beeline for the drawer labeled *T*, for Terra Isle, and thumbed through the folders alphabetically: TACK ROOM, TAXES (ten years' worth), TAXIDERMY, TECH MANUALS, TERMITE CONTROL, TESLA RECEIPTS. No Terra Isle.

In the *V* drawer, she searched for Vaughn Capital Group. Nope. Then the *J* drawer for Jayden. Nothing. And that was odd, because Dylan had said Hilda and Vaughn had been working on a moneymaking venture for a few years. Why no file for him or his business?

She flipped through the *Q* drawer, and holy shit, there QUINN, GIA sat tucked away between QUICKEN 14 LEDGERS and QUITCLAIM DEEDS. She plucked out the folder and opened it. Inside were a dozen or more three-by-five photos of Gia, photos Hilda had likely handed out to her search goons.

Gia's face looked drugged and terrified. Someone had written the numbers *0187* in black ink on her forehead. *Why?*

A squeaking sound at the door nearly buckled her knees. No time to run, and no way to explain this boundary violation. She took one of the photos and crammed it into her apron. Goodbye, Bronze Access Card, goodbye, college…

"Abbie?"

She spun around to find Dylan standing there, his mouth hanging open. "We gotta stop meeting like this," he whispered, the trope befitting. "What are you doing in here?"

Her face grew hot. "Same thing you're doing: looking for clues about Gia and what your mother did to her." She stopped a moment, and added, "Are you angry?" Not that she cared in the least what he thought. Unless maybe she did?

A slow smile lifted the corners of his lips. "Only that you didn't lock the door behind you," he said, injecting a little levity into an untenable situation. He locked it.

Reaching into her apron, she pulled out the photo and met him at the workstation, where she handed it to him.

Narrowing his eyes, he examined it. "My God. What have they done to her? What's with the numbers on her forehead?"

She shrugged. "I searched the file cabinets, but couldn't find anything."

"Not surprising," he said and handed the photo back to her. He whipped out his wallet and pulled out a QDAC, a high-tech thumb drive like the one Uncle Jesse's assistant had given her when she visited the auto shop. "This gem will hold Hilda's entire hard drive."

Hilda's dark energy filled the room. "But where's her computer?"

Dylan plopped down at the workstation, and when he triple-tapped the glassy black surface, an embedded keyboard lit from within. Then a flap opened and a monitor rose, so paper-thin it looked like the slightest flick would shatter it. The monitor read, UNKNOWN USER. PLEASE ENTER PASSWORD, and a dialog box popped up.

The entire desk surface *was* the computer! *Incredible.* "You have the password?" Abbie asked, still amazed at what she was seeing.

"Maybe," he answered uncertainly. He opened the drawer above his legs and pulled out a diamond-studded business card case. He lifted the lid and flipped the case over, the cards falling into his other hand. Hilda had handwritten the password on the card facing up.

"What are you up to, mother dearest?"

After he typed *Gold.4.leafclover@89*, dozens of colorful icons materialized on the screen. Then he pushed the QDAC into a slot on the glass surface.

This computer was way beyond Abbie's understanding. She looked on as he feverishly typed.

"Of course," he said with an air of disappointment.

"What?"

"I can clone the hard drive to the QDAC, but the files are more secure than Fort Knox."

"Well, what are *we* gonna do about it?"

"When we get back to our rooms, I'll go online and search for hacking software." A few more taps on the keyboard, and the monitor read, APPROXIMATE UPLOAD TIME: SIXTY SECONDS. A countdown widget began.

When a doorknob jiggled somewhere nearby, Abbie flinched, a lightning bolt shooting through her body.

"Shit," Dylan whispered, his lips tight. "Someone from the carriage house is trying to get in."

From underneath the door, a shadow flickered. Hilda shouted, "Grab my key from the center console. We're locked out."

Abbie swung her head to the widget. Forty-eight seconds remaining.

Dylan pointed across the room. "Hide in the closet, and I'll meet you in there."

She ran for it and closed herself into the dark space of hanging coats, a mink, and something itchy. How stupid, thinking she'd get away with it. *Hurry, Dylan, please hurry!* She pictured Skyla on the terrace burning sage, yearning for Gia to come home. Abbie was a terrible friend; she should've told Skyla yesterday as soon as she'd overheard the conversation.

Finally, yes! Dylan squeezed in next to her. As he closed the door, muted voices spilled into the library. His warm body felt good pressed against hers, like it had while they'd waited for rescue in the tree stump. But damn, her armpits had stunk up the closet.

"It'll be fine," he whispered.

"Did the cloning finish?"

"Yes, but I forgot to push the chair back under her desk."

There was a foreboding lull. Abbie imagined Hilda as a bloodhound, her snout leading straight to them.

"What's wrong, darling?" Ben asked.

"Somebody's been in here. I always push in my chair when I leave my desk."

"Nonsense. You must have forgotten last time. Grab whatever you needed and go to bed."

"Have a drink with me first," she insisted.

"Of course, dear. What's your fancy?"

"Vodka martini, light on the vermouth."

"For Christ's sake," Dylan whispered, finding Abbie's hand and gently squeezing it.

After a half hour of Abbie and Dylan listening to his insufferable mother bitch about how HR Enterprises was suffering because the state had cut housing assistance to the citizens of Humboldt County, his parents left.

"Well, that was stressful," Abbie said, exhaling with relief.

"Try living a lifetime with her," Dylan quipped.

"Can't imagine. Listen, I'm telling Skyla about Gia tonight. She's going out of her mind with worry."

"I think you should wait until we learn more. There's no sense getting her hopes up, right?"

It didn't feel right, but she agreed.

CHAPTER TWELVE

Days earlier

As Gia Quinn lay on the bed, naked and cold and plotting her escape, she counted the days since the blurry figure had thrown her in the loony bin. Three days? Four? It was hard to pinpoint.

The pasty-faced man was dumber than a thief in a bright-orange jumpsuit. She overheard him telling a new orderly the pass code to exit the building. *020189* which she recited to herself until she had it memorized.

Someone stopped outside her room, the shadow filtering through underneath the door. A tray of food slid through the slot. Starving, she scurried to it and devoured the mystery sandwich. And pudding! Forget the spoon; she frantically scooped her fingers into the cup and filled her mouth.

In an instant she grew woozy, and the room began spinning like a merciless amusement park ride. Before she could make it to her bed, she crumpled to the floor, paralyzed.

Pasty-Face stood over her and grinned. His bottom incisor had rotted out, and plaque coated the rest of his teeth. He hurled her onto the bed. Gawking at her body, he ran his index finger up her leg, past her groin, over her breast, and up to her cheek. "You're one juicy peach," he said with a lecherous grin.

She wanted to knock those nasty teeth right out of his skull.

As he wheeled her down the hall, passing patients' rooms, their doors and windows open, the stench of bodily excrement mixed with the ocean air rushed across her bare skin. She listened. The sound of sloshing water. This wasn't Eureka's Harbor View West psych ward—too close to the ocean.

When Pasty-Face pushed her through another set of double doors, there was a *thunk*. At the far end of a long white hall, he shoved her into a room labeled ONCOLOGY. *Why?* She didn't have cancer.

He stopped in the center of the room, parked her under a brightly lit ceiling-mounted medical lamp, and left her alone, waiting. Waiting for what? When she tried to pinch her eyes closed, she couldn't, so she stared at the ceiling, tears coursing down her cheeks.

After several never-ending minutes, the nasal nurse rolled in the medical cart. She tied a tourniquet around Gia's arm and drew blood. After filling the glass vial, she checked her watch, wrote something on a sticky label, and affixed it to the vial, then dropped it into her scrub's shirt pocket.

A guy who looked too young to be a doctor hovered above her holding a chart. He inspected the papers. "All set. Attach the oximeter and administer the first round."

First round? The vitals monitor beeped wildly.

"But she's awake."

"I'm well aware. Just do as you're told."

When the nurse plunged in the needle, the icy liquid burning, the walls and ceiling started rippling as if made of water. The motion sickness lingered as her lungs grew heavy as if liquid were filling them.

"Okay," the nurse said, "we're at fifteen seconds."

"Next round," he ordered, sweat streaming from his forehead onto his cheeks.

Another syringe, burning worse than the first. Then *bam*—her limbs curled inward.

"Blood pressure two forty over one twenty," the nurse reported. "She's going to have a heart attack or a stroke."

"Next round," he ordered without acknowledging her concern.

In a split second, vomit launched up Gia's windpipe, but with her next breath, it suctioned down into her lungs. Teetering on the edge of death, she silently screamed, *Help me! Please, someone help me! I'm dying!*

Oblivious, he continued writing on his chart while the nurse watched the monitor.

Finally, the nurse glanced at Gia's face. "She's turning blue! She's asphyxiating!"

Without a hint of emotion, he said calmly, "Get her in the Trendelenburg position and get her suctioned out. We're not done with this one yet."

Then the room faded until it dissolved into a pinpoint.

CHAPTER THIRTEEN

Sunday, December 23

Dear Journal,

Was up most of the night tossing and turning. Breaking into Hilda's library—Jesus. And yesterday, when I dropped off my car after meeting with Dylan at the beach, I watched Mom through the window. She was hanging Liza's and my Christmas stockings on the mantle. I could've stopped in for coffee, asked if she's enjoying her new book club. How hard would it have been to give her a little of my time?

Ms. B is letting us off at 3:00 on Christmas. Mom will be thrilled to have the family together. I'll make it up to her then.

Love,
Abbie

IT WAS NEARLY NOON as Abbie stood at the kitchen sink and clipped red rose stems and dropped them into a crystal vase.

She hadn't immediately noticed the blood pooling on her fingers. And Clem was singing annoying Christmas carols. How could she feel the holiday joy with the world coming apart at the seams?

When Dylan walked in, she tensed, her heart thudding into her feet. She was about to put her acting skills to the test. It wasn't going to be easy.

"Good morning, everyone," he greeted. He wore blue jeans and a fitted black T-shirt, and his hair was still wet from showering. He grabbed an apron from the drawer and tied it behind his back.

Skyla looked him in the eyes, ignoring the compliance rules, and dropped what she was doing as she said, "Good morning, Dylan, have you met Abbie Spencer, Gia's replacement?"

Dylan turned to Abbie without a glimmer of recognition. "Hello, nice to meet you."

As he walked toward her, Kristine intercepted him. "Welcome home," she cooed, shamelessly flaunting her assets.

"Thanks." When he curtly brushed past her, the humiliation on Kristine's face sent waves of glee through Abbie. As he shook her hand, his eyes glimmered their secret. His scent was delicious. And was he purposefully torturing her with those tanned biceps?

"How are you enjoying working at Redwood Manor?" he asked.

She was his subordinate, and addressing him felt awkward. "I like it very well, thank you."

Clem chimed in. "Enough lollygagging around, Dylan. Please fill the dishwasher. Chop-chop."

Wow. Dylan must not be the guy living in the ivory tower she had imagined him to be. She lifted the vase, and as she carried it to the other side of the kitchen, she passed Clem, who had arranged crêpes suzette and melon wedges on two plates, placed them on a rolling cart, and covered them with a sterling silver dome. On top of the silverware, wrapped in napkins, he crisscrossed two roses he took from Abbie's vase.

"Looks beautiful," she complimented.

"Come," Skyla said. "Every Sunday morning, Mr. and Mrs. De Young eat breakfast in the dining parlor between their bedrooms. I'll show you the ropes."

Bedrooms, plural? As Abbie backed away at the prospect of seeing Hilda, Dylan said, "I'll do it. I haven't seen my parents since I came home."

Ms. B, who had walked into the kitchen and overheard the conversation, said to Dylan, "You'll see them soon enough. Abbie needs to learn proper room service protocol."

He glanced at Abbie, his expression saying, "I tried." Back to loading the dishwasher.

What a nightmare.

As Abbie and Skyla rode the wood-paneled elevator to the second floor, Skyla looked at her and gasped. "Oh my God, look at you! There's blood spots on your apron!"

Abbie looked down and could practically feel Hilda's wrath cramming her into that portable coffin. "Shit. Let's go back so I can get a fresh one."

"No time." Skyla untied hers and handed it to Abbie. "Wear it over yours."

"Then you won't have one."

"Don't worry about me. I can handle her."

This new friend had her back. It felt pretty good. A shame Abbie was such a shitty one.

When the elevator opened, Skyla pushed the rolling cart down the hall and stopped before the dining parlor. "You *must* knock twice, then say, 'room service.' Don't be nervous. It's a cinch."

Abbie whispered in her ear, "Yeah, it's a cinch to knock, but once we're in there, that's a different story." She rapped twice softly. "Room service!"

"Enter!" Hilda responded.

Skyla walked in first, with Abbie following close behind. Hilda was sitting at the mahogany table reading the morning paper, her readers perched precariously on the tip of her nose. Inspecting Skyla's attire, she said sternly, "Where is your apron?"

Abbie's face reddened at the idea of Skyla taking the heat for her own carelessness.

"I apologize, ma'am," Skyla said like an obedient soldier, dropping her head. "I forgot it."

"One more strike, and out you go." Hilda stood, sashayed over to Abbie, and analyzed her face. "I swear I've seen you before."

And that face of yours appears trapped in a high-velocity wind tunnel. Those lips—Luscious Linda, the blow-up doll. Abbie's instincts made her step back as Hilda's presence violated her space, but she held her tongue.

Ben walked in from his attached bedroom, wearing a tailored navy-blue suit. He sat and opened the business section of the newspaper. "Please roll the cart to the table, Skyla."

"Yes, sir. Is there anything else we can do for—?"

"No," Hilda interjected. "Get back to work."

"Yes, ma'am," Skyla replied, smiling politely. She took Abbie by the elbow, and they exited the room.

In the hallway, Abbie leaned against the wall and took a deep breath to collect herself. "My God, she's a miserable woman."

Hilda's and Ben's voices filtered through the door. Skyla grinned, tiptoed over, and cupped her ear to it. Abbie followed like a naughty schoolgirl.

"…cannot imagine spending one's life as a servant," Hilda said. "What a pair, those two. They'll never amount to anything. But I swear I've seen the new one somewhere before. So help me, I'll figure it out."

"You do that," Ben said to humor her. "Let's eat before the crêpes get cold."

"Come on," Skyla whispered. "I think I'm going to be sick."

A loud clearing of someone's throat made the girls jump. It was Rex, standing at the far end of the hall. With his index finger, he beckoned them his way.

"Don't worry, he has no authority over us," Skyla whispered.

When they stepped closer, they flanked the wall opposite him.

Almost past him, almost past…

He grabbed Abbie's arm. "I've been watching you. You're trouble, little missy."

Trouble? Had he spotted her breaking into Hilda's library? At this point, she realized this creepy butler was to be avoided at all costs. She wrenched her arm away.

As the girls hurried back to the kitchen, Abbie plotted ways to taint Rex and Hilda's food. Not to kill them, of course, just to make them suffer a little. Maybe Ex-Lax-laced chocolate chip cookies? How entertaining to watch them lose their bowels in a room full of uppities.

The second they got back to the kitchen, Clem said to Skyla, "I need for you and Dylan to run to the market. My shopping list is extensive. I sent it to both of your phones."

Dylan, sitting at the farm table, set his coffee cup down and stood.

"That's right," Skyla said and began folding a pile of hand towels. "The Christmas Eve party's tomorrow night."

Ms. B, who was entering staff schedules into the planning monitor, stopped what she was doing. "Skyla can't go with Dylan. She has an evaluation in a half hour."

"How about Abbie, then?" Clem said. "She should familiarize herself with the market anyway."

"I'll go!" Kristine piped up, her head popping out of the pantry.

Apparently, this one-dimensional psycho wasn't going to give up.

"No," Clem said. "Abbie's going. You get to the dining room and start dusting the furniture. And when you're done, the downstairs toilet bowls need scrubbing."

"The toilet bowls? Seriously?" she asked, aghast, as Abbie relished every second of the disgusted look on Kristine's face.

Alone with Dylan. Perfect opportunity to ask him about his luck with the hacking software.

In the seven-car carriage house, with its high-pitched ceiling of hand-hewn beams spanning from dormer to dormer, Abbie and Dylan approached a row of expensive cars, mostly makes and models she had never heard of. Dylan headed left to a black Lamborghini Roadster at the end of the row.

"We're not taking that thing, are we?" she asked, her arms limp at her sides.

Amused, he opened the passenger door for her.

"But where are the groceries supposed to fit?"

"The trunk's bigger than it looks, trust me. Hop in and buckle up, and get ready to feel seven hundred fifty horsepower!"

A flashback to Ty racing down Myrtle and almost killing them bounced through her head like a stone skipping over water. One thought led to the next, and then the next…

"Okay, okay, I'm teasing," he conceded. "I promise, I won't drive fast."

Had her fear been that obvious? He walked around and climbed in. Although this was their fourth meeting, she still couldn't shake her sense of unease in his presence. It didn't help she was attracted to him. She had thought Ty had snuffed out any hope of her ever feeling amorous again. And Dylan felt the same way about her—she could sense it. But it didn't matter. She needed this job, and she wouldn't do anything to jeopardize it, or worse, end up in jail. Of course, she thought, she had already jeopardized it by breaking into Hilda's office, but that was worth Ms. B firing her over. Regardless, distancing herself from Dylan at this point seemed disingenuous.

He backed them out of the carriage house, and as the sports car rumbled slowly along the cobblestones beneath the canopy of ivy-covered oak trees, Abbie asked if he'd found the hacking software needed to crack Hilda's hard drive.

He nodded. "Wasn't easy. On the dark web, I found a company in Germany specializing in encrypted data. They won't send me the upload link until my payment goes through, and that won't be until Wednesday morning. I still haven't figured out how I'm gonna intercept the credit card bill, though. If Hilda sees it before the software arrives, I'm in deep shit."

"But that's three more days," she said with alarm. "We can't wait until then. Her thugs might find Gia, if they haven't already."

"They haven't," he said confidently and cranked up the heat. "I managed to mirror all texts delivered to Hilda's phone."

"So, everything she receives, you get on your phone, too?"

"Yep," he said with a sly grin. "Didn't read anything damning, but in her most recent text exchange with Jayden, he asked if she had found Gia and she said no. And there's no sign of her at the barricades leading out of Humboldt County, so she's gotta be close."

The good news relaxed Abbie's knotted muscles a bit. As they approached the iron gate, Dylan pushed a button on the overhead console, and the gate opened. But seriously, what was the point when the entire city was already a fortress?

He revved the engine a few times and pulled the car onto Waterfront Drive.

"Not again," he moaned, peering into the rearview mirror.

Abbie swung her head around to find a black car moving in fast. "Who's following us?"

"My chaperones." He stomped on the gas, leaving the other car swimming in a cloud of exhaust.

CHAPTER FOURTEEN

GIA FLUTTERED IN AND OUT OF CONSCIOUSNESS. She willed her aching eyes open. *The hospital... The cameras... The ticking clock... How much time has passed?* Her throat and lungs burned, and her temples pounded in unison with her heart. She shivered, her bare skin wet and sticky.

The nurse backed into the room, pulling the evil cart toward the bed. "You should be plenty relaxed for your next treatment. If you're a good girl, I won't strap you down this time. You think you can be a good girl?"

Gia nodded. "Please, what day is it? How long have I been here?"

"The passing of time should be of little relevance to you."

"We're probably close to the same age," Gia pleaded. "You could be me, having this done to you. Doesn't it bother you?"

"Not one iota," said the nurse casually. "You're here because you broke the law. Did you think you'd go unpunished?"

Broke *what* law?

Out of nowhere, an ear-piercing alarm sounded. When a frantic man bellowed over the loudspeaker, "Escapee, escapee!", the nurse bolted out the open door into the hall and slipped on the freshly mopped floor, right before Gia's eyes. *Thunk!* Her head hit the floor hard.

Sweet justice. Gia smiled wickedly.

A woman zoomed in and knelt before the nurse. Through the caterwauling, she yelled, "She's knocked out! Get a gurney, quick!"

Gia reached for the water pitcher; too bad it wasn't popcorn, because the show was about to get exciting. Then something more satisfying than the water pitcher caught her eye. The nurse had left the hypodermic needle on the cart. She hoped it was the instant-paralysis variety.

In the hallway, orderlies were rounding up a few roaming zombified patients. A man in scrubs showed up with a gurney, lifted the nurse onto it, and wheeled her away.

Hoping nobody was monitoring her room during the emergency, Gia took a gamble, grabbed the needle, and parked the cart outside her room. Any drugged-up zombie could've stolen the needle, right?

But where to hide it? She shut herself in the bathroom. The toilet tank? Nah, too obvious. Under the sink? She reached in and felt around the wooden frame. Just as she suspected, there was a three-quarter-inch ledge above the cabinet door, like the one she hid her weed on—in a house she could no longer visualize. But her memory was slowly coming back…

CHAPTER FIFTEEN

Monday, December 24

Dear Journal,

First note to self: Always check shoes before leaving bath-room. (Three feet of trailing toilet paper as you serve break-fast disgusts Hilda and causes Skyla and Carter to bust a gut.)

Second note to self: Always check ingredient labels when making cocktails. (I accidentally made Ben's Bloody Mary with one tablespoon of ghost pepper sauce, not Worcestershire sauce, which set his mouth on fire and left Hilda laughing hysterically.)

Third note to self: Don't let your guard down just because Hilda lowers hers.

Love,
Abbie

THE CHRISTMAS EVE PARTY commenced outside under the brick-and-ivy-covered "porte cochere," as Clem called it. The staff called it the covered porch. Most everyone, except Abbie and Skyla, was getting their cigarette fix in before the dinner bell rang. As staffers flocked outside to mingle with each other, Skyla introduced Abbie to the gardeners and stable hands she hadn't yet met.

An engine roared down the cobblestone driveway, then headlights filtered through the night fog. A brand-new black Ford truck came to a screeching halt in front of the porch. "Oohs" and "aahs" filled the air.

"Damn, look at that shiny beast!" Skyla exclaimed.

The truck door swung open, and out jumped Carter. "Look what Daddy bought today."

"Carter, what the hell!" Skyla said, dazzled. As she hopped inside, the rest of the group gathered around the truck and fondled it.

"Hey, hey, fingerprints, peeps, fingerprints," Carter scolded in jest.

On a sous-chef's salary? But if anyone was deserving, it was him. He'd worked hard for it.

After several minutes of Abbie delighting in his joy over his new toy, the bell rang, summoning the twelve spirited staff members to the great room. The buffet spanned multiple tables, each bedecked with blue spruce branches and holly. On the first table sizzled two juicy prime rib roasts, a spiral ham, prawns, and scallops. On the other was the usual fare of mashed potatoes, fresh salad, and a dozen or more side dishes Clem had prepared.

At the opulent dining room table, lavishly garnished with an assortment of fresh flowers and the finest silver, Abbie, wearing the black formfitting dress Skyla had lent her, settled next to Skyla on a blue-velvet-upholstered chair as the crystal chandeliers sparkled above everyone's eager faces. At one end of the table stood Clem, and at the other, Ms. B.

Abbie scanned the room for Dylan. What had happened to them in the forest had forged a bond that would forever connect them. But if she didn't get her feelings under control, she might do something foolish. As Ty used to say, *A guy has needs.* Well, so did the ladies. But she cast the carnal thoughts from her mind. She whispered to Skyla, "Are Hilda and Ben home?"

"They're hiding in their bedrooms. You think they'd mingle with us genetically inferior paupers?"

Abbie chuckled. "Suppose not."

When Dylan sauntered in, Abbie nearly choked on an olive. He sat beside Carter, and the two fist-bumped. He smiled at everyone, but his gaze lingered on Abbie. If she didn't break the spell, curiosity would rouse suspicion. She glanced at Kristine who had witnessed her and Dylan's furtive connection. Talk about flying daggers. When an involuntary chuckle burst through Abbie's lips, Skyla shot her a questioning look.

Dylan and Carter began talking about their next fishing trip, and how they wanted to spend the night on the open sea. Carter promised he wouldn't puke on the boat again. Dylan said they'd better hit the gym if they were going to reel in another four-hundred-pound halibut. Did they actually get that big? Not the ones she beheaded at Pacific One Fishery, that's for sure.

"You look ravishing, Ms. B," Clem complimented from across the table.

Ms. B blushed. Her long auburn hair hung below her shoulders and curled away from her face. "Why, thank you, Clem. You don't look so bad yourself."

Abbie had already sensed the sexual tension between them: the coy brushes against each other, the secret smiles only they understood. Earlier, she had seen them leaving the pantry looking flushed and disheveled. Treasonous, according to the manifesto.

Ms. B tapped her wine glass with a spoon. "Excellent. We're all here. I have a few words to share with you before we dine. First and foremost, thank you for tolerating Clem's and Carter's ridiculous dance moves."

The whole group burst out laughing, Carter being the loudest with a honking sort of snort.

Clem stood and bowed. "Thank you, thank you very much," he said, Elvis-style.

Carter sang, *"You ain't nothin' but a hound dog."*

Abbie was laughing so hard her gut hurt, and Skyla claimed to have peed herself.

"Okay, everybody, one more thing," Ms. B continued, wiping away her tears. "Because of your collective efforts, this has been the best staff in the history of my tenure here at Redwood Manor. Thank you dearly for your loyalty and hard work. You make me look good."

Everyone stood, the room filling with joyous applause.

When they sat back down, Dylan remained standing. "I have a few words to share, too. First, a special thank you to Ms. B and Clem, who pretty much raised me from a small boy. Without your love, your friendship, I...I don't know what would have become of me. As William Shakespeare once said, 'A friend is one that knows you as you are, understands where you have been, accepts what you have become, and still, gently allows you to grow.'"

"Cheers to that," Clem said, raising his glass and everyone clinked their glasses together. "Now, let's dish up, my friends."

After ample delicious food and good conversation, the partygoers, bloated and half drunk, took to the dance floor. The sound system played an eclectic collection of pop, classic rock, and country music.

Abbie scanned the room for Dylan as she sat alone at the bar. He had disappeared after dinner. Not letting it bother her, she watched her co-workers whooping it up, enjoying themselves.

Carter danced toward her, swaying his head to a song she had never heard before. He held out a hand. "Heavy hearts need to dance. Shall we, Ms. Abbie?"

Apparently, she'd make a lousy poker player. "We shall," she said, taking his hand and lifting it high enough to perform a spin underneath.

"Look who has the moves!" He pulled her in close for a slow dance.

"Twinkle Toes Spencer here," she joked.

As they danced in leisurely circles, she caught sight of Dylan walking in, his piercing eyes sending the butterflies fluttering. Their visual foreplay brought a flush to her face.

Carter whispered in her ear, "You know he has a thing for you?"

Abbie tensed. "Yeah, right. He told you that?"

"Didn't have to. I pick up on stuff," he said hushedly and winked. "The two of you awkwardly avoid each other, and he acts different when you enter the room. No worries, I won't tell."

She whispered back, "There's nothing to tell."

After a moment, he asked, "You happy here? I mean, working at Redwood Manor."

"Yeah, I guess. The money's incredible. You're obviously doing well, buying that shiny truck."

"Can't wait to show it off to the fam-bam in Compton. I'm leaving in the morning—be gone for a week. Usin' my vacation time before it expires."

"Are you nuts?" she said. "You're gonna get carjacked driving it down there!"

"Nah, I pack heat."

"Well, that's reassuring. But I can't imagine how you can afford the payment."

"How can I afford it on a sous-chef salary with meager second and third side jobs?" His face reddened, and he grew nervous, like he regretted what he had said. But why?

"You have a third side job? What is it?" she pressed.

A god-awful rock song blasted, relieving him from answering her question. She stared at the back of his head curiously as he scurried to the keg, where everyone had already gathered. As she sat at the bar, wondering where Skyla had gone, Carter took the hose spigot and sprayed beer directly into his mouth.

"Chug, chug, chug!" the crowd cheered.

Her social battery depleted, Abbie dropped her head to the bar top and rested. What a crazy, fun evening! If only Mom could experience this side of life. She thought of her parents living their sad lives over the wall, unable to move on. The dichotomy between Abbie's new life and her former—

A pleasant aroma filled her nostrils… *Dylan.* Her eyelids fluttered, and when she opened them, there was a folded note next to her ginger ale. She glanced around and spotted him leaving the room.

The note read, *Library, midnight. Don't be followed.*

CHAPTER SIXTEEN

AT MIDNIGHT, ABBIE INCONSPICUOUSLY backed down the hall toward Hilda's library. When she entered, Dylan stood from the hearth, flames crackling behind him. The aroma of burning oak conjured memories of spending time at Grandma and Grandpa Spencer's house in Sandpoint.

"You made it," he said, smiling warmly, and her eyes dropped to a bottle of red wine and two wine glasses on the hearth. *Shit. With alcohol comes expectations.*

She closed the door, locked it, and leaned against it. "I'm tempting fate here. Your parents are home."

"They won't find out. When I passed Hilda's bedroom, her drunken snoring sounded like a broken foghorn."

"But why meet here, when other rooms are safer?" she asked, sauntering toward him.

"You'll find out soon enough," he answered, pouring a glass of merlot and handing it to her.

So damn tempting. "No, thank you. I quit a while back."

Surprised, he retracted the glass and set it down. "There's a story there."

"Yeah—a big, ugly one. A conversation for another day. But please, you go ahead."

"I'm fine without."

She appreciated his thoughtfulness. "Tonight was wonderful. One of the best Christmas Eves I've ever had."

"Ms. B and Clem are the best."

"Yeah, Clem was so damn funny, telling stories about his Paris days during dinner. Can you imagine dropping a plate of food on the prime minister's lap?" The visual made her laugh almost as hard as she had at dinner.

On the hand-hewn mantle, she studied the framed photographs of Ben and Hilda posing with famous politicians and movie stars. When she spotted a photo of Dylan taken around the time they'd first met on Valentine's Day in Lake Tahoe, she picked it up. "My God, you look so young and innocent."

"I'm not innocent anymore?" he said playfully.

She set the photo back down. "You know what I mean." Then another photo caught her eye, and she picked it up. "Who are these people?"

He leaned in. "The little girl is Hilda when she was, I dunno, maybe eight or nine."

"Should've known, with the fancy tutu. And the man with the bowl cut?"

"Her adoptive father. My *so-called* grandfather."

"What's his name?"

"Walter Rhodes."

He looked familiar. "Is he an actor?"

"No. He was a professor at Cornell."

She set the photo back and sat on the hearth, and Dylan sat beside her. "You two close?"

"We were. Then we weren't. I don't know what happened. As a kid, I looked up to him, loved him. I spent the summer after third grade at his home in Ithaca, New York. Best summer of my life. Then when he retired to Malibu, he stopped answering my calls."

"That must've been incredibly painful."

"It was, yeah."

A flash of Hilda unlocking the door, barging into the room, and burning her Bronze Access Card made her jump to her feet. "I'm feeling nervous about being here."

"Please, don't go. What if I told you there was a way for us to see each other without anybody knowing—and there would be no expectations other than friendship?"

His statement took her aback. "Do you believe guys and girls can be just friends?"

He shrugged. "I haven't been in this situation. But I'd like to try. How about you?"

Not a good idea. Her attraction to him might prove fatal to her entire future. But after little thought, she caved—a controlled cave, she convinced herself. "Friendship I can handle. But what's your plan?"

"Come with me," he said as he stood, eyes gleaming mischievously. "I have something to show you."

At the far end of the library, he led her through a wide arched passageway into a miniature room with a blue-striped velvet wing chair and a walnut coffee table with matching side tables. On the ceiling, a gifted artist had hand-painted cherubs that hovered in a pale-blue sky amid fluffy clouds.

"This was my favorite room as a kid. I'd sit in that chair and stare at the ceiling and dream."

"I can see why," admitted Abbie.

He narrowed his eyes. "I have a story to tell you, and you're the first to hear it. I've kept it secret since I was a kid."

"Sounds intriguing."

"When I was little, I spent a lot of time in here reading, mostly so I could be closer to Hilda. I was constantly trying to get her attention, but she was usually too busy at her desk to notice. One evening—God, I must've been about seven—I was goofing off, totally bored. And I discovered this." With the tips of his fingers, he nudged one of the wainscot panels twice, and it opened.

"You're kidding me!" she exclaimed, awestruck. "This is my childhood fantasy come true!"

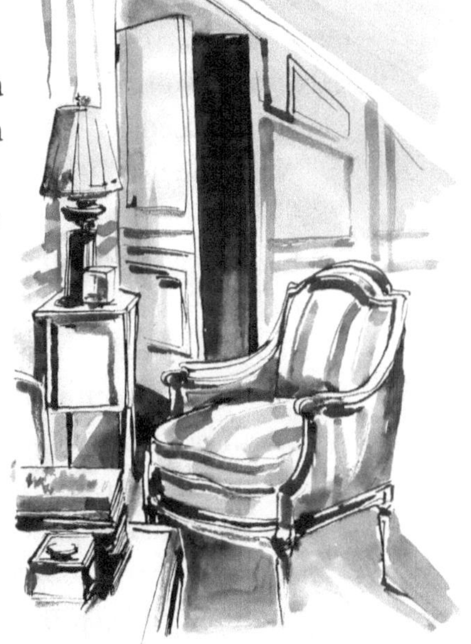

He slid inside and flicked on the light. "Come on in. We're on an adventure."

Brimming with wonder, she entered the musty space. Dylan shut them inside, their bodies pressed together. Cobwebs and dust clung to the plaster that oozed through the lath. To the left was a narrow passageway, maybe two feet wide, looking like it continued between the walls. And to the right was a set of stairs going down. Dylan explained the passageway led to the rarely used tea parlor in the east wing, where a secret panel opened next to the fireplace.

"You ready to check out these stairs?" he asked, brushing away the cobwebs.

"Never been readier," she said enthusiastically.

Dylan ducked to avoid hitting his head on the low-hanging rafters. Abbie followed, grabbing tight to the back of his shirt. Like Alice, she found herself falling down the proverbial rabbit hole.

At the bottom of the narrow creaking stairwell that seemed to continue down deep into the earth, they stopped at an iron door. He slid the latch and stepped through. The large room housed a row of three bunk beds on one side, and on the other, old maps and newspapers covered the wall. In one corner sat two hand-carved Edwardian padded chairs. Dusty boxes lay strewn about with mounds of paperwork pouring out of them. At the foot of one of the bunks rested an over-sized trunk stuffed with dust-covered clothing and blankets. On the exposed ceiling joists, more dust and cobwebs.

"What the heck is this place?"

"A World War II–era bunker," Dylan answered as he made his way to the back of the room and sat at a round quarter-sawn oak table. "In 1942, after a Japanese submarine lobbed sixteen shells at the Ellwood Oil Field in Santa Barbara, down south, the invasion sparked panic in the American populace. It was the first shelling ever on US soil. From reading through the home builder's notebooks, I gathered he had become paranoid and thought the Japanese were gonna bomb here, too. So, he built this home for his wife and children to keep them safe. And here we sit, in a paranoid man's hideout."

"What a story," Abbie said. "History was one of my favorite subjects in school."

"Funny you should say that," he said. "It was mine, too. Oh, if you need to use the restroom, it's through the door between the bunk beds."

She walked over to it, flicked on the light, and peeked in. A pillbox toilet, a white porcelain sink, and a claw-foot tub filled the small space in the white-subway-tiled room, nearly identical to the bathroom she shared with Skyla and Kristine. After checking her makeup in the mirror, she sat at the table with Dylan. "No one knows anything about this?"

"Nope. Only me, and now you. And what I'm about to tell you is even crazier."

She leaned in closer; he had her full attention.

"When I was fifteen, I rearranged the furniture down here, to make this space my own." He pointed. "I found that iron door after moving the bookshelf next to it out of the way. There was a key hanging from a nail."

"Okay…"

"Nobody had opened the door in years, and it took me a while to free the lock, but with a little oil, I finally loosened it. On the other side is a long brick tunnel."

"No way!" she said, the mysterious image implanted in her brain. "Sounds a bit like *The Lion, the Witch, and the Wardrobe.*"

"In a way, but not that magical. At the end of the tunnel is a ladder. I climbed it. It took a while to pry open the lid, but when I opened it, I was standing outside, looking at the night sky. I had no idea where I was, and as silly as it may sound, I was scared shitless, so I ran back to my bed, and had some insane dreams, as you can imagine. I returned the next morning, and found out it comes out between an old, abandoned red farmhouse and St. Mary's Church. I figured it was about several hundred yards from the wall."

Abbie thought for a moment, and pieced it together. "And that's how you met me the day we walked to the beach: you used the tunnel! I wondered why you didn't have a car."

"Couldn't have Hilda's spies notifying her that I was meeting up with someone secretly. Remember, she has me followed."

Abbie nodded, still disturbed by this clear violation. "How could I forget? So, just curious. How did the builders of the wall not dig into the tunnel?"

"Luck, I suppose," he said with a shrug. "It's pretty deep. I'm sure your head is spinning about now."

"A little. But you can go on with your story." She couldn't wait to hear the rest.

He took a deep breath. "I closed the lid behind me and covered it with branches, then explored a bit. I used to worry someone might find it, but the farmhouse is so run-down, and squatters don't go out there anymore. And that's the end of my story."

"Well, it's incredible. Thank you for trusting me with your secret, Dylan."

"The truth is, it's a relief to tell someone. Carrying a secret can make you feel alone," he said, a sadness filling his eyes.

She felt an overwhelming urge to hug him, but restrained herself. "I know about secrets. Some can eat a person alive." Her mind traveled to the foggy bluff where she and Uncle Jesse had disposed of Ty. What they had done with his body, she'd take to her own grave.

"Wanna share?" he asked.

"Not really."

He nodded. "Not to be more of a downer, but I have news about Gia. I wanted to wait to tell you until after I showed you this space, because I didn't want to ruin the moment. Plus, there isn't anything we could've done about it anyway."

She dropped her head back, alarmed. "What?"

"One of Hilda's guys found the nursing scrubs Gia was wearing."

"Where?"

"In a back-alley dumpster in Eureka."

Instantly, a plan came to her. "After my shift ends tomorrow, I'm gonna hit the streets to find her."

He looked at her with concern. "First, it's too dangerous, and second, tomorrow's Christmas."

Sure, Dylan wasn't Ty, but the presumption she couldn't take care of herself made her jaw clench.

"I've offended you again," he said.

"I know it's dangerous, Dylan." She shook off her irritation. "But tomorrow's the best time because the people searching for her will be home with their families, don't you think?"

"I'm guessing people like that don't have families."

"Well, some might," she retorted.

He rapped his fingers on the table, his thoughts churning as he studied her.

Finally, he relented. "If you're set on going, I'm coming with. You need me; you know you do."

No, she didn't need him, but it would be nice to have company. A huge yawn escaped her lungs. "We're gonna find her, I know it. I can feel it. But now I've gotta get to bed. I'm beat."

He agreed. "I'll guide you to the tea parlor's secret panel, where you can get out. I'll go out through the library, so nobody sees us together. After your shift tomorrow, use the tea parlor to meet me here, and we'll go through the tunnel to Eureka. I'll have a car waiting for us at St. Mary's."

With the amber wall sconces lighting Abbie's way down the stairwell to her bedroom, Gia plagued her thoughts. They had similar facial features, worked in the same house—it was as if they were the same person.

In her bedroom, feet aching, she kicked off her heels. A hot bath sounded good. The metal shower stall was fine, but the deep claw-foot tub, which she had yet to try, was sure to beat the cold, rust-stained tub back home.

As she was about to slip out of Skyla's black dress, Kristine barged in.

"Where'd you vanish to earlier, Abbie Flabby?" she asked, the vodka cranberry in her hand sloshing onto the hardwood floor.

Oh. She. Did. Not!

Squinting, Kristine moved in closer and took a swipe at Abbie's hair. "Cobwebs, huh? Dylan had cobwebs in his hair, too. You were off fucking him, trying to get yourself knocked up! One determined little seed, and you'll be basking in luxury for the rest of your life. That's been your plan all along, hasn't it?"

Kristine couldn't project any harder if she tried. After deciding a throat punch might be a little harsh, Abbie said calmly, "You're pathetic. You know that, right?" She took Kristine by the shoulders and drove her into the foyer. "Come in here again without knocking, and I'll hog-tie you with your tits."

Abbie locked herself in her room, her body quaking inside. Intentionally getting pregnant? She needed a long, hot bath.

Wearing her blue terry-cloth robe, she knocked on the bathroom door across from her bedroom. She was relieved nobody was using it and doubly relieved by the door's sturdy lock.

While the tub slowly filled, she dropped her robe and ran her hands over her "flabby" body. *Calm down*, she told herself. Kristine had no power to make her feel any more insecure than she allowed herself to feel.

She looked down at her legs. By this time, the stubble had grown into a forest, and she'd need a hedge trimmer to groom her more intimate areas. Unfortunately, she only had a razor, so at the sink, she lathered up with shaving cream and dehaired herself.

As she settled into the steaming tub, her body floated weightlessly, as if in space. She gently tapped her finger on the placid water, watching it ripple and imagined a colossal finger tapping the sea. How long before the wave would hit the next continent?

Holding her breath, she slipped beneath the water. The rhythmic thumping of her heart filled her ears. An occasional droplet of water escaped the faucet and plunked into her imaginary sea. No going back to the cold, rust-stained tub back home. Not ever.

When she came up for air, she gazed at the white globe ceiling fixture hanging above the tub. Something about the black finial in the center looked amiss. She squinted.

A flicker of something…

A hidden camera?

She launched out of the tub and wrapped herself tightly in her robe. Where had she put her cell phone? On the sink. She opened the camera and zoomed in on the finial, her eyes narrowing.

What the—definitely a camera!

I've been watching you, Rex had said. She had never trusted him, and she hated the way he treated Skyla. But apparently the butler was a dyed-in-the-wool pervert. She thought back to the things he must've seen her doing. The violation made her stomach turn.

The bathroom doorknob rattled, and again more violently. *Rex?* It sounded like his key was stuck in the keyhole and he was trying to free it. Maybe it was Kristine? Either way, she needed to call Ms. B for help.

Speed-dial one. She brought the phone to her ear. *No answer, no answer. Dammit!*

The rattling continued.

Speed-dial two: Ben's phone.

Keith Urban's "Blue Ain't Your Color" sounded from right outside the bathroom door.

An instant cold sweat. If terror and disappointment could kill, she'd be dead on the floor. Thinking on her feet, she swiped from photo to video on her cell, hit record, and hid it behind a few toiletries on the sink.

Click. Ben sauntered in, wearing sweatpants and a black polo T-shirt. He locked them both inside. "That damn lock. Finally, we're alone. No Skyla."

Her chest heaved, the pain razor-sharp. She backed into the sink. "Whaddoyou think you're doing, breaking in like that?"

"What do you mean? We have a connection," he said, genuinely confounded. "The way you look at me, the way you smile. C'mon, Abbie, you want me as much as I want you."

The thought of wanting him made her gag. It felt almost incestuous. "Whatever you think I feel, you're dead wrong. You're my boss, and I respected you. I can't believe you think there's something between us. There's not, I promise you. Now leave, you're freaking me out, Ben!"

The turning gears in his brain reflected in his eyes. Then his upper lip quivered. Agitation swelled to the surface. It was a look she'd seen on Ty's face, right before he—

"You know, Gia—" He shook off his careless error. "I mean, Abbie. I was kind enough to hire you, and this is how you repay me?"

Gia? So, that's why he'd hired Abbie: because they looked so much alike. Gia was his muse, and now she was gone. Had she been having a consensual relationship with Ben? Abbie doubted it. She sidestepped closer to the door. "Putting a camera in my bathroom? It's sick, Ben. Sick."

He glanced at the fixture above the tub. "You're a smart one, aren't you? I'd wager the video footage of you doing *very* personal things would go viral if I uploaded it to the net."

Abbie's eyes widened. Her boss was a psychopath, like his wife and Kristine. Had he hidden a camera in her bedroom, too? She searched for something to hurl at him. At once, he started toward her.

Her mind crumbling, she darted to the door. As she fumbled to unlock it, Ben grabbed her by the neck and shoved her against the wall. He lifted her onto the tips of her toes, his lecherous sneer so close she could smell the devil on his breath. His tongue inched out. *Oh God, no!* He moved in closer and skimmed the repulsive thing across her lips. Bite if off? She considered it. Finally, his iron grip released, and she gagged and coughed.

In a bizarre twist of emotion, his face softened. "Quid pro quo. Do you know what that means, Abbie?"

Wiping her lips clean, she shook her head.

"It means you do something for me, and I won't upload that footage. A fair bargain, wouldn't you say?"

The proposition sent waves of nausea through her. "What exactly do you want?"

With his thumb and index finger, he pinched her cheeks together. "Meet me in the sauna Thursday morning at ten. One second late, and I'll ruin your life so fast, it'll make your asshole pucker."

"What's your deal, Ben?" she croaked from between his fingers. "Can't get it up without abusing women?"

His shameful truth. He squeezed harder, and her upper lip crammed into her nose. "Shall we sample the hors d'oeuvres before Thursday?"

She fought to twist her head free, the burn searing her skin. No place to escape. She was a caged animal, and he would have his way with her. "So help me God, you touch me, I'll—" With a quick jerk, she pulled away and ran for the drain cleaner under the sink. A quick flip of the cap, and she squirted it into his eyes and up his nose.

Dropping to his knees, he covered his face, screaming in pain.

She grabbed her cell phone and raced across the hall to her bedroom, her neck vertebrae throbbing. *The sauna? Is raping women in steamy places his deviant fetish?* Somehow, she had to fight her way out. But how? Kill him? Could she? Her life would be effectively over!

How to secure her bedroom door? Searching the room, her eyes stopped on the wing chair. *Perfect!* She dragged it to the door and crammed the headrest under the knob. She didn't have Dylan's cell phone number to call him for help. Ms. B wasn't answering—probably in bed sleeping. It was after 1:30 a.m., after all. Had Skyla heard the commotion? She was probably upstairs in the great room, still partying. Had Kristine heard? She must have...

The door rattled. The bastard was persistent, she'd give him that. After a few seconds, he growled, "Little cunt, you'll get yours." Then his footsteps pounded up the stairs.

Abbie needed a disinfecting shower. Or better yet, a boiling-hot bleach bath. *Goddamn you, Ben, you sicko!* She rocked back and forth on her bed until her heartbeat settled a bit. Where had he hidden the camera in the bedroom? She'd find it later. For now, she needed a safe place to watch the video she had recorded on her cell phone. Had it recorded the entire assault?

Burrowing into a dark corner of the closet—likely no camera there—she hit the play button. There it was as clear as day: Ben breaking in and assaulting her, and even better, him threatening to upload her private moments online.

The idea hit hard…and it was brilliant. On her cell phone, she clicked SEND VIDEO BY TEXT, and in the comment box, she typed, *CHECKMATE,* and sent it to Ben's cell phone.

Delivered.

Because Ben would surely disable her phone, she took the Jesse's Auto Repair QDAC from her wallet and airdropped the video onto it.

The cell screen lit up with a response from Ben: *TRUCE. WE'RE EVEN.* Then the message dissolved and disappeared. He wasn't going to make it that easy.

CHAPTER SEVENTEEN

Days earlier

Gia's decision to escape that night might end in her death, but the alternative was a death not of her choosing. Through her barred window, a burst of clouds filled the night sky. Exhilaration filled her. She could taste freedom. But if she made it out alive, where would she go?

A memory cleared the fog bank. The sweltering sauna, the reoccurring nightmare, a flash of a blurred-out face, the image grew clearer, until…

Ben De Young sprang up on the other side of the window, their eyes locking. She hurtled backward and landed on the bed, blinking over and over until *poof*, he vanished. The room constricted into a black speck, and she allowed her body to sink into the mattress. Just a hallucination.

Her brain's floodgate opened, churning up the memories of the abuse he had inflicted upon her. *Skyla…oh my God, Skyla!* Had Ben assaulted her, too? The one person she'd lay down her life for? Her stomach heaved.

Focus on escape. Deal with him later.

The clock read 8:51. The nurse, who'd recovered from her concussion way too quickly, had never been late for her rounds. Right now, she'd be arranging the evil medical cart with blood-testing supplies—something she administered every two hours, on the hour, from eight in the morning until eight at night. *For what purpose?* In nine minutes, she'd barge in and whip out her rubber tourniquet.

Hobbling to the bathroom, the camera trailed her. *Patient in room 122 is heading in to take a crap.* After shutting herself inside, she retrieved the needle from under the sink. How could the dumb bitch not remember leaving it on the cart?

Gia knelt before the toilet, the needle practically salivating in the palm of her hand. With her free hand, she crammed a finger down her throat and rhythmically probed, her body writhing until the vomit came. She flinched when the nurse barged in. Wearily lifting her head, she begged, "You gotta give me something. Please, I'm sick." The dollop of puke on her chin was a nice touch.

"Get in bed," the nurse ordered impatiently. "I need your vitals and blood."

Head hanging inside the bowl, she heaved for effect. "I can't get up. Please..."

"Fine, then. I'll do it here." She rolled in the cart. "Hold out your damn arm so I can get in there."

"Let me be," Gia whimpered.

The nurse dropped to her knees and grabbed Gia's left wrist. "Don't make this harder on yourself."

This evil bitch is going down! Gia plunged the needle into the nurse's neck and watched her life force evaporate into full-body paralysis.

CHAPTER EIGHTEEN

The next morning, Christmas day, Abbie awoke feeling as though a speeding semitruck had plowed into her. Aching body, sick gut. Like her hangovers from the past, but tenfold worse. As she shielded her eyes from the morning light filtering through her window, the nightmare of Ben blundered in like the shards of a broken mirror. She sat up quickly, her back against the headboard.

A few remnants of frosted glass lingered on her duvet. Last night, when she discovered he'd hidden a voyeur camera in the ceiling light above her bed, too, she tossed the Port Allegiance Manifesto into it. Her attention swiveled to the wing chair. *Good.* It was still wedged under the doorknob where she had placed it for protection.

He had also threatened to upload her most personal moments onto the internet. If Uncle Jesse, Mom, or Dylan accidentally stumbled upon it, she'd crawl into a cave and die.

Speaking of Dylan, traveling with him through the secret tunnel tonight to find Gia couldn't come soon enough. She'd use the opportunity to tell him what his father had done to her.

Her cell phone was sitting on her nightstand. No doubt Ben had disabled it. She clicked the side button and the screen lit up. She'd texted herself, *TEST.*

Your cell is out of service. Please call (707) 903-5768 for customer service.

There was a knock at the door. "Abbie?" Skyla said. "Merry Christmas! Wake up. It's past six."

Shit! She had forgotten to set her alarm clock last night. After tossing the cell in the wastebasket, she scurried to the chair and moved it away to let Skyla in. "Be ready in a sec." She ran to her closet, and as she dressed in her uniform, she noticed Skyla was holding a Christmas card in her hand. Abbie hoped it wasn't for her, as she hadn't gotten one for Skyla.

"Slow down," Skyla said as she sat in the wing chair. "You're not late yet. We're scheduled to help Clem with Christmas breakfast for Ben and Hilda. After, we're preparing a full meal for the soup kitchen in Eureka. Clem and I are delivering. You can join, too, if you want. Totally optional."

"No Kristine?"

"Nope. She's not interested."

No surprise there. Feeding the homeless was a venture Abbie would normally jump on, but she had already made plans with Dylan, and had also promised Mom she'd stop by for a visit. She declined the invitation.

"Just me and jolly ol' Clem, then," Skyla said. "After Ben and Hilda eat, they're flying to Vegas for the night. Jayden Vaughn gifted them front-row tickets to see Criss Angel, who's broken the record for the longest residency in history."

Welcome news; she wouldn't have to fear Ben for a while. "I thought Criss's and Houdini's ghosts got forever trapped in their virtual reality trick."

An unbridled snort escaped Skyla's lips. "Criss made it out, but Houdini wasn't so lucky." She held out the envelope. "Someone taped this to your door."

Abbie took it tentatively. "Why didn't they put it in my mail cubby?"

"No idea. Outta here, darlin'. Meet you in the kitchen. You have five minutes." She blew a kiss as she left.

Abbie liked the "darlin'" bit. It reminded her of Uncle Jesse. She missed him. Should she tell him what Ben had done to her? No, it was time to become more independent, get herself out of her own messes. Even if she did tell him, there wasn't anything he could do about it. But was she replacing Uncle Jesse with Dylan as her savior now? The thought unsettled her.

She opened the envelope. The front of the card read *Peace, Love & Joy*, surrounded by mistletoe and holly. When she opened it, what appeared to be a gift card in its own little envelope fell out. *From who?* She read the inscription:

My dearest Abbie,

Please find enclosed a very special Christmas gift. So cold here out at sea. I miss your warm body. Say hello to my dad for me.

Love,
Ty

Her spine turned to ice, the crackling extending to her limbs. Who would know what she and Uncle Jesse had done? She slid the gift card out with trembling hands.

A Jesse's Auto Repair Quick Data Access Card? What the hell? She dug through her purse, removed her wallet, and—oh my God! Her QDAC wasn't in the credit card slot where she had placed it last night. Ben had stolen it while she slept. But why send it back? And most importantly, how had he gotten into her room with the chair blocking the entrance?

She ran for the French doors, the floor seeming to buckle under her feet.

Unlocked—and the cording of the curtain next to it was stuck in the doorjamb. She remembered a few days ago opening the door to let in fresh air, but she had locked it, she was positive.

The QDAC. She inserted it into her computer, booted it up, and looked into the eye scanner. A dialog box popped up: How do you want to open this file? She chose the default media player app.

An aerial view of her family's house? Classical music played tranquilly in the background. Confused, she stared at the screen, waiting. Dead bushes swayed in the wind, and there, the neighbor's pit bull. He stopped and relieved himself on their back screen door.

Then, Uncle Jesse backed out the door. He was dragging her hope chest, with Ty's body inside!

Night vision now. The background violins feverishly picked up in tempo as she and Uncle Jesse hoisted the chest onto the tailgate.

No! The chest crashed to the ground, and out spilled Ty, the camera zooming in on his mangled face. The bloody baseball bat rolled to the side of the alley—a detail Abbie hadn't known, but there it rested, right before her eyes. She let out a gasp and watched as Wendy the drone zoomed in on her tortured face staring into the night sky.

It transitioned to an aerial of Scoop Hawkins pulling them over. Then to Sue-meg State Park, where she and Uncle Jesse had scurried to the bluff's edge, dropped to their butts, and catapulted the chest into the abyss.

"'New employee vetting proved invaluable,'" she muttered, remembering Ben's words when she had first met him. In the moments after she had applied for the job, he had launched Wendy to see where she lived. He had known all along about the entire traumatic episode with Ty's body, and that she and Uncle Jesse had shoved it off the bluff, but how had he found out it was Ty?

She thought back. Ben's hat, the one he wore to hide his hair loss; the Keith Urban ringtone on his phone; it was all a ploy to groom her, to make her feel safe with him. And he'd erased the only evidence she had against him. Now, without proof of what he'd done to her, she was at his mercy. She needed to find where he'd stored the video. Was it on his computer, on his cell phone, in the cloud? All the above, she figured.

When she and Skyla had created the Envision Plus presentation for his benefit gala, they'd been in his tiny office off the south wing. She'd break in later and try to find and erase any trace of what she and Uncle Jesse had done.

Her thoughts jumped to the QDAC. How had he accessed it without her eye recognition? The only way would've been for him to hold her laptop to her eye as she slept.

That's exactly what he had done. The scumbag had drugged her, which explained the hangover feelings she still had. She needed to call Uncle Jesse and tell him everything, but she didn't have a phone now, and she'd bet her life Ben had bugged the upstairs phone. She'd have to wait until she and Dylan were in Eureka tonight and tell her uncle in person.

"Abbie, what are you doing in there?" Skyla hollered as she banged on the door. "Ms. B is pissed!"

Shit. Twenty minutes had passed. Abbie scurried to let her in. "I'm so sorry. I must've lost track of the time."

"You'd better get a handle on it before Ms. B fires you," Skyla warned.

"I will. I promise." Terrified at the prospect of running into Ben, Abbie bustled into the kitchen under Clem's and Kristine's disapproving eyes. She lowered her head and stepped up to the scheduling screen to check her duties.

"You're late," Ms. B said quietly, startling her.

Abbie spun around. "Yes, ma'am. It won't happen again, I promise."

Anger had engorged the vein in Ms. B's forehead. "I'll hold you to that. Now, Mr. and Mrs. De Young want a pot of coffee delivered to their dining parlor upstairs. Grab a serving platter, the silver pot, some sugar and cream, and a few spoons, and bring it to them. And make sure the coffee is piping hot."

No way she could face Ben, no way in hell. "Ms. B, c-could someone else deliver it? P-please?"

Handing her a fresh apron, Ms. B answered sternly, "Skyla has already taught you room service protocol. Now get moving before Mrs. De Young rings the buzzer again."

"Blue Ain't Your Color" played perversely in Abbie's head as she approached the dining parlor. She fantasized about grabbing the Visine from her bathroom and emptying the bottle into the coffeepot. Hopefully lethal enough to kill them both.

She was certain Hilda hadn't a clue what her lecherous husband had been up to, which meant she was safe from him, for now. Sweat beading her upper lip, she knocked twice. "Room service."

"Enter," Hilda said.

They were at the table, Hilda's face buried in the newspaper, and Ben's in his laptop. How should she play this? *Keep your cool; don't allow him to see you break.*

"Took long enough!" Hilda barked.

Avoiding eye contact, Abbie rolled the cart to the table and set the porcelain saucers before them. Ben ignored her. Casually, he said to Hilda, "Remember the article in last week's paper about that cop in Eureka whose son went missing?"

In danger of losing her footing, Abbie gripped the rail on the cart, her skull about to blow.

"Mmm," Hilda replied, entirely uninterested. She addressed Abbie: "You expect *me* to pour the coffee?"

Taking the silver pot by the handle, Abbie filled the porcelain cups, a little splashing onto the white linen napkins. Hilda hadn't noticed, but she would.

Ben continued, his frenzied excitement burning a hole through his monitor. "There's been a breakthrough in the case."

"Who cares?" Hilda said. "Focus on completing your speech for the benefit gala." She brushed Abbie away.

"I've completed it, darling," he said, pacifying her. "It's ready to go, so, please, relax."

As Abbie turned to leave, Ben read the online article aloud just to torture her. "'A beachcomber at Centerville Beach in Ferndale found a decomposing body believed to be that of Ty Hawkins of Eureka, CA. The coroner suspects foul play. Cause of death: blunt force trauma to the head. Scoop Hawkins, the young man's father, identified the remains as belonging to his son, after recognizing his dental crowns. Officials won't know for certain until they receive dental records and the results of a DNA analysis.'" He closed his computer and grinned at Abbie.

Ben De Young, you so need to die.

Skyla and Clem had already left for Eureka to deliver the meal to the soup kitchen. Abbie checked the kitchen clock. It was 2:57—three minutes until the end of her shift, then off to meet Dylan in the bunker. He'd been out of the house all day, and being unable to tell him what Ben had done to her was raking her nerves raw.

Finding Gia now seemed secondary to Ty's body washing ashore. What if the authorities found DNA evidence linking her and Uncle Jesse to his death? No mention of her hope chest. It had likely sunk to the bottom of the sea when Ty's body floated out of it. Uncle Jesse had not taken the news well when she had called and told him earlier.

She pulled the hand sprayer from the sink and rinsed the rest of the food debris into the garbage disposal. Ms. B approached her and turned off the water. "Good job today, Abbie. I'm sorry this morning got off to a bad start."

Abbie sighed. "Don't feel bad. I'm sorry for showing up late and disappointing you."

"Something's been troubling you. Would you care to discuss it?"

Three o'clock. She needed to get to her bedroom to pack a bag and grab her purse. "Ms. B, you're a wonderful boss, and yeah, something's bothering me, but I'm not ready to talk right now. Spending the rest of Christmas with my family will help."

Ms. B's concern turned to understanding and she nodded. "You do that. Spend the night with them, and enjoy yourself."

"Thank you, ma'am."

Ms. B turned away, and Abbie hurried to her bedroom, praying she wouldn't have another run-in with Ben.

At a quarter past three, unnerved from sneaking through the secret panel alone and skulking inside the old walls of Redwood Manor, Abbie reached the bunker to find Dylan wearing hobo clothes, looking the bona fide Eureka resident. She wished him a Merry Christmas, then changed into her own street clothes in the bathroom. When she came out, she said they needed to talk.

"Sounds serious." He pulled out a chair for her.

"You have no idea." She sat and buried her face in her hands, trying to hold back her tears. Through open fingers, she peered at him.

"What is it, Abbie?" he asked, leaning in, his expression one of grave concern.

"This is super rough."

"I can see that."

Dropping her hands, she gathered herself a moment. "Okay, here we go. As I was lying in the tub last night, I noticed something odd on the light fixture above me. I grabbed my cell phone and took a picture, then zoomed in, and I found a spy cam." She let it sink in for a moment, and Dylan's eyes widened. "Then the doorknob rattled—"

He stared at her incredulously, too stunned to speak.

"I was scared out of my mind, so I called Ms. B for help, but she didn't answer. She had programmed your dad's number into the cell as well, so when I called it, it rang in the hallway outside the bathroom door! I was in a panic, so I turned on my cell's video recorder and hid it. Then Ben pushed through the door, saying some crazy shit like 'we have a connection' or something. I told him we didn't, and that's when he got crazy scary. He lifted me off my feet and pinned me to the wall. He said if I don't meet him in the sauna tomorrow morning at ten, he's gonna ruin my life."

Dylan was silent and stared at her for what seemed like an eternity. Then he slammed his hand onto the table, his jugular looking like it was about to burst. He jumped up and paced the room, both hands clenched into fists. "What the fuck, Abbie! I'm gonna kill the son of a bitch!"

Relief washed over her that he was having the reaction she'd hoped for. It was his father she was accusing, after all. "But, Dylan, there's more," she said, taking a deep breath. "I locked myself in my bedroom and put the video footage onto a QDAC, like yours, for safekeeping, because I figured he would disable my phone, which he did, by the way. I sent him the video as leverage, to protect myself, and he texted back that we had a truce, but I knew he was lying."

Dylan was visibly shaking. He gulped hard, as if trying to choke down a mouthful of Saltines without milk.

Abbie continued, "Last night when you brought me here, I felt honored you trusted me with your secret place. And if we are to be true friends, I need to be honest with you about my past. I wish I'd been honest sooner."

"Honest about what?" He frowned, his rage toward his father turning into confusion over her words.

"Okay, here we go," she said determinedly, and fanned her face. "When Skyla got to my bedroom this morning, she handed me a Christmas card someone had taped to my door. When I opened it, my QDAC fell out, and at the bottom of the card was my dead ex-boyfriend's signature."

Dylan shook his head, completely mystified by this new revelation and not knowing where to begin with his many questions, so he let her continue.

"I knew it was mine because it said JESSE'S AUTO REPAIR on it. Your dad broke into my bedroom last night, somehow drugged me while I slept, stole my memory card, and used my retina to gain access to the card through my computer. Then he uploaded another video onto it to blackmail me."

Dylan, exasperated, ran his fingers through his hair. His piercing eyes were looking at her for elaboration. "What in God's name was on the video?"

She'd make it short and not so sweet, like ripping off a Band-Aid. "Here's where I know I should've been honest with you sooner. My uncle Jesse killed my abusive ex, Ty… in self-defense. He and I drove to the ocean together and pushed his body off a bluff, and your dad's drone captured the entire thing, including when I dropped the chest and Ty's body rolled out, his face clear as day to the drone. That's what was on the memory card he left me. Now I have no proof of what he did to me, and I need to get the video of Uncle Jesse and me so I can destroy it."

Dylan plopped down beside her and dropped his head to the table.

"Please say something," Abbie pleaded. "Kick me out, call the cops, whatever." Had telling him been a mistake? Sure, Uncle Jesse's and her actions were beyond the scope of moral behavior, but it was self-defense, she was sure of it. And Ty was a monster who'd almost killed her.

Dylan lifted his head and peered at her. "I can't believe you've been living with this. And to have no one to share it with. It's tragic, Abbie. I don't know what else to say. But we're gonna find the drone footage, and the videos of you, and burn them. I promise, Ben will pay for what he's done to you."

Hope settled in, and it felt good.

Now it was time to travel through the mystical tunnel to Eureka.

When Dylan opened the iron door and shone his flashlight down the arched brick tunnel, a gust of subterranean air rushed Abbie's face, so exhilarating that she imagined spreading her arms and soaring into the unknown.

He stepped in first and reached out his hand. "You ready?"

She nodded, feeling lighter since releasing her beast of a secret about what she and Uncle Jesse had done. They were going to find Gia, figure out why Hilda and her henchmen

had kidnapped her, and most importantly, reunite her with Skyla.

As they trekked through the darkness for several minutes, icy-cold droplets of water from the fissures above dampened their hair, and moss clusters and tiny mushrooms grew along the aging walls. The tunnel showed no sign of ending.

Dylan broke the silence. "Did you tell anybody about the drone footage?"

She wiped away a drip of water from her cheek. "No. But whether we find Gia or not, I'm going home to spend the rest of Christmas with my family, so I'll tell them then."

He stopped. "So, if we find her, I'm bringing her back to the bunker alone?"

The disappointment in his voice made her feel bad, but what could she do? "I need to see them, Dylan. It's Christmas."

"Of course, you do," he agreed and continued walking. "Whaddayou think the odds of finding her are? I mean, if we come up empty, how would you feel if I—" He stopped himself. "Oh, never mind."

"What? Say it."

"Well, if I joined you and your family tonight? I'd love to see your mom and uncle again. I've thought about them a lot over the years."

The idea suited Abbie perfectly fine. And Mom, oh, Mom. Seeing Dylan again would make Christmas even more special for her. She pulled Dylan along. "You'd best prepare yourself for Mom kicking your ass again at Monopoly."

"Ah yes, I remember she was a ruthless land tycoon," he joked.

After a while, he slowed, and the ladder appeared. He pointed his flashlight to the top, but the darkness swallowed the light, blurring it into obscurity.

"I'll head up first. The lid at the top takes a little finagling. Follow me, and hold on tight." He set his foot on the first rung and began climbing.

Step after step, Abbie, breathing heavily, imagined losing her grip and plummeting to the bottom. The fear was so intense, she had to fight the urge to turn back. But by then, they had probably climbed more than halfway up, and she had no intention of giving up now. She thought about how much she missed Liza. The image of the silly hog bucking her back legs over her head made Abbie smile. They'd see each other soon.

"We're here," he announced. "Stay put 'til I climb out."

"Not goin' anywhere," she said with a white-knuckle grip on the cold, rusty rungs.

After some grunting and the squeak of rusty metal, he called her up, his hand reaching down to take hers. Back on solid ground, she moved away from the hole and plopped down in the dead weeds, the northern winds icy and nipping at her face.

Sirens, the sound of a woman screaming. *Eureka's theme song.* But in a curious way, it was a comfort to be back in her native environment.

"Let's get to our ride," Dylan said and helped her to her feet. They made their way through a field of weeds and pampas grass. No telling if they'd come upon a bum's nest.

"Where'd you find your ratty clothes?" Abbie asked with amusement.

"In the stables. I know, I reek of manure."

"Well, I wasn't gonna say anything," she teased.

He chuckled, then grew serious. "When I was little and got into trouble, Hilda would banish me to the stables, where she made me sleep in a stall. Clem would sneak me in a blanket, food, and water. Then he'd get up early the next morning and take it away so she wouldn't find the evidence."

Abbie remembered what Dylan had said when they were at the beach three days earlier. *The grass isn't always greener on the other side.* How shortsighted of her to believe Port Allegiance was the cure for what ailed her. "It sucks you went through that. Have you thought about moving away someday?"

"Yep. To Ithaca, New York."

"Where you spent the summer after third grade with your grandfather Walter, right?"

"Wow, you remembered!"

"Of course. You seemed so sad about losing touch with him. I'm tuned in to other people's misery. It's a curse."

"Yeah, I remember when we were in the hospital, and Hilda started screaming at me for ruining her ski vacation, you stood between us, trying to protect me."

"Did it work?" she asked, prodding to see if he remembered what happened next.

"You know it did," he said in a tone that told her he knew what she was fishing for. "Hilda was about to shove you away when your uncle tossed his coffee in her face. The glue on her fake eyelashes melted, and they slid down her cheeks!"

The memory made Abbie snort. As they reminisced more, she had lost track of time. Before them stood St. Mary's Church, its white steeple towering into the gray, billowy clouds. There was one vehicle in the parking lot: a beat-up blue Sprinter van at least twenty years past its prime.

"Your carriage awaits, Ms. Spencer," Dylan said, gesturing.

She chuckled. "Where'd you find the time to car shop?"

As he strode over to it, Abbie following, he explained, "This afternoon while you prepared dinner for the shelter, I used the tunnel to come here. I searched a few neighborhoods until I found a 'For Sale' sign in a car window. That's when I came upon this beauty. The owner told me he didn't have any money to buy Christmas gifts for his kids, so needless to say, he was psyched to sell." Dylan unlocked the passenger door and opened it for her.

Cigarette-burned plastic seats, trash scattered across stained carpet, and there was a musty odor of mold. She slid inside. "She's a beauty, all right," she mocked sarcastically.

Snickering, he closed her door, walked around, and slid in. "There's a little something for you in the back." He flicked on the dome light, then dragged a plastic shopping bag over the center console. "Merry Christmas," he said with a devilish grin.

She arched a brow. "What's this?"

"Open it."

She reached in and pulled out several baseball caps and a handful of blonde hair. Two wigs, actually: one long hair, and one short. "Smart," she said. "Miranda's Thrift Store?"

"Yep." He took one of the caps and put it on.

She picked the short wig and adjusted it over her head, her own hair already in a bun. "How do I look?"

"It's on backwards," Dylan said, chuckling.

"Duh, bangs go in the front." She plucked it off and tried again, then twisted the rearview mirror to look at herself. "I look like an old woman from a wig catalog. Damn thing's itchy." She slipped a finger underneath and scratched.

"You look adorable," he said, his deep-brown eyes swallowing her up.

The intimacy provoked disconcerting feelings in her. Excitement? Fear? She couldn't tell; both emotions felt the same.

Dylan sighed. "When we met in the kitchen that night," he took this opportunity to confess, "I was surprised, of course, but mostly terrified Hilda would figure out who you were. I wasn't sure if I could hide my feelings. I think you feel something, too, Abbie. Do you, or is it my wishful thinking?"

She thought carefully before speaking. "I am attracted to you, but my mind tells me to back off. This whole fantasy life is just that, a fantasy, Dylan. I won't let anybody hurt me again. And I'm still trying to fix myself, if it's possible."

"Anything's possible," he said softly, his expression making her almost believe him. He reached into the plastic shopping bag and pulled out a small pink velvet jewelry box.

"What's this?" she asked, squinting at him.

"See for yourself."

She flipped open the lid and gasped. A gold necklace! Lifting it closer to her face, she examined it. Engraved on the pendant was an ancient man wearing a smock and holding a walking stick.

"It's Saint Christopher," Dylan explained. "He's the patron saint of travelers. It's to keep you safe throughout your life."

Shaking her head vehemently, she handed the box back to him. "I…I can't accept this. It's way too extravagant."

Moving closer to her, he took out the necklace and gently draped it around her neck, his warm hands grazing her skin, melting her into the seat. Tears pooled in her eyes, but she wiped them away before they could roll down her cheeks. Had he not pulled away from her and started driving, she would have made love to him right then and there.

CHAPTER NINETEEN

As Abbie and Dylan trolled the decayed streets of Eureka in the van, they passed telephone pole after telephone pole plastered with missing person flyers with Ty's face on them. Was his corpse in a fridge at the coroner's office? Had the authorities found any DNA evidence?

On the corner of Fifth and Main, they came upon a prostitute wearing a miniskirt and fishnet stockings. When they stopped, a cold gust of air carried her bouquet of Jungle Gardenia perfume and unwashed sex through the open window. She dusted her finger across Dylan's cheek and said suggestively, "Two for one. Your girlfriend can join, no extra charge."

Breathing through his mouth, Dylan pulled out a hundred-dollar bill from his jacket pocket, along with the photo of Gia. "Recognize this girl?"

The prostitute shook her head dramatically. "Not again. I already told you people, no."

Out of nowhere, one short siren bleeped, and when a patrol car pulled up behind them, the prostitute tore down the alley, keeping Dylan's money.

Abbie swiveled her head. "It's my ex's dad!"

"Jesus. The ex you and your uncle—"

"Yeah, keep your cool." Abbie frantically wedged herself behind the driver's seat as Scoop's clunky footsteps moved in closer. Why the hell was he working the day after a beachcomber had found his son's body?

"Hello, Officer. What's the problem?" Dylan asked, the window still rolled down.

"Penal Code 647. Soliciting a prostitute is illegal and punishable by six months in jail and a five-thousand-dollar fine."

"Not what you're thinking, sir." His voice cracked like an adolescent boy's.

"Better explain, or else I'll haul your punk ass to jail."

"A friend of mine is missing. I'm trying to find him."

"What's your name?"

A painful pause. "John Fisher."

"Show me your ID," Scoop ordered.

"I forgot my wallet at home."

Scoop laughed in a taunting way. "Get out of your vehicle, boy."

"But, sir—"

"Now!"

As Dylan opened the door, his wallet dropped onto the floor beside Abbie.

Brilliant. She strained to listen in.

"Place your hands on the vehicle," Scoop instructed.

There was a giant *thunk.*

"Sir, please, please… Jesus, seriously?"

Scoop's CB radio crackled. The dispatcher said a distraught mother had phoned in, claiming to have found a baggie of fentanyl pills, a potent synthetic opioid, in her sixteen-year-old son's closet. She wanted an officer to stop by to confiscate it and teach her boy a lesson. Without another word, Scoop returned to his patrol car, sped off, and left Abbie and Dylan trembling in their shoes.

"Your first taste of Eureka," she said as he took the driver's seat and she climbed back up front. "How'd ya like it?"

"Tastes like shit," he replied unnerved. "Nobody has ever frisked me before, let alone has a man ever groped my package."

"Welcome to a system that allows a druggie cop to violate innocent people. Happens all the time, and he gets away with it."

"'Druggie cop'?"

"Yeah. I guarantee you Scoop left to steal that kid's drugs. He'll find a dark alley and get apogee-bent."

"What's that mean?" he asked, his sheltered life apparent.

"Baked. High. You know, to check out from reality."

"Lovely." He cranked the ignition.

With Scoop riding the fast track to oblivion, Abbie and Dylan drove to the abandoned Bayshore Mall unmolested, and parked at the periphery of the lot, to which the homeless had laid claim by creating a makeshift tent city, like the one behind her house. Folding themselves inward, careful not to trip on garbage, they weaved through clusters of people huddled by trash-fueled campfires, the bitter coastal winds bearing down hard now, blowing noxious smoke and debris to the east. Off in the distance was the sound of a harmonica playing a sad man's tune.

Gia's photo in hand, Abbie showed it to anyone willing to look. "Go to hell" was the universal response, sometimes more harshly expressed.

Powering past a row of smelly portable toilets and losing hope, Abbie stopped by an elderly couple huddled against a dumpster. "Hello," she softly greeted.

The man, skeleton-thin, his skin dripping like wax off a candle, stopped rocking himself, and when the woman slid the wool blanket off her head, it fell into the dirt. She had clearly once been beautiful, but time had ravaged her features.

"Peggy?" Abbie said, astonished.

The woman looked at her blankly, then her face lit up. "Abbie? Well, I haven't seen you in a dog's age," she croaked, her voice ragged and steaming in the air. "Not so Merry Christmas, is it?"

"Not at all," Abbie said, shaking her head sympathetically. She knelt and adjusted the blanket over Peggy's shoulders. "Why aren't you and Barney at the shelter, keeping warm?"

"They're at full capacity."

"Only taking in families with children," Barney added.

"Are they at least providing enough food for everyone out here?" Abbie asked.

"Rations are low," Peggy told her. "They're serving one small meal a day."

"I'm so sorry to hear that. I wish I could help." She introduced Dylan, then told them she was looking for a friend and showed her the photo of Gia. "Have you seen this girl around?"

Peggy took it, her cracked fingernails caked with grime. "This is the same photo some men were showing around a few days ago. I'll tell you the same thing I told them: can't say we have. Hundreds of people pass through here every day, honey."

"Okay, I understand. We'll keep asking around," Abbie said. She wished she had something to give them—a granola bar, anything. After they said their goodbyes, she pulled Dylan away, his body rigid.

"You okay?" she asked, noticing his troubled expression.

"I'm not. I knew people had it rough this side of the wall, but this… Jesus. How do you know that couple?"

"When I was in ninth and tenth grade, Uncle Jesse and I volunteered at the shelter. He stayed an hour, sometimes longer, and I stayed through dinner service. That's where I met them. And when I decided I wanted to attend college, I knew it would cost a lot, that I'd better get a paying job. So, I quit and started working at Pacific One Fishery full-time during my junior and senior years."

"You worked full-time *and* went to school?"

"Wasn't a problem. Schoolwork came easy to me. So did helping these people."

"You're amazing. Really, you are."

She smiled up at him. "I can be."

After showing the photo of Gia around some more and having no luck, they entered the shelter, where Abbie came to an abrupt stop. The space, formerly a cosmetics retailer, had expanded into the food court. Before them was a sea of sleeping bags under mostly burned-out lights. Entire families gathered, the life in their faces drained, and off in the distance, by the spindly Christmas tree blinking blue lights, a band of kids was running amok, burning off pent-up energy.

No shreds of ripped Christmas paper or new toys anywhere in sight.

"Merry Christmas," she said solemnly and turned to Dylan, whose bottom lip was trembling. His look was one of utter disbelief.

"This is Hilda's doing," he said simply. "So many children. I'll never be able to unsee this. Ever. I wish I'd known…"

"It's rough, I know," she agreed.

A little girl with knotted black hair, maybe five, tugged at Dylan's pants. "Mommy said Santa was busy giving gifts to children on the other side of the world who needed them more. Next year, he'll come see us." She beamed.

"Yes, he will." Dylan knelt in front of her, pulled out his wallet, and tucked a hundred-dollar bill into her tiny hand. "Give this to Mommy, and tell her to keep it for a rainy day."

The little girl thanked him and ran off, but he remained on his knee, looking as if he might cry. His visceral reaction pained Abbie, but he needed that moment. It would serve as a catalyst to undo Hilda's deeds.

As they made their way to the management office, he stopped dead and pointed to two men sitting at a table, looking entirely out of place. One wore pressed khakis and fancy shoes, and the other, nice jeans and a black leather jacket.

"That's what's-his-name from HR Enterprises," he said. "He's Hilda's eviction specialist. The other guy I don't know."

"Gia's obviously not here," she said, feeling glum.

When the specialist turned toward them, Dylan grabbed her arm and escorted her toward the door.

Abbie stopped abruptly and pulled her arm free.

"What is it?" he asked.

"The twins, they're here! Just to the left of the specialist." Her heart ached. They were huddled together against the wall. One of them brandished a black eye, and the other a laceration across his cheek. Dirt and grime covered their clothing, and they were clearly in desperate need of a shower. She moved to speak with them, but Dylan stopped her.

"We can't, Abbie. It's too risky."

As much as she wanted to run to them and apologize for assuming they'd had anything to do with cheating, Dylan was right. Tomorrow, she'd withdraw money from her bank, come back, and give it to them.

Next stop: the bus station.

Unsurprisingly, the bus station was a bust, and after they'd checked their fourth motel, nightfall had set in. Only two motels remained on their list before they surrendered to the fact that Gia was nowhere to be found, at least not tonight.

With Abbie running short on hope, and Dylan short on cash, they walked into the Diamond W Roadhouse. At the front desk, she rang the bell, and an emaciated old woman wearing a floral bathrobe emerged from behind pink beaded curtains. In a raspy voice, she said, "Cash only. Is this by the hour, or y'all staying the night?"

On the cracked glass countertop, Abbie slid the photo of Gia to her. "Please, ma'am, have you seen this girl?"

The woman threw her arms up and shouted, "Are you cockamamie crazy? Get the hell out!"

Slipping her a fifty, Dylan said, "She's a friend of ours, and she's in trouble."

Leaning forward, the woman scoped out the parking lot. "That fifty won't get you jack shit, pretty boy."

He slipped her another. "This is all I have, ma'am." He turned his pockets inside out.

The woman glowered at him and flopped her dentures around in her mouth.

Distracting herself from the carnival sideshow, Abbie opened her wallet and emptied her bills onto the counter. "Please, I have nothing else to offer."

"Hmmm. Okay, that'll do." She picked up the photo and eyed it. "Yep. She was here, beggin' for a room. Not sure what day it was. Didn't have no money. A guy named Dwight showed up and paid. Expectations, of course." She winked, grinning nastily. "The girl left next day. Don't ask where she went, 'cause I dunno."

"You know this Dwight?" Abbie asked her.

"Sure. He's a regular here. Sings karaoke over at Roxie's. And you better not tell him I told you so."

"We promise, ma'am," Abbie said. "Anyone else been here looking for her?"

"Yeah. Didn't tell 'em jack shit."

Cars lined the street in front of Roxie's. People were whooping it up by the door, smoking cigarettes and weed. A guy in a tasseled biker jacket pressed some floozy up against the building, his hand inching up her red miniskirt.

Inside, Abbie and Dylan gingerly stepped across the sticky, uneven floor, the cigarette smoke and the stink of stale beer hitting hard. On stage, a man sang karaoke to a heavy metal song while a half-naked woman gyrated her hips on a corner table. The guys around her hollered, "Take it off, baby, take it off!"

As Abbie made her way around the tables to the bar, Dylan in tow, she ignored the catcalls and ass slaps. The bartender was shaking a cocktail with one hand and filling a pint glass of beer with the other.

Abbie leaned over the bartop. "You know where we can find Dwight? Family emergency."

He gestured to a man and woman sitting by the jukebox. She thanked him and made a beeline for the middle-aged man wearing a backwards baseball cap.

"Dwight?"

"Who wants to know?" he asked, scowling.

"We're not cops," Abbie assured him, then showed him the picture of Gia. "She's in trouble. Have you seen her around?"

"Never seen her before. Now scram." He brushed them away.

"Please." She sat across from him. "We can help her."

Dwight told his companion to leave, then studied Abbie's and Dylan's faces, questioning their sincerity. "What kinda trouble you talkin' about?"

"Some bad people kidnapped her," Abbie said. "She escaped, but we don't know where to. We're trying to find out. Please, it's super important."

Dwight swilled his beer. "How do I know you ain't the ones who took 'er?"

"Come on," Abbie pleaded. "Do we look like kidnappers? We're her last hope, I swear it."

"I'm not selling that girl out. I promised her."

Yes! He's seen her!

"Look, I appreciate your loyalty to her. It's admirable," Dylan said as he sat beside Abbie. "But please hear me out.

Her parents died a few years back in a car accident. She's been working her ass off for a better life and has her future planned out. This is a girl who's going places. But she doesn't have anyone helping her except for us. We really are her only hope at this point."

Dwight downed the rest of his beer, then signaled to the bartender for another. "She said her name was Robin, had no money. I got her set up in a motel room, paid for a few nights, and brought her some of my wife's clothes." He glanced at the ceiling and made the sign of the cross.

"Where's she now?" Abbie pressed.

"I wanna get one thing straight," Dwight said. "I never had sex with her. She's not that type of girl. I was just helpin' her out."

"That's awesome," Abbie said. "You did a good thing, but we need to know where she is."

"I gave her my phone number and told her to call from the motel phone if she needed anything. She called the same night and said bad people were in the parking lot looking for her, so I picked her up in the back alley and drove her to one of them abandoned Victorian houses. I gave her a little cash and that was that." He scrawled something on a bar napkin and handed it to Abbie: *278 W. Grotto St.*

Dylan patted Dwight's arm. "You may have saved this girl's life. If anyone comes by looking for her, I hope you'll tell them you don't know anything."

"You can bet yer ass I will," Dwight assured them. "Good luck to you folks. I hope you find 'er and help 'er."

CHAPTER TWENTY

Potholes riddled West Grotto Street. As Dylan dodged them, Abbie, her window rolled down because the van's defrost didn't work, watched the numbers on the houses go by. The acrid stench of vinegar and acetone from the meth labs mixed with the fog and misted down like nuclear fallout.

"What a hellhole of a neighborhood," Dylan rightly observed.

"There it is!" She pointed to an abandoned ramshackle house, the porch support posts having rotted through, leaving the roof dangling precariously on the verge of collapse. The second-floor windows remained intact, but most of the windows on the lower level had been busted out, no doubt by kids or other troublemakers.

He made a U-turn, parked in front, and released his seat belt. "Wait here."

"Not a chance." She climbed out, stifling the urge to get cranky with him.

"How about the person with the flashlight leads, then?"

"Sounds fair enough," she agreed. Dylan was tall and strong, but in a hits-the-gym sort of way, not the streetwise sort. Still, she appreciated his intentions.

The beam of light guided their way along the uprooted path to the house. They carefully climbed the front steps, moving deliberately so as not to fall through the rotting slats. The doorknob was missing, so Dylan pushed on the door. Past the foyer, they stood in the barren living room and listened. The only sound was the whistling wind through the shattered windows. With its ornate moldings and classic Victorian feel, the house must've been stunning in its day, but now druggies had littered the floor with garbage, empty liquor bottles, and syringes.

"There's no way she's here," he whispered. "This place isn't fit for an animal."

"You'll have to check out my place sometime," she quipped.

"Seriously?"

"Minus the litter and drug paraphernalia, yeah. We do have the luxury of working windows, though."

Grabbing her arm, he whispered, "You hear rustling?"

"From where?"

"There it is again!" He directed the light to a partially open six-paneled door.

"I heard it." She tiptoed toward the sound, her heart hammering.

Out rushed a mischief of rats scurrying their way to safety. As Dylan hopped around like lava filled his shoes, a few rodents disappear through a hole in the baseboard.

"Did you see the mangy one?" he whispered in a frenzy. "It almost climbed up inside my pants!"

"'Mangy'?" Suppressing a snicker, she guided him around the rest of the main floor, the kitchen being the last room they checked. Cautiously, she stepped inside, and the floor beneath her caved in. As her body plummeted through the floor like she was in a dunk tank at a carnival, she threw out her arms, supporting herself from plunging into the basement.

The flashlight hit the floor. Dylan ran to her and crammed his hands under her armpits from behind. Grunting, he hoisted her up, and they fell backward, Abbie landing between his legs.

"You okay?" he said, breathing hard.

"Yeah. This is only slightly awkward." She took a long, calming breath, then got to her feet.

Dylan shone the flashlight into the cavernous hole. Ten feet below was an old coal furnace with a pointed iron rod sticking out the top.

"Holy shit," he said and gulped.

"I almost impaled myself! You saved my life!" Rubbing the Saint Christopher pendant he had given her, she thanked him, the shock hitting her hard. She'd been cocky to think she was any more street savvy than he was. This attitude was becoming a theme in her life, she noted. They needed to find Gia and get the hell out of there.

After carefully climbing the main stairs, they stopped on a landing that opened onto four rooms. All the doors were open except for one.

"Call her name," Abbie whispered. "She knows and trusts you."

Dylan sucked in a deep breath. "Gia, you in there? It's Dylan from Redwood Manor. I'm here to help you."

A moment passed. He called out her name again. No response.

"Just go in," nudged Abbie.

He nodded and gave the knob a twist. The door was locked. "What now?"

Abbie shrugged. "Kick it in?"

"Yeah, guess it's our only option." He stood a leg's length away and firmly planted one foot on the floor. A swift kick, and the door made a dull thudding noise. A second attempt, then a third. The door wasn't willing to budge.

"Lemme help," she said and stood at his side. On the count of three, they kicked hard, ripping the door clean off its hinges.

As Dylan combed the barren space with his flashlight, Abbie crept to the soiled twin mattress on the floor and ran a hand under the blanket. "It's warm," she whispered. She pointed to what looked like the closet.

"Gia, it's me, Dylan. I'm sorry for scaring you. I'm with a girl named Abbie. She overheard Hilda and a man named Jayden talking about kidnapping you. They're out there looking for you, but we won't let them do it, I promise."

Still nothing. He slowly twisted the knob, and the door flung open. Out jumped Gia, a shard of glass raised above her head. She came down hard, shrieking, as Dylan grabbed her wrist in midair and plucked the weapon from her hand.

Backing into a dark corner, Gia, dressed in filthy blue-and-white-striped overalls, dropped to the floor and recoiled into a ball. Like a hunted animal, she stared at them wild-eyed, the numbers *0187* on her forehead peeking through her curly blonde hair, which hung in matted ropes. After she gave Abbie the once-over and Abbie introduced herself, Gia squinted at Dylan suspiciously.

"You and Carter are best friends. How do I know you're not here to bring me back to him?"

He frowned, confused. "What are you talking about?"

"Don't play dumb with me!"

"I'm not, I swear."

"Carter's the sicko who abducted me and brought me to that place, whatever the fuck it was."

Abbie stepped back, as she and Dylan locked eyes, neither able to process Gia's shocking revelation. She remembered Carter telling her, as a side job, that he supplied the manor with fresh seafood. Then at the Christmas Eve party, when he had mentioned a third job, he grew oddly nervous. Maybe abducting people *was* his third job!

"Everything makes sense now," Dylan said to Abbie, the betrayal striking him hard. "Carter was reporting back to Hilda personal things I told him. It explains how her spies knew about the private places I visited, the girls I dated, everything." He turned to Gia. "I'm so sorry. I didn't know, I swear to God."

She stared at him, assessing his words, and the feral animal in her visibly relaxed. "I believe you." Then her eyes rounded. "Skyla. Please tell me Carter didn't take her, too."

"No, she's fine," he assured her.

She got to her feet and sobbed. "I tried to contact her, but someone's blocked unknown callers to her and Redwood Manor's phones."

"She's been searching for you," Abbie said. "She never gave up, never believed you up and quit like everyone else said."

"When can I see her?" She brushed the tears from her cheek.

"Tonight," Dylan promised and took her arm. "Do you need a doctor?"

"Are you insane?" She jerked away. "They're out there looking for me! Anyway, other than being cold and starving, I think I'm okay."

"No doctor, then," he said apologetically, then asked Abbie where they could get some fast food.

"I hear Burgers-To-Go is pretty good. It's only a few blocks away. They take credit cards. You have one?"

"Yup. Burgers it is." He turned to Gia. "After we eat, if you're okay with it, I'd like to take you to a bunker underneath Redwood Manor. Nobody knows about it except Abbie and me. I'll bring you clean clothes, and if you want, you can take a hot bath."

She thrust her arms in the air. "A hot bath! Hallelujah."

After leaving the drive-through vending machine, Dylan parked in the Clyde's Market parking lot, where he and Abbie climbed in the back with Gia, the three now facing each other. Dylan doled out the food: supersized double bacon cheeseburgers and fries for everyone. Gia tore into the burger like a ravenous animal, barely chewing each bite. Mayo and beef fat were dripping down her chin, but she didn't bother wiping it away.

Abbie diverted her eyes from this private carnal moment. She thought back to the last time she herself had eaten. Must've been last night at the Christmas Eve party. No wonder she felt weak and cranky. She sunk her teeth into the greasy burger, hoping it wouldn't wreak havoc on her gut.

"Wish Clem would cook some diner food like this once in a while," Dylan said and let out a slow, rumbling belch.

Abbie wiped her mouth with a napkin. "They don't teach the fine art of vending-machine food at the Le Cordon Bleu in Paris."

After they'd gorged themselves sick, Abbie half attempted to clean up their trash, but there wasn't much a girl could do to tidy up this dump Dylan was driving. Didn't matter, of course; the point was that Gia was safe. The lengths she and Dylan had endured to find her gave Abbie the sense of purpose she'd been seeking. When she sat back down, she caught Gia staring at her, eyes darting around her face.

"Is everything okay?" Abbie asked.

Gia nodded. "I've heard no one can truly know what they look like to other people, but you and I—we could be sisters." Her eyes widened. "Who hired you?"

Abbie stopped sucking the food from her teeth. "Ben, because apparently he has a type, and with you gone, he needed a new victim."

"That's what I figured," Gia said. "Has he hurt you, too?"

"Yes," Abbie replied, but she wanted to keep the focus on Gia. "I've told Dylan the entire sleazy story."

"I'm so sorry," Gia said to her.

"He's a monster," Dylan said. "And you don't need to worry about what you say around me. I'm on your side."

Gia sighed. "Thank you, Dylan. He's dangerous. We need to destroy his credibility and get the bar association to revoke his license."

"Better yet," Dylan added, "have him sent to prison."

"Good luck with that," Gia said, rolling her eyes. "He's great at pretending to be this passive guy, but it's just a facade to hide how ruthless, vindictive, and power-hungry he really is. And his lies are so convincing, it's scary. You wouldn't believe what I've been through."

"Do you wanna share with us what happened?" he asked.

Gia gnawed on the peeling skin on her bottom lip.

"You don't have to," Abbie said sincerely.

She took a deep, cleansing breath. "I'm ready to talk. It took me a while to remember what he'd done to me, because of the drugs the nurse had me on. But slowly, the past has come into focus, and now I remember everything. Him taking me under his wing so I could learn about law was an incredible opportunity. That is, until he broke into the bathroom and forced himself on me. And I couldn't confide in Skyla, because he threatened to kill her if I told anyone. What was I supposed to do? I had to comply with his every sadistic whim. I won't get into details, but I'll say this: that man is a sick motherfucker, and if I have anything to say about it, he will never hurt another girl."

"He won't," Dylan said. "I promise."

"And Carter's equally as demented, by the way." Gia cleared her throat and mentally weighed what she'd been through. "Dylan, you know how he and I were such good friends, how we clicked, the fun times Skyla and I had when we went fishing with him? But then he began avoiding me when I told him I wasn't into guys and that Skyla and I were a couple."

She paused when Dylan gave her a surprised look. "Nobody knew, Dylan. We had to keep it secret."

"Or Hilda would make your life hell. I get it, totally get it," he acknowledged.

"Exactly. Well, Carter dissing me was no big deal. I figured, screw him if all he wanted was a piece of tail. Then one day he asked me to meet him at the bunkhouse by the marina. I agreed to stop by before volunteering at the Boy's and Girl's Club. He said he was sorry for ghosting me and that he was dealing with personal issues." She shook her head, looking furious he had duped her.

"He can be a real charmer," Dylan said. "How could you have known his intentions?"

"Yeah, well, then he gave me an iced tea. I got so damn dizzy. Then I fell on the sofa, completely paralyzed. I barely knew what was going on around me." She held back tears. "Then he pulled a condom out of his wallet, and he raped me until I passed out. I woke up strapped to a gurney in what I thought was a mental hospital."

"Oh my God," Abbie said, tears trickling down her cheeks. "I can't imagine what that must've been like."

Dylan looked ready to kill. He had tensed his whole body, his hands balled into a fist.

"To have no control," Gia continued, "arms and legs strapped down, a needle coming at you, and there's not a goddamned thing you can do to stop it."

"And for what?" Abbie asked breathlessly. "Who were these people? Who are they? What do they want?"

Gia shrugged. "They were sadists, every one of them. The nurse, the orderly. The only doctor figure couldn't have been one; he was too young. I remember he was tall, super tall. Brown hair. Must've been in his mid-twenties. I never heard any names, though. The worst of it was when they injected me with this burning liquid and I tried to vomit, but it came back into my lungs, and I couldn't cough it up, because the drugs paralyzed me. They didn't notice until I was almost dead."

Gia continued recounting more horrifying details of her imprisonment, and Abbie's mouth hung open. She turned to Dylan, who had the same reaction. How had this poor girl survived?

"The only thing keeping me alive were my thoughts of Skyla, seeing her again, being with her."

"She burns sage on the terrace every night," Abbie said quietly, "to let you know she hasn't lost hope."

A smile lifted her cheeks. "I know. I felt it."

"But how did you escape?" Dylan asked.

She held a hand to her mouth. "Oh my God, it was insane! Terrifying. I thought they were holding me on an island, because of the conversations I overheard between orderlies, plus I could hear boats coming and going."

"The place was called Terra Isle," he told her.

"So that's what it was called." Gia continued. "Anyway, I learned a supply shipment was due in a few days, and I was gonna stow away on that damn boat somehow, no matter what. I had already stolen and hid a hypodermic needle filled with a medication that knocks out its victim. When it was time for me to escape, I injected that whacked-out nurse. After she fell unconscious, I dressed in her uniform. Once I was outside, though, I could barely see five feet ahead of me because a storm had hit. It took me a second to realize I wasn't on an island but somewhere else. Somewhere so terrifying that I almost turned back."

"Holy shit," Abbie exclaimed.

"What was it?" Dylan asked Gia.

"I don't know, like one of those offshore platforms, like the ones oil rig workers use for deep-sea drilling? Anyway, I ran blind, hoping I wouldn't fall into the sea. After a while, a ladder appeared next to a massive cargo elevator. I climbed down, not knowing what waited at the bottom. The freezing ocean water kept spraying me, and the wind nearly blew me into the water." She paused and shook her head. "God, I was so cold. After what seemed like a lifetime, my feet landed on a dock or something, where I hid behind a piling and waited for the boat to pull in. When it did, some men unloaded supplies and caught the elevator to the top. That's when I climbed aboard and hid in a crawlspace under a bench. It took forever for them to come back. Probably only ten minutes, though. Finally, we made it to shore. When it had been quiet long enough, I climbed out. Thank God they'd moored in Eureka and not in Port Allegiance; otherwise, I would've never made it out of the city alive. So, there you have it: that's my story. No one will believe it, though."

Abbie sat there stunned. "I believe you. What a gutsy escape."

"That's about the most terrifying story I've ever heard," Dylan added.

"It *was* terrifying," Gia replied. "The idea of never seeing Skyla again was the worst of it. I need to see her now."

"You got it," Dylan said, then turned to Abbie. "Let's get you home to celebrate the rest of Christmas with your family."

CHAPTER TWENTY-ONE

DYLAN PULLED UP TO ABBIE'S HOUSE, the Christmas tree lights inside casting an array of festive colors into the front yard. Her beautiful mom was inside doing what she did best: creating a sense of home, a sense of shelter from the storm.

She turned to Gia, who looked like a small lost child sitting in the back seat. "I'm glad you're okay. I can't wait to get to know you better."

"Me, too, Abbie." Gia moved in and hugged her. "Thank you for caring so much about someone you'd never met. The world needs more people like you."

Abbie squeezed tight, then pulled away. "I'm learning there are a lot more good people than bad."

"Hopefully I'll get to that place in my head one day."

"You will," Abbie said, her throat throbbing. "I wish I could be there to see your reunion with Skyla, but I hope you enjoy celebrating the rest of Christmas with her! I'll see you both tomorrow." She looked meaningfully at Dylan and got out and closed the door.

As she walked toward Liza, the pig bucked wildly. "Poor, poor girl. You're so neglected. You were expecting veggie scraps, but I'm showing up empty-handed."

At the front door, she used her key to get in, then waved goodbye to Dylan and Gia, who had waited to make sure she made it inside safely.

Hanging her purse on a hook, she stood motionless in the silent house. No warm hellos, only a chilly breeze passing through the hallway.

She wandered to the Christmas tree, the gifts unopened. Picking up a few, she read their labels. *To Abbie, from Santa. To Brodie, from Ana. To Jesse, from Ana and Brodie.* It was odd they hadn't opened gifts yet. They must have waited for her so they could open them as a family. But why had they gone to bed so early? It was only 7:30.

Maybe she'd prance into her parents' bedroom and jump on their bed like she used to do when she was a child? *"Santa came! Santa came! Get up!"* Yes, absurd, but she itched to do it. Mom's face would beam brighter than the tree angel's halo.

Footsteps sounded in the hallway. "Hello?"

Uncle Jesse stepped out, looking disheveled, a real mess. His eyes were red and bloated; clearly, he'd been crying. "Just me, darlin'."

She gulped and stared at him wide-eyed, a sense of doom descending on her. "What's going on? You're freaking me out."

He took a deep breath. "Abbie, sit down. We need to talk."

She studied his eyes, looking for answers. Despair engulfed him, like on the day she'd watched him fish out Sammie's lifeless body from the pond behind their house in Sandpoint.

"No!" she screamed and ran down the hall to her parents' bedroom.

Slumped in a chair next to the open sliding glass door, Dad had a beer in his hand. The bed covers were in disarray. The bed was empty.

"Where's Mom?" she demanded.

Dad shook his head, his face blank.

"Dammit, answer me! Where is she?"

"She's dead, Abbie."

What?! No way she had heard that right.

As Dad burst into sobs, Uncle Jesse shuffled in and clutched her in his arms. She wasn't having it and pushed him away. "You're a liar," she yelled to Dad. "Whaddya do to her, you piece of shit?"

"He's telling the truth, darlin'," Uncle Jesse said. "She passed away early this evening, at the hospital." He dropped his head.

The weight of a ton of bricks raining down on her sent her crumbling into a pile at Uncle Jesse's feet. He dropped to the floor and rocked her back and forth while she absorbed the pain. This had to be a nightmare! It couldn't be true. Mom, dead? Through the delirium, she searched the deepest crevices of her brain for understanding.

After a few minutes, she lifted her head from his lap, wiped the snot from her nose, and pleaded, "Why didn't you call me to come home? I texted you my cell number, and the main Redwood Manor number, too."

"When I called your cell phone," her uncle said, "it said your service had been disconnected."

She'd forgotten. *Ben.*

"Then I called Redwood Manor and told the woman who answered that we had a family emergency, and you needed to get to the hospital right away. She said she'd let you know. When you didn't show up, I called back, must've tried a hundred times, but the damn line was busy. Still is."

When his words settled, she sprang to her feet. "*Who* did you talk to at Redwood Manor?" she demanded.

He searched his memory. "Misty, Christy, maybe? No, it was Kristine. Yeah, that's how she answered."

Rage exploded inside her, and she stomped maniacally around the room. "That wicked bitch! She'll pay, so help me God, she's gonna pay."

Confused, her father asked, "What's going on?"

Abbie didn't feel like explaining. "How? How did Mom die?"

Her father looked up and said, "Well, she'd spent the day in bed." He took a swig of his beer. "Later, when I checked on her, she was on the bathroom floor, passed out."

Uncle Jesse added, "That's when he yelled for me to call an ambulance. Damn 911 guy said they didn't run the ambulance on Christmas day, so I called Dr. Xavier, and he said he'd meet us at the hospital. Your dad carried her to my truck, and we drove her in."

Abbie rubbed her burning eyes. "But what happened to her? I don't understand."

"Heart attack," Dad said.

Uncle Jesse wiped his own tears away. "The doc worked hard to save her, and when he couldn't, he was pretty torn up."

Her knees buckled. Mom now lay alone in a refrigerator somewhere. The coroner would inject her with formaldehyde, then carve her up. "Dead at forty-two," Abbie said in a daze. "It's not fair."

"Dr. Xavier said you can see her if you want," Dad said.

"But you don't have to," Uncle Jesse offered.

She held her gut. "I need some time to myself. Can you both please leave me alone?"

"Of course," Uncle Jesse said as he helped his brother out of the chair.

"I loved your mom," Dad said as he approached her, "more than you'll ever know, Abbie."

When she rejected his hug, he hung his head and stumbled to the door. Then he stopped and peered into her eyes. "I love you, too, Abbie. Always have. I haven't been the best at sayin' it, but it's the truth."

She had long hated her dad, but now she wasn't so sure. His words threw her into a tailspin. This declaration of love—was it a manipulation? Something he expressed freely now but would later take back when the alcohol wore off? The grudge she'd been carrying for years had grown far too heavy, but she wasn't willing to shed it yet.

Beaten, Dad nodded and left.

She wandered around the room, sobbing as she touched her mother's belongings. In the closet, she brought the clothing to her nose and inhaled her scent. Lavender.

She sat on Mom's side of the bed. On the nightstand, on a pile of *Woman's Day* magazines was a prescription bottle. Curious, Abbie picked it up. The label read, OMAX 0136— QTY: 1—DIRECTIONS: TAKE WITH WATER BETWEEN NOON AND 1:00 P.M. ON DECEMBER 25, 2040.

When Abbie jiggled the bottle, something inside rattled. She twisted off the lid and a metallic silver pill the size of a pellet rolled around at the bottom. Mom had hated pills. Abbie set the bottle down and opened the drawer of the nightstand. There was an envelope addressed to Abbie! She leaned back against the pillows and tore it open. Inside was a letter, and a key.

December 25, 2040

To my dearest daughter,

There's so much I want to tell you. I'll start with the key. It goes to the blue carry case I keep in the closet. Grandma and Grandpa's wedding rings and photographs are inside, along with other items I know you'll appreciate.

What I'm about to tell you, I wish I could've been honest about sooner; it would've saved everyone a lot of grief. Your dad is not the only one to blame for our crumbling lives. After Sammie died, I punished him; I withdrew my affection. I stopped being his lover and friend. It was wrong, and my lack of moral support for him, I believe, led to his alcoholism. Yes, he has free will, but I was awful to him, and after I was done punishing him, the guilt set in over what I had created, so I compensated by defending him.

Sammie's death wasn't his fault. I'm to blame. I had removed the back door lock and the doorknob because I was going to repaint the door. It happened after I left for work at the dress shop. Your dad had fallen asleep on the couch, and Sammie woke up early from his nap. He grabbed Dad's fishing pole and snuck out that door. Your dad never pointed his finger at me; he blamed himself because he'd fallen asleep. I'm sorry we never gave you the details before, but now you know. Please see it in your heart to forgive him/us. I know he has been awful to you, and he should apologize, but he's damaged, sweetie. But the man I fell in love with is still in there somewhere, I know it.

I'm writing this letter because I've become very ill, and I'm afraid my final days are near. Yes, melodramatic, and I'll rip up this letter if I get better. But in case I don't, I need for you to know how much I love you, my precious daughter. Be bold. Now go get 'em.

Love, Mom

The heartfelt words were as insightful and honest as any Abbie had ever read. She had never truly known her mother, and now her death had stolen the opportunity. And the bit about Dad was heartbreaking. The rest of the letter faded in her mind, like disappearing ink. The swell of her heart came as a surprise right out of left field. Maybe she wasn't dead inside. She wanted to be in Dad's arms, but this time, she'd console him and apologize for adding to his misery.

As she was about to go look for him, she hesitated. The shame of having added to his grief stopped her. She couldn't look him in the eyes; she was a coward.

After reading Mom's letter again, an irrepressible rage ignited within her. She swiped the items from Mom's nightstand onto the floor, then kicked them out the sliding glass door, where they scattered into the mud.

Footsteps in the hallway again.

"Let her be!" Uncle Jesse yelled to his brother.

Gasping for breath, she spotted the framed photo hanging on the wall of her, Mom, and Sammie, taken in Sandpoint two days before he died. It had been a sweltering summer day. The cool pond glistened in the sunlight as Sammie played on a black inner tube, a little boy with curly brown locks of hair, his face brimming with excitement.

The morning of his death—if only she hadn't yelled at him for barging into her bedroom holding his new dinosaur toys. All he'd wanted was for her to play with him. He had left brokenhearted—the back of his slumped little body was the last she'd seen of him as he exited her door.

She ripped the photo from the wall and chucked it across the room.

Both dead.

She got to the kitchen, where she opened the cabinet with Mom's recipe box. To her surprise, it sat next to a bottle of Jack Daniels. She stared at the bottle, then at the recipe box, and back at the bottle again. A tortured choice. *Bring the bottle to the table, too?*

The old Abbie—the one she thought she'd buried—grabbed both and sat. But somehow, thumbing through Mom's recipes didn't feel as comforting as she'd thought it would. She plucked out a handwritten recipe for tamale pie. A phantom aroma of seasoned ground beef and buttery cornmeal filled the kitchen. The memories, oh, the memories… Mom would never see another day on earth, attend her wedding, or be a grandma.

"I'm so sorry, Mom. Just one drink," she cried.

She unscrewed the bottle cap and took a giant swig. Another wouldn't hurt. She gulped and gulped and gulped until the burning filled her stomach, and fuck, it felt good. Closing her eyes, she questioned why she had ever quit drinking. This was her destiny: a sloppy loser drunk. The shame plunged in deeper than a butcher knife, and as she chugged more, Dad and Uncle Jesse walked in. The disappointment in Uncle Jesse's eyes nearly killed her.

CHAPTER TWENTY-TWO

THE NEXT DAY, Abbie wallowed in bed mourning her mother's death and the not-so-sobering truth that she'd never walk the earth again. *Four p.m.* She buried her head under the covers, her skull feeling like someone had hammered it on an anvil. Nausea, the bed spins, her old familiar self-induced misery. She was a hypocrite, placing higher standards on everyone but herself.

She thought back to when Mom had asked her if she wanted to help decorate the Christmas tree, and Abbie had declined. She had vowed to make it up to Mom, but that chance had died, along with Abbie's worthless promises. Indeed, she was her father's daughter. And now, she and Mom would never decorate another tree together again.

Her dreams of college were dead, as dead as Ty, but he had been right about one thing: girls from Eureka never got ahead. Now that she and Dylan had found Gia, she had no reason to ever set foot in Port Allegiance again. It'd been a silly schoolgirl fantasy to think she had a chance. Hilda was right: Dylan had no business associating with "her type."

Uncle Jesse knocked on her door. He was persistent. She had ignored his previous attempts to enter her bedroom, but she couldn't hide away forever, so she allowed him in, dreading the conversation about her bingefest last night.

"Got coffee and a banana for you," he said, sitting on the bed beside her.

"Put them on the nightstand."

When he moved the covers away from her face, she pulled them back over. "If you're here to counsel me on the dangers of—"

"I'm not, Abbie, but you can't hide in here forever."

Pressure built up behind her eyes, and the tears came. Then anger hit her. She slapped the covers away and sat up. "Why not? There's nothing left."

"That's bullshit, and you know it," he said sternly. "Now get out of bed, take a hot shower, and get back to work in Port Allegiance. It's what your mom would want."

The gall of him using Mom like that! "Don't you dare pretend to know what Mom would want. I'm never going back—*never.*"

"And don't *you* dare piss away your future," he said, shaking a finger at her.

He was fighting for her when she hadn't the will to fight for herself. Mom's face filled her mind, as clear and beautiful as the day she'd joined her new friend's book club—Abbie's first day working in Port Allegiance. Mom's final words to her: *Go show Port Allegiance what you're made of, my beautiful, capable daughter. I love you. Now get going before you miss your bus.*

The emotions overtook her, and she sobbed, the despair unbearable. Uncle Jesse clutched her in his arms.

"God, I love you," she said, sobbing her eyes out. "You never judge. I couldn't do that with my own parents."

"You're young, Abbie. There are no mistakes, only learning moments."

"What are you, some sort of philosopher now?"

"Not even close."

Learning moments. Kristine Mallory, you're about to receive the lesson of your lifetime.

At five p.m., during the dinner shift, Abbie burst through the Redwood Manor kitchen door and scoured the room for her prey. When she spotted Kristine, Abbie charged, drew her arm back, and clocked her flawless face with such force that Kristine stumbled over sideways and hit the floor. When Abbie went in for another round, Kristine whelped and scooted backward, her once tidy brunette bun flung loose, leaving a clump of hair dangling over one eye. Wet mascara trickled down her ivory cheeks.

"Holy shit!" Clem exclaimed as Ms. B looked on in shock.

As Dylan ran into the kitchen, Abbie lunged, snatched a fistful of Kristine's hair, and hoisted her to her feet. As she drew back her arm again, Ms. B dragged Abbie aside and shouted, "What the bloody hell is going on?!"

Kristine tucked the rogue hair behind her ear, venom oozing from her eyes. She attempted to charge Abbie, but Dylan grabbed her around the waist and restrained her. She kicked and screeched like Satan's spawn.

"Never has such a thing happened on my watch!" Ms. B shouted. "Abbie, you had better explain yourself right now, and it had better be good."

Abbie inhaled and gathered herself. "My uncle called here yesterday because my mom was in the hospital. He told Kristine that I needed to get there right away. She promised him she'd tell me." She cupped her mouth, fighting back tears. "Now my mom is dead, and I wasn't with her! She died without me!"

The group gasped in unison and turned to Kristine, their jaws hanging open.

"That's sad, but you're lying," Kristine insisted, still clamped in Dylan's arms. "I never talked to your uncle."

Incredulous, Abbie yelled, "Then how did he know your name? I've never mentioned you before. 'Hello, Redwood Manor, Kristine speaking.' Ring a bell?"

Kristine smirked and tried to wriggle away from Dylan.

"Lord help me, it's true," Ms. B said, glaring at Kristine, then directed her attention to Abbie. "I am so sorry about your mother, my dear. You have spoken so warmly of her, and I know how close you two were."

"Thank you, Ms. B, I appreciate that." But Abbie didn't want sympathy; she needed to unravel her brain alone.

"I can't believe this, Abbie," Clem said, heartbroken.

"Kristine, to my office, now," Ms. B ordered, her calm tone masking a fury she was too professional to allow the rest of the staff to witness. "Clem, you, too, please."

"By the way," Abbie said to Ms. B, "Kristine's the one who cheated at paintball by stealing one of our helmets, not either of the twins. She lied to Mrs. De Young."

Talk about lighting Ms. B's fuse. She snatched Kristine by the hair and pulled her away, Clem close behind.

Now Abbie was alone with Dylan, and his face showed the same expression as the day his dog, Pete, had died in Lake Tahoe. He pulled her into the pantry and wrapped his warm arms around her, but she felt numb to his comfort.

"I'm so sorry, Abbie," he said. "I can't imagine what you're feeling right now. And Kristine, I can hardly believe she's so fucking evil."

"I can," Abbie said angrily and pulled away. She paused a moment and said, "How's Gia?"

"Sleeping in the bunker. She's sick. Skyla's with her now."

"Doesn't surprise me. She probably caught pneumonia staying in that cold, disgusting house. I wish I'd been here for their reunion."

"Seeing them together was a beautiful thing."

Mom. Abbie imagined her lying in the fridge at the morgue, her body gray and cold. Dad was going to have her cremated today.

Dylan set a hand on her shoulder. "It's been an awful couple of days, hasn't it?"

She held back from crying.

"You wanna talk about her?"

"Not yet," she said, a hand over her heart. "But thanks."

"When you're ready, I'm here for you."

She smiled weakly. "Just like you were there for me six years ago."

"You were there for me, too, remember?"

"I guess we have a symbiotic relationship, huh?"

They gazed at each other until the intimacy pushed Abbie's attention to a fifty-pound sack of flour.

He saved her the discomfort. "The hacking software came last night, earlier than expected."

A spark lit. With the shock of her mother's death, she had forgotten. "And?"

"A whole lot of people are either looking at life in prison or the death penalty. I wanted you to be the first person I told, but I couldn't keep it from Skyla and Gia. Meet us in the bunker, and I'll tell you everything." He peeked out the door. "Give me a ten-minute head start."

As Abbie strode toward the tea parlor, she pictured Mom hanging her and Liza's Christmas stockings alone. No final "I love you." Regrets, oh, the regrets. They seared a hole in her heart.

The sound of pounding footsteps ahead. Hilda rounded the corner, wearing jodhpurs and a white polo button-up. "Abilene Spencer." Her shrill voice reverberated in the central cortex of Abbie's brain.

With a clawlike hand, Hilda waved a piece of red stationery before Abbie's face. "I didn't put two and two together until some brave soul just slipped this under my library door." She read the letter aloud. 'It has come to my attention that Dylan has been carrying on a sexual relationship with Abbie Spencer. She's nothing but a grifter trying to infiltrate your society. Signed, a friend.' She gave Abbie a "Gotcha!" look. "You're the scummy little thing who was responsible for Dylan losing his ear and toe in Lake Tahoe!"

Abbie's heart drummed in her chest. *Red stationery, Kristine Mallory's signature color. Satan's spawn strikes again.*

Hilda continued, "The authorities will be here shortly to arrest you for violating the laws of the Compliance Society."

Fuck this bullshit. Enraged, Abbie shoved her. Hilda's body slammed into the wall, sending a priceless oil painting crashing to the ground.

As Abbie ran, Hilda screamed for Ben and Rex, her voice an explosive backdraft rushing her from behind. Rounding the corner to the east wing, she burst into the tea parlor, and to the right of the fireplace, she double pressed the panel and climbed inside the wall.

Footsteps thumped closer to the panel. In the darkness, Abbie listened.

Hilda's muffled voice: "Where the hell are you and Ben? He's not answering my call."

She's on her phone.

"I don't care," Hilda continued. "You need to find Abbie and deliver her to Carter, NOW!"

A lull. "On vacation? This can't wait a few hours until you get back! I'll call the enforcers to find her."

The parlor door slammed.

Still quaking inside, Abbie pushed through the bunker door to find Dylan at the table before his laptop, and Gia sleeping in bed, a Band-Aid covering the tattoo on her forehead. Skyla came rushing to Abbie and hugged her tightly. "Dylan told me about your mom, and Kristine. I'm so sorry."

"Thanks." She settled into Skyla's embrace. "It was wrong not telling you about Gia the second I heard about her abduction. I wanted to find out more so I wouldn't give you false hope."

"It's okay, I understand, Abbie. All that matters is now." Skyla pulled away, smiled sincerely, and lay down with Gia. She brushed a few curly blonde strands from her face.

"You're good to her," Abbie said, watching the tender moment.

"So good that I couldn't find her myself. I should've searched harder."

"Dylan and I got lucky, that's all."

Still wading through the hangover from last night's binge, Abbie took a seat next to Dylan, anxious to learn what the hacking software had uncovered.

"You ready?" he asked, his nervous energy setting her on edge.

"Not really." She peered at Skyla, propped up on one elbow. "Dylan said you already know."

A somber nod. She wiped away a tear.

"It's super complicated," Dylan said. He tapped his keyboard a few times, and a report popped up. "And I don't fully understand what I read, but here's the gist of it. I found out that Hilda's company, HR Enterprises, is a front corporation for a company named Genome Sphere, which she and Jayden Vaughn created two years ago."

"What's a front corporation?" she asked.

"It's a group that represents themselves one way, but in actuality, they serve another hidden party who is unknown to the public. HR Enterprises is a legit property management company, but its true identity as Genome Sphere is hidden."

She drew in her chin. "Is it illegal?"

"In this case, yes. Genome Sphere is intermeshed in a shit ton of morally reprehensible activities."

"But why create a front corporation?"

Dylan stood and paced the room, then peered directly at her. "It's about illegal drug testing for what Hilda and Jayden have named the Pacifica virus, which Genome Sphere's scientists manufactured in their laboratories. Their heinous goal is *to create and own the only cure*."

Abbie looked over at Skyla, who nodded it was true. Dylan's story was straight out of a science fiction movie. Abbie sat with his words a moment and thought. The threat of a released virus traveling around the globe, infecting people, killing innocent millions, made her shudder.

"It's also about the bottom dollar," he said as he sat back down at the table. "When the CDC scientists eradicated every variant of the coronavirus two years ago, and the economy recovered somewhat, the governor stopped relief payments to business owners and private citizens. As a result, lots of people in Eureka couldn't pay their rent to Hilda's company, HR Enterprises. Hilda and Ben have a certain lifestyle to maintain, so they started looking for a new revenue source. That's when Hilda and Jayden Vaughn hooked up." Poor Dylan looked and sounded completely disgusted and shell-shocked by what he'd learned about both his parents.

"Jesus," Abbie said. "A match made in hell."

"From the bowels of hell," Skyla added.

Dylan said, "Plenty of residents of Port Allegiance have their hands in the revenue jar, and Ben's doling out shareholder checks to them."

"No surprise there," Abbie said.

Pounding feet on the floor above them sent her into fight-or-flight mode. *The enforcers!* She briefly explained her confrontation with Hilda, who had called them to search the house.

"We're safe down here," Dylan assured her and continued with his story. "Are you familiar with the claim that the Rancho Seco Nuclear Generating Station, six hours from here, is potentially giving the residents of Galt and the surrounding areas lung cancer?"

"Sure," Abbie said. "My mom and I watched the breaking news about it. And yesterday, while Skyla and I helped prepare the meal for the homeless, we listened to a new report. The EPA conducted an evaluation of the plant and found nothing wrong. We didn't believe it for a second."

"Well, you can believe the EPA on this one," he said. "Get this: the Pacifica virus has migrated outside of Humboldt County to Galt, and caused those lung cancer deaths. Local doctors don't know why these people developed cancer, but Hilda and Jayden's doctors—not actually doctors yet, but medical students from Port Allegiance University—know exactly why they died."

"Students?" The conversation she'd overheard at the coffee shop about viruses came back to her.

"Yep."

Unnerved by the crashing noises upstairs, it was impossible to concentrate. "So how did those people die?"

"A group of these students stole a victim's corpse from the morgue and conducted their own autopsy." He explained they had two test groups: one in Eureka, to observe how the virus behaved within the general public; and the other on Terra Isle, in a controlled environment, where the students used the tattoos so as not to confuse the bodies. For half the test subjects, the antidote had failed, and they died. The other half, for whom the antidote had eradicated the cancer cells, the students drown them in the sea because they knew too much. As for the guinea pigs still in Eureka, the test was over. They were either back to living their normal lives, or dead, but not to worry, the virus wasn't contagious. And Terra Isle, nine miles off the coast from here, was as Gia had described: an oil-drilling platform. When the oil had run dry a few years back, Dylan's parents had purchased the structure and converted it into a research laboratory. From what Dylan gathered, no victims were there anymore, but Hilda planned for it to be at full capacity come Friday night, two days from now, for experimentation with a new type of female sterilization drug.

"This is insane!" Abbie tried to piece her thoughts together. "But I don't understand. How does the virus turn into lung cancer?"

Skyla jumped in. "Through sexual contact, blood transfusions, or injecting it into someone's body."

Dylan added that only certain connective tissues in the lungs, and no other place in the body attracted the virus. Once an infection was present, it behaved similarly to the human papillomavirus, or HPV, but grew at lightning speed.

Abbie's mind raced with a million questions. Then she remembered the sex-ed talk she and Mom had had years ago. "Like venereal warts, the sexually transmitted disease that causes cervical cancer in women?"

"Exactly," he said. "And get this, most of the people in Eureka who have died or gone missing didn't die at the hands of the East Bay Serial Killer. He never existed. It was either the Pacifica virus that killed them, or Carter abducting them and boating them to Terra Isle."

"Even the coroner's office is involved," Skyla said.

"Of course," Abbie replied, feeling like she was in a daze. "Otherwise, they would've told the CDC about the unusually high number of lung cancer cases that had been pouring into his office." This nightmare was getting crazier by the second. "Gia? Is that what's wrong with her?" Abbie asked, and Skyla nodded morosely.

Dylan explained that Hilda had ordered Gia's abduction after discovering Ben was having his way with her. She couldn't risk Gia going public. The data showed from the time the students injected the virus into someone's body, without the antidote, they had only ten days before the cancer killed them. They had injected Gia ten days ago; she'd be dead by eight that evening.

Abbie checked the time: 6:33 p.m. "And she knows about this?"

"Yes," Dylan said quietly.

His story was so inconceivable that Abbie wondered if she was asleep and trapped in a lucid nightmare. Then it dawned on her. She shouted, "Why the fuck are we talking about this when we could be finding Gia's antidote? She only has ninety minutes!"

"The only antidote is on Terra Isle," Dylan explained, then went on to say boating there would be impossible. Two dozen armed enforcers surrounded the sea structure, along with twenty-four-seven satellite surveillance. The obstacles were insurmountable.

"We just let her die then?"

"What choice is there?" Skyla asked. "We can't take her to the hospital; she's refused. We need to respect her wishes."

Abbie was about to explode. "Why can't we get her to a hospital outside Humboldt County, where Hilda's goons aren't standing guard?"

"So the doctors can do what?" Dylan asked. "There isn't enough time." Judging by the pained look on his face, Abbie suspected he was about to drop another bomb, and she pressed her back against her chair.

Reluctantly, he opened a folder on his laptop labeled TEST SUBJECTS. He scrolled to 0136 - SPENCER, ANA. Abbie's mother. "I am so sorry," he whispered.

Mom's name filtered in and out of her vision. Couldn't be…no way…had to be a mistake. She scooted to the edge of her seat, Dylan's paraphrasing launching at her like bullets from a machine gun: *Ana Spencer, a well-nourished forty-two-year-old woman with no history of illness or disease… dated eleven days ago… to inject the Pacifica virus into a healthy woman… Once in the bloodstream… travels directly to lungs…cancerous tumors forming… Patient given antidote to be taken at a specific time…*

"It's not true," Abbie snapped, cutting him off. "My mom never had a tattoo. The file's wrong."

"They only tattooed the victims on Terra Isle," he said regretfully. "I'm sick the Orthromax didn't work for your mom, Abbie."

"Orthromax?"

"The name of the antidote."

Abbie thought back to last night, when she had read the prescription bottle on Mom's nightstand: OMAX 0136— QTY: 1—DIRECTIONS: TAKE WITH WATER BETWEEN NOON AND 1:00 P.M. ON DECEMBER 25, 2040.

0136? Mom's case file number! She remembered Mom saying Dr. Xavier had given her a vitamin B_{12} shot to help her depression. But it hadn't been a vitamin shot at all! "Oh my God!" Abbie blurted out. "Our doctor injected my mom with the virus! That lying bastard said she died from a heart attack, but she died of cancer!"

Skyla jumped up and sat at the table, and Dylan leaned in hard.

"The silver pill on her nightstand," Abbie cried. "It was her fifty-percent chance for survival."

"What are you talking about?" Skyla pressed.

Too good to be true. "My mom never took the pill…but Gia can!"

"Are you saying the antidote is right over the wall at your house?" Skyla asked.

"That's exactly what I'm saying."

"Then what are you and Dylan waiting for? Go and get it!"

Abbie mentally tracked the quickest way to her house. Gia only had a little more than an hour left. It would take too long to trek the tunnel to get the Sprinter van at St. Mary's, then drive home and back. But she couldn't risk the enforcers catching her upstairs. Then she remembered Hilda's library shared a door with the carriage house. They could take Dylan's car.

She listened carefully. No more stomping feet upstairs.

CHAPTER TWENTY-THREE

Current time: 6:47 p.m.
Deadline: 8:00 p.m.

IN THE LIBRARY, as Abbie and Dylan rushed to the door leading to the carriage house, Ben entered, holding what she recognized as the flame-throwing rifle from his gun cabinet.

Ben stood there, too stunned to speak at first. "What the hell do you think you're doing in here?" Something clicked in his mind, and he engaged Abbie in a stare-down. "And fraternizing with the help, Dylan?"

She stared at the flamethrower. "What have you done?"

Ben sashayed over to Hilda's desk, where he sat and rested his weapon on the glass top. "What I've done is no concern of yours, my dear. Let's just say I've taken care of some unfinished business. Exterminated the roaches."

"Kinda like Gia, huh, Ben?" Dylan said impulsively, bungling the timeline of their mission, if not blowing it all together.

"Gia?" Ben looked confused, then realized they'd caught him.

At this point, for them, the only way to get out alive was to kill or disable him. They had to rile him up, give them an excuse. She moved in closer to him and dropped the second bomb. "And guess what? She's here in your house, the house where you raped her. You nearly destroyed her life, and holy shit, does she have a story to tell."

Ben tugged at his collar, looking like he might collapse. "Here? Where did you find her?"

"That's no concern of yours, you sadistic pervert," Dylan said, disgust contorting his face.

Ben's panicked expression turned into a sneer. "One phone call to the judge, who owes me a favor, by the way, and he'll make sure Abbie and Jesse Spencer are sentenced to death for the murder of Ty Hawkins."

"The fuck you will," Dylan hissed, spraying spit.

"No gumption, boy. Nature versus nurture. From the moment Hilda birthed you, it was obvious you never shared my genes."

Judging by the blank look on Dylan's face, he was trying to process Ben's cryptic words. "What are you talking about?"

"Are you dense?" Ben asked, looking eager to mortally wound him. "You're not mine. I have a low sperm count. Doctors conceived you in a petri dish. You are your grandfather's little squirt. Walter Rhodes. Get it now?"

Dylan nearly fell backward, the color draining from his face.

Abbie had forgotten Walter had adopted Hilda. But she remembered Dylan saying that spending the summer after third grade at his grandfather's home in Ithaca, New York, was the best summer of his life. He loved his grandfather, but Walter had ceased contact with Dylan, and Dylan never learned why. But why use his sperm?

After a moment of reflection, Dylan said, "It makes sense now why you and I have never been alike, and if you think I'm hurt, you're sadly mistaken. This is the best news I've ever heard. And by the way, I have news for you, too, Ben."

Abbie checked her watch. Time was running short.

"This oughta be good," Ben said, and rolled his eyes.

"All those millions of dollars you and Hilda have stashed away for human medical testing, I've moved it to a secure location, away from your greedy hands. It'll help the families whose lives you've ruined."

Ben's face dropped, and his nostrils flared. He jerked forward to grab the flamethrower, but Abbie got to it first and tossed it as far away as possible.

"You're dead, bitch!" He launched himself over the desk, then wrestled her onto her back, and sat on her. Hands gripping her neck, he lifted her head and banged it repeatedly on the hardwood floor.

Through a kaleidoscope of riotous colors, the flamethrower whizzed past her vision.

A gruesome *thunk*.

Ben's hands loosened, his eyes rolled back, and he fell over sideways, unconscious.

"Jesus Christ, are you okay?" Dylan dropped to his knees, his hands trembling.

She wiped away the salty blood splatter from her lips, then rubbed the back of her head, but she wasn't sure if she was okay. Two Dylans drifted in her vision. She rubbed her eyes until he and Ben came into focus. *Dammit!* Ben was still alive, his breathing shallow. Dylan hadn't whacked him hard enough. Could she snuff the life out of him? No, she wasn't a killer, and neither was Dylan. Her head throbbed as she scanned the library. "Where can we hide his body until we figure out what to do with him?"

He tossed the weapon aside and thought a moment. "The secret passage. We'll gag him and tie him up there."

"Tie him up with what?" She threw up her arms helplessly, thinking about how much time they were wasting.

"I dunno. Fuck!" Dylan thought a minute, then ran to a tall cabinet and opened it. Inside were fishing poles and supplies.

After dragging Ben inside the wall and clearing away any evidence in the library, Dylan confiscated his cell phone and bound his limbs together with fishing line. As he secured him to a vertical iron waste pipe, Abbie crammed a handful of Kleenex into his mouth, then wrapped his head repeatedly with Scotch tape.

7:14: forty-six minutes left.

Abbie, now a stowaway in the ridiculously tiny trunk of Dylan's Lamborghini Roadster, would remain there until he parked in the alley behind her house. Would the enforcers stop him outside and search his vehicle? He was late for his evening class, he'd say calmly. If they didn't believe him, he'd plow through both the blockade and the Port of Entry. *Balls to the wall,* he'd promised.

The sound of the automatic door opening… A rev of the overpowered engine, then a jerk of her body as he backed out of the carriage house. The rumbling of tires over cobblestone. An audible shifting into gear…rumbling forward… and forward… Then, a hard slamming on the brakes.

Shit!

The engine was too loud for Abbie to hear voices. Sweat saturated her clothes as her thoughts dissolved into the worst-case scenario. What the fuck was happening? Gia was going to die! The confined space squeezed her, seeming to deplete the space of any remaining oxygen. If a full-blown anxiety attack came on, she'd go crazy; she might begin screaming and kicking to get out. The trunk would trap her here until the enforcers pried open the latch.

Breathe, she told herself. She thought back to Grandma and Grandpa's house in Sandpoint, her happiest and safest place. The aroma of the guest room sheets…

A quick rev of the engine, and the car rumbled forward. If it was the enforcers who had stopped them, Dylan had outwitted them.

He breezed through the Port of Entry. They'd arrive at her house at approximately 7:23, five minutes from now. How could this nightmare have happened in 2040? Had the Holocaust not taught humankind anything? Of course, this didn't compare to that horrific time in history, but still, Port Allegiance's very existence, its unchallenged laws, were a complete breakdown of governmental checks and balances. How were she, Dylan, and Skyla going to expose to the world this manufactured virus that Hilda and Vaughn and every co-conspirator had created? They were simply three tiny fish in a sea of sharks. If they survived this, she vowed to avenge her mother's death, and potentially Gia's, along with all the other poor souls.

After a few minutes of her calculating their location with Dylan's every turn, the car skidded in the gravel behind her house. The trunk latch clicked, and the door flipped open to the caustic stench of burning tar paper and plastic. Smoke filled the dim alleyway.

Confusion set in. Something awful was happening.

In an instant, Dylan pulled her out. Horrified, she watched as menacing flames tentacled out of every busted window of her house, snapping and crackling, the heat on her face palpable.

Uncle Jesse, Dad, Liza! As she bolted to the backyard, Dylan grabbed her around the waist and yelled, "It's not safe, Abbie!"

"My family!" she screamed, clawing at him. She pried herself free and raced to the side of the house, shielding her face from the heat. Jumping over a pile of chicken wire, she caught sight of Sideshow Bob lying feet up, dead, his glorious feathers ruffled. The grief hit her so hard her mind crumbled.

Gotta move on, gotta move on.

Dylan grabbed her again, pulling her to the sidewalk in front of the house, where spectators lined the street, and where no fire truck was in sight. Dad had parked in his usual spot, but Uncle Jesse's truck was missing. Had the two of them escaped the flames? Liza's pen door was open, but no Liza. Abbie called up and down the street for her. Struggling to breathe, she plucked Dylan's phone from his shirt pocket and dialed Uncle Jesse.

She exhaled hard when he answered on the first ring. "It's me," she said flat out. "Our house is on fire! Where are you two? Where's Liza?"

"Jesus Christ, Abbie, I haven't been able to get a hold of you. The phone line at your job's still out. We're at our camping spot. Your dad sprained his ankle, and I opened Liza's pen and shooed her out before we ran. Don't worry about her. She'll come back."

Sobbing, she dropped to her knees and told him she was so glad they were alive, then ended the call. With the smoke moving in heavy, she coughed and sputtered.

Then it hit her: *Ben's flamethrower!* He had burned down her house because she hadn't shown up for their 'date' in the sauna. *One second late, and I'll ruin your life so fast, it'll make your asshole pucker.* Had he also made good on his threat to upload the video to the web? Or given the enforcers the video of her and Uncle Jesse pushing Ty off the bluff?

As Dylan cradled her in his lap, she pictured Gia, who'd be dead soon after they returned. Mom's gift had been wasted. Abbie envisioned the pill bottle melting into the nightstand.

A flashback. After last night's tantrum in her parents' bedroom, she had knocked everything from the nightstand onto the floor, then kicked it all out the door. Had the pill bottle been one of the items?

Fighting the smoke, she raced to the sliding glass door at the side of the house. As she rounded the corner, she lost her footing and face-planted into the wet mud. A clumsy swipe of her eyes, and she crawled the rest of the way, ten feet maybe, her knees sinking into the mud. Dylan was close behind.

Through the light of the flames, she spotted Mom's alarm clock, her magazines, her water bottle, the tiny picture of Sammie. Where was the damn pill bottle? Was it the one item she had failed to kick out the door? *Fuck!*

Frantically, she patted the mud in every direction, her eyes watering, the burning getting worse. Pain in her lungs. Oh, the pain.

Something hard under her hand. As she gripped it, consciousness faded into a pinpoint, then nothingness.

"Wake up, Abbie, come on, wake up."

Dylan's voice came filtering through the haze, like years ago when he had roused her to stay awake in the hollowed-out tree stump in Lake Tahoe. She cracked her eyelids, her upper lashes peeling away from the lower. Where was she? In her backyard, her house still ablaze.

"You're gonna be okay," Dylan said breathlessly, the flames flickering in his eyes.

The memory struck with a start. Mom's scattered items, the pill bottle, *the hard object in the mud!* Bolting upright, she peered at her clenched fist, a ball of caked mud. Slowly, she worked her fingers open, hoping... *Yes!* She'd done it!

"You've got to be kidding me," Dylan said, and dug it out.

She got to her feet, her lungs baked from smoke and heat. "What time is it?"

"Almost eight." Swooping her up, he carried her to the back of his car, where he propped her against the trunk. As he walked around front to pop the latch, the roof of her house collapsed, the flames swallowing it whole.

There was a thunking sound, then something dragging along the gravel. "Dylan?" she called out.

No answer. She peered up and down the alley, the trees lining it making it too dim to make out any shapes. "Dylan, where are you?"

She stood in the center of the alley, turning around and around.

Footsteps approached through the dark. The hair at the nape of her neck stood erect.

"Sentimental girls like you always come home," a familiar man's voice said.

In a second, he'd finagled her into a choke hold, and as he dragged her down the alley, the stench of Drakkar Noir filled her nose.

Rex!

Feet spinning backward in the gravel, she beat at him with her arms. If he got her inside his vehicle...

The terror induced a rush of iron will. She wedged her chin under his arm and bit into his flesh, his hair filling her mouth and getting stuck between her teeth. He swore, loosening his grip, and she fell to the ground, gravel boring into her kneecaps. She scuttled away like a crab, maybe five feet.

Ahead, a hint of light shone on an empty liquor bottle. Her weapon. Inches away, almost there, *almost there...*

Rex grabbed her by the ankles and dragged her, the gravel raking her belly and breasts raw. In one fell swoop, he chucked her into the trunk of his vehicle. There was a body beside her. It was Dylan!

Rex slammed down the hatch, leaving them in complete darkness. Like a manic mime, she searched with her hands for an escape route, but all she found were cold metal bars. Rex had sealed their fate, reducing them to nothing more than caged animals, and as for Abbie, another human test subject. She imagined herself strapped to a gurney on Terra Isle, simply another missing girl from Eureka. No big deal.

She tried to rouse Dylan, shook him hard. Why hadn't Rex driven off yet?

A guttural scream came from outside. It didn't sound human.

Dylan was waking up, a groaning sound escaping his throat.

The interior lights flashed, then came a blaring alarm, so loud it disoriented her.

"What's happening?" Dylan asked, raising himself up and holding his head.

"No idea. You okay?"

"Something hit me over the head, and—"

The back hatch opened, and she burrowed into the corner of the cage. The first thing that came into view was a key fob dangling from filthy hands.

Tony Wilkens! Her veteran friend who lived in a tent across the alley. He stuck in his head. "These new remote controls are space age. Fancy-pants got away, but I got a piece o' him." He held up Rex's wallet. "You kids wanna go to Denny's and have ourselves some chicken-fried steak? My treat."

Having declined Tony's insane offer, Abbie, again in the trunk of Dylan's car, dialed Ms. B, the harsh reality hitting: it was after eight now, and Gia might well be dead.

"Dylan," Ms. B said, sounding flustered. "The house is in chaos. Why are the enforcers storming the house looking for Abbie?"

"Just answer yes or no, ma'am. It's me, Abbie. Dylan lent me his phone. Are you alone?"

A pause. "Yes."

"Can't go into detail, but I beg you, please keep the enforcers and Hilda away from her library. It's a matter of life or death."

"Whose death? I'm bloody confused."

"Please, please, promise you'll keep the library clear. Dylan will be home soon."

"Oh, Abbie. I don't know what kind of a mess you kids have gotten yourselves into, but yes, I promise."

"You're the best!" Ending the call, she dialed Uncle Jesse.

"Sorry for hanging up. What happened at the house?"

"First, tell me what's going on with you. You're in trouble."

"I'm fine. I'll tell you about it when I see you. The house?"

"How much time ya got?" he asked.

"Only a few minutes."

"Me and your dad were in the living room, fixing that old Briggs and Stratton engine for the lawn mower, when some crazy SOB kicked the front door in, holding what I thought was a gun, but it turned out to be a flame-throwing rifle! I mean, Jesus Christ! Behind him was a man with silver hair, holding a can of gasoline."

Rex.

"I grabbed my pistol from the end table, and as I went to shoot, flames shot at us and burned the hair off my knuckles, and I dropped my gun."

"Jesus," Abbie exhaled.

"The flames followed us to your parents' bedroom. When we got out and ran into Bum Jungle"—the burned-down city block scattered with tents directly across the alley from their house—"your dad sprained his ankle. We hid there 'til it was safe to grab the camping gear from the shed."

"Oh, Uncle Jesse, that must've been horrifying."

"It was dammit! And don't worry about Liza, darlin'. She's probably chowing down somewhere near where we hid. And as for your dad, well, I told him I killed Ty."

There was silence for a moment.

Shit. She still hadn't told Uncle Jesse about Ben's video of them pushing Ty off the bluff. No time now. She told him she'd call soon, and not to worry. After saying "I love you," they hung up, their lives a chaotic mess.

She adjusted herself in the cramped space, her raw belly and breasts burning from the gravel that Rex had raked her over. A sticky wetness saturated her shirt—*blood.* She tried to hold back from sobbing, but she succumbed.

Mom. Abbie needed her like she needed oxygen. The fire had left her, Uncle Jesse, and Dad homeless. The blue carry case holding Grandma's jewelry and invaluable photos had surely burned along with everything else. Add arson to Ben's list of crimes. He needed to die, there was no doubt about it. Now she was certain she could snuff out his miserable life. It would be easy. A hard pinch to his nose when they got back, and he'd be dead in minutes.

And in a few days, new test victims would arrive on Terra Isle. Wasn't gonna happen, not a chance. She imagined Skyla lying with Gia, crying over her body, wondering why she and Dylan had failed at such a simple mission. And Hilda, when she had ordered Rex to find Abbie and deliver her to Carter, Abbie had assumed Hilda meant to locate her in Redwood Manor. She had been naive. Never again.

When Abbie entered the secret panel in Hilda's library and stopped abruptly, Dylan crashed into the back of her. *Oh God, Ben!* Something was finally going right. He sat there lifeless, his head slumped over his shoulder. His eyes were partially open, and his skin held a bluish tint. Spit had considerably swelled the Kleenex she had crammed into his mouth. The psychopath was dead, no doubt. Had the tissue swollen into the back of his throat, cutting off his intake of oxygen through his nose?

"What're you doing?" Dylan said anxiously and nudged her further inside. He closed the panel behind him.

"I think I killed him."

He pushed past her and stopped cold, his face turning ashen. "Oh fuck." He put a hand on the wall to stabilize himself.

In the shadows, there was a glint of a viscous substance where the wall behind Ben's head met the floor. She moved in closer. Blood, a river of it snaking straight for the bunker. Ben had bled out from Dylan whacking the flamethrower over his head. That's what had killed him. No time to allay his horror.

With Mom's muddy pill bottle firmly in her grip, she careened along the narrow passageway and down the stairs, her feet slipping around as if she were on ice. At the bottom, the air was balmy with the taste of salt, and the iron door had dammed the pooling blood.

Abbie pushed through, Skyla oblivious to the mess seeping in. She was hopping up and down, the palm of her hand pressed into her forehead. "She's still alive! Please, oh please, tell me you got it!"

When Abbie handed her the bottle, Skyla burst into tears and hurriedly sat at Gia's side. Hands shaking, she unscrewed the bottle cap and out rolled the metallic silver pill into her palm. "Open your mouth, baby. Come on, you can do it."

As if she had survived a week stranded in the Mojave Desert, Gia parted her cracked and bloodied lips, and Skyla set the pill on her tongue, then rested the rim of a water bottle on her lower lip and poured in a little. Gia's throat gurgled as she worked it down.

"Good girl," Skyla praised, stroking her hair. "Imagine the pill hitting your stomach and splitting into thousands of micro-warriors, every one of them fighting the cancer until it's dead, until you're cured."

"I love you, Stilts," Gia croaked, barely audible. "I'm gonna be okay, right?"

"Of course. I love you, too. I won't leave your side. You *are* strong, and you *will* make a full recovery."

With Skyla's reassuring words, the drug flicked Gia's lights out rather quickly.

In a panic, Skyla rested two fingers on the side of Gia's neck, the silence deafening. She sighed in relief. "Whatever powers there be, please save her," she begged.

"It's a waiting game now," Dylan said.

"How long will it take to kick in?" Skyla asked him.

"The literature said between six to eight hours."

"That's too long!" she cried and stretched out beside her, nuzzling her head into Gia's neck. "You're gonna be okay."

It was an agonizing moment. If loyalty could be patented, Skyla would own the rights.

After Abbie and Dylan offered some comforting words, Skyla fell into much-needed sleep beside Gia. As Abbie covered them with the blanket, she considered the possibility of Skyla ending her own life if Gia died.

She turned to Dylan, his usual positive disposition having died along with Ben. What were they going to do with his body?

She led him into the bathroom and set both hands on his shoulders. "How are you coping?"

"I'm not," he replied and paced the small space. "This is a goddamned nightmare. When Ben was banging your head into the floor, I swung the gun at him with the intent to kill, to get him out of our way. Now that he's actually dead, the reality of what I've done is fucking with my head. I killed a human being!"

She set a hand on his chest and stopped him. "No matter what horrible things your father did, it doesn't negate the fact you loved him. You're going to grieve, naturally."

"I don't know if it's grief or anger," he said, shaking his head. "Probably both. His and Hilda's crimes will be a shit stain smeared across the history books."

"You're right. But what are we going to do with his body?"

He moved to the sink and splashed cold water on his face. "I have a temporary plan. Later, when everyone's asleep, I'll drag him into the meat locker until I decide what to do."

A gruesome image. "But Clem will find him. He's in and out of that locker several times a day. Why not ask him for help? Tell him everything. We trust him, don't we? He won't betray us."

His eyes narrowed. "Including what Ben did to you and your mom?"

"Yes. Give him *all* the sordid details."

As Dylan considered the idea, his spirit slowly rebounded. "I'll do it," he said, nodding. "But Hilda's shipping new test victims to Terra Isle the day after tomorrow. How are we going to stop it?"

The same question had been hounding her mind. Then an idea struck, clear in its unfolding. Screw the tiny fish in a sea of sharks bullshit. Tomorrow night at nine was the benefit gala at the De Young Theater for the Arts. With Ben on an unexpected business trip, Hilda would have to recite his speech instead. *Yes, that's it.* Dylan would text her from Ben's phone pretending to be Ben and explain why he couldn't attend.

Abbie pitched her idea to Dylan, and after some discussion, they agreed nothing in the world would ever be the same again. It was time to call Uncle Jesse to enlist his help.

CHAPTER TWENTY-FOUR

THE NEXT MORNING, Abbie's sleeping brain, a camera in burst mode, was capturing snapshots of Mom merrily decorating the house, then the undertaker pushing her body into the furnace, then a flash of Ty's and Ben's corpses, then Sideshow Bob's feathered carcass. The pain came out in a silent scream: "Make it stop!"

There was a clanking sound, and the images turned to dust. Addled, she cracked her lids open, her vision like peering through murky water. She blinked a few times.

The bunker! Had Dylan and Clem disposed of Ben's body? The antidote! Had it worked for Gia? She checked the bed where Gia and Skyla had fallen asleep together last night. Empty. After everything she and Dylan had gone through to save her life, had Gia fallen short of the fifty-percent chance of survival? As grief settled her head back into the pillow, there was another clanking sound.

At the table, Skyla was arranging a platter of breakfast goodies, juice, and a pot of coffee. She didn't look distraught;

in fact, there was a peace about her Abbie had never seen. Her body even moved differently, had a jovial hop to it.

"Abbie!" Skyla said with a slight flinch. "Good morning."

"The antidote worked?"

"Yep," she answered, her smile stretching wide. "You guys saved her life."

Abbie sprang to her feet. "Where is she?"

"In the bathroom, soaking in the tub."

"Why didn't you wake me?"

"You've had a hard go of it. Dylan and I thought you needed some sleep. He told me what happened with Ben, how he and Clem stored him in the meat locker. Geez, it's a bloodbath out there."

Abbie peered at the open door. There was an area rug draped over the blood, a little seeping out the side. She gagged. For the first time in her life, the coffee would have to wait. "How's Dylan doing?"

"Surprisingly well, considering."

"And Gia? How's she feeling?"

"A hell of a lot better than last night." Skyla poured herself some orange juice. "Her lungs aren't on fire anymore, and she's breathing more easily now." She lowered her voice. "But I'm worried about her mental health. She's changed; she's different. I mean, how could she not be, after what they did to her? The torture. She's talking about revenge. I can't let her do it, can't let her go to prison. No way."

The enormity of what Gia had suffered was hard to imagine. "What now?" Abbie asked. "Where will you two go?"

"Haven't thought that far ahead."

"I imagine anywhere other than Port Allegiance."

"The grass isn't always greener, right?"

Dylan's words, too. If only Abbie had known how prophetic the saying would come to be for her. Her family's burned-down house, the house she had once despised, was like an aching hole in her heart.

The bathroom door opened, and Gia appeared, her hair wrapped in a towel. Some of the color had returned to her face, but she still looked haggard, the black rings under her eyes pronounced. But she was a living miracle, really. Their gaze connected in a sisterhood unlike anything Abbie had ever experienced, other than with Skyla.

Gia approached and embraced her tight, not letting go. "I'm alive because your mother isn't. I'm so sorry for your loss."

It was as if Mom were embracing her, promising this nightmare would soon end and everything was going to be okay. God, it felt right, like coming home.

They separated when a herd of footsteps tromped down the stairs.

Dylan entered, holding what Abbie recognized as her laptop, and behind him was Clem, a leather bag over his shoulder. His eyes were darting around like he'd entered a foreign world. For him, it was; he had known nothing of the bunker.

"Good morning," Dylan said to Abbie and handed her the computer. "Grabbed it and all your belongings from your bedroom. Hilda ordered Rex to clear it out for your replacement."

"You're awesome. Thanks." It was wonderful seeing him. She tried to read his face.

"I'm okay," he said to her. He pulled out an envelope from his shirt pocket and handed it to Gia. "For you and Skyla. Inside are new identity cards and one-way bus tickets to San

Diego. Ms. B has scheduled you an appointment with an oncologist."

Clem jumped in. "There's also a prepaid credit card, and some cash, too. It's enough to keep you both afloat for a few months. After the appointment, you can both stay at my time-share on Bainbridge Island up in Washington State until you come up with a plan." He dug into his bag and handed Abbie, Skyla, and Gia each a cell phone with charger. "The phones are untraceable. I've already programmed our numbers into the contacts. In the itinerary app, you'll find detailed instructions about the appointment, where your hotel is located, et cetera." He handed the leather bag to Gia. "Ms. B's clothes, a few hats, and cosmetics for you both to disguise yourselves. It's nine o'clock. Your bus leaves in ninety minutes."

Gia took a step back, looking uncertain. "Ninety minutes? I'm grateful for what you've all done, but things are moving too fast. I'm not leaving until these animals pay!"

"Gia," said Dylan softly, stepping forward, "let someone else take the reins." He turned to Abbie. "Tell them about our plan."

After a few minutes, Abbie finished with, "See Gia? You can move on knowing justice will be served, and that every despicable act they inflicted upon humanity will dominate the internet."

DE YOUNG
12/27 9PM
BENEFIT GALA FOR NEEDY

CHAPTER TWENTY-FIVE

THE ATMOSPHERE UNDER THE retractable cargo cover of Hilda's white Cadillac Escalade was as combustible as a slow-ticking time bomb, thanks to Uncle Jesse's nervous energy. "An hour 'til showtime," he said to Abbie as they both lay curled up on the floor. "Where the hell are they?"

"They'll be here," she assured him. "You stressing out won't make it happen any sooner."

"Exposing one of the biggest crimes of the century doesn't stress you out? Or how about the enforcers shooting us dead, or a one-way ticket to San Quentin? Why not? Free room and board. We'd never have to dumpster dive again."

"Shh! Listen. You hear that?"

Echoing voices in the carriage house. High heels clicking on concrete.

"They're coming," she whispered.

The doors opened, and the Escalade bounced as Dylan and Hilda climbed in.

"Why must we take this tank?" Hilda carped. "You know how I hate it. And turn on the damn heat, it's freezing in here."

"I know you wanted the Jag, but Clem said there's something wrong with the steering column," Dylan lied, sparing Abbie and her uncle from its cramped trunk. "I'll make sure it gets to the auto shop tomorrow."

"Why didn't you warm this thing up first?"

The engine fired up. A screech of spinning tires pressed Abbie against the back hatch.

"How old are you?" Hilda bitched. "You're going to scrub those skid marks off the concrete when we get home! And your father. I could wring his neck. He knows how critical it is for us to show a united front tonight. Everybody who's anybody will be there. We're making a huge donation to the cause, and now I must give his damn speech for him. You know how I hate public speaking."

"I know. Take a Valium or something. Ben's grateful you're standing in for him."

"I bet he extended his trip to hook up with that Kate Loveland hussy from Vaughn Capital. They had a thing once, you know."

"Please, spare me his indiscretions."

The SUV stopped. Then the iron gate opening. She peeked out the back window into the night fog, visibility ten feet at best. Skyla and Gia had been on the bus now for ten and a half hours, putting them close to Los Angeles. Saying goodbye had been hard. Abbie had promised by the night's end, they'd have wreaked vengeance for every victim.

After the short stint to the theater, Hilda's lips still flapping, Dylan stopped before the grand art deco De Young

Theater for the Arts, the marquee lit with a cache of flashing white bulbs.

"What are you doing?" Hilda asked, annoyed. "This isn't the valet."

"I'll be in in a minute. Last time the valet parked for us, they scratched the car. Ben was furious, remember?"

The slamming of a door shook the SUV. As Dylan sped away, Abbie watched Hilda, wearing a skin-tight white gown that flared at the ankle, shuffle to the theater entrance, where an usher wearing an old-Hollywood-style red velvet uniform and tasseled fez escorted her inside.

"God, she's awful," Dylan growled. "Please tell me you guys are back there."

"We are," Abbie replied.

"No time to waste. You both ready?"

Uncle Jesse answered, "Ready as a two-bit buzzard shitting out an ostrich egg."

"Keep up the humor," Dylan said. "We'll need it."

He raced behind the theater, and as planned, parked by the service entrance. He released the back hatch, and Abbie inched out, a pistol strapped to her ankle. Uncle Jesse followed, then got to his feet and tugged at his collar as if he was miserable dressed in Dylan's expensive black tuxedo and ruby-red cummerbund. He'd vowed never to wear one, yet here he stood, albeit sulking a little. Lugging around a man-purse with Abbie's laptop inside had almost been a deal breaker for him. In the bunker that afternoon, she had cut his hair short and shaved off his goatee. *I feel like one of those little hairless Chihuahuas,* he'd complained.

Dylan walked around the SUV to them. His eyes widened. "Wow," he mouthed. "You both look so, so different. I'd never recognize either of you on the street."

Abbie contorted her face; the caked-on foundation itched like poison oak. She had styled her hair into a fancy updo with a diamond brooch comb poked into the back. Ms. B's ruby-sequined gown, a size too small, squeezed her butt, but the pumps fit as perfectly as Dorothy's in *The Wizard of Oz*. She imagined clicking her heels together and traveling anywhere but here.

And Dylan wore a tailored black tux that highlighted his broad shoulders. He had clipped on his bow tie crooked, so she adjusted it and told him he looked handsome.

"Not so bad yourself," he said, grinning.

His gaze stayed fixed on her, unleashing the butterflies in her stomach, their flutters only described in sappy romance novels. "Am I worth the half-million-dollar reward Hilda put up for my return to the authorities?" she asked sassily.

"You're worth a hell of a lot more than that."

"Come on, kids," Uncle Jesse said. "We gotta hustle."

"Hold on a sec," Dylan said softly, his eyes still glued on Abbie. He reached into his pants pocket and tucked a packet of Sour Patch Kids into her hand.

He'd remembered the candy helped stave off her anxiety attacks. Could the guy be any more thoughtful? After tonight, if their plan went haywire, she might not ever see him again. The fantasy came on hard. As she pressed her lips into his, he cupped her neck with hands that desired her. And his taste, like the aroma of his skin, earthy and sweet, like his cologne. She slipped her hands under his silk cummerbund, his waist contoured and hard.

When Uncle Jesse cleared his throat, she snapped back to reality. Dylan was grinning at her like he'd been reading her mind.

She needed a cold shower, but Sour Patch would have to do. She popped a few into her mouth, then zipped them into her evening purse with her cell phone. Like a true gentleman, Dylan crooked his arm and lifted his elbow for her to slip her arm around.

Spearheading their way to the theater's back entrance, they approached several large Piercy's Catering vans backed up to the double steel doors, a handful of men unloading food and beverages. In the wide service hallway, giant ducts and pipes infiltrated the walls, and dozens of worker bees buzzed about preparing for the epic event. Dylan, sensing her discomfort, squeezed her forearm gently.

"Dylan, my boy, how are you?" a distinguished man wearing a white suit greeted from out of nowhere. He beamed when he turned to Abbie.

Shit. The bounty for my head.

"Hello, sir," Dylan said, then turned to Abbie and Uncle Jesse. "I'd like to introduce you to Marlon Langley, the event coordinator."

Fight-or-flight launched Abbie into the Southern accent Uncle Jesse used when telling the story of Guillermo, the vicious gun-toting cat. "I'm Daisy, sir, Daisy West, and this is my father, Jeb West. Such an honor to attend this event."

Stunned by her performance, Dylan gawked at her.

"A Southern belle!" Marlon took her hand and kissed the top of it, his lips not actually touching her skin. "Don't come across many of you in these parts. It's my pleasure to meet you both." He shook Uncle Jesse's hand.

"The pleasure is ours," Uncle Jesse said, his drawl spot-on. "The De Youngs have told me what a sensational job you've been doing, coordinating and all."

Marlon's chest puffed up like a dove in mating season. "Oh my, what a compliment! I look forward to seeing them this evening." He turned to Dylan. "I understand your father is going to give a speech."

Dylan checked his watch. "I'm afraid he's on a last-minute business trip, so my mother will be giving it instead."

"Well, that is unfortunate." Marlon paused before correcting himself. "Not unfortunate your mother will give his speech; I meant unfortunate your father will not be attending."

"I understood what you meant, sir."

Marlon patted Dylan on the back. "At any rate, please enjoy the evening. Perhaps I'll see *y'all* in the ballroom later."

"Looking forward to it," Abbie said, annoyed by his use of "y'all." She curtsied lightly. "And please, Marlon, save a dance for me."

"It would be my pleasure, Ms. West."

With Dylan leading, the trio climbed the fire escape stairwell to the balcony level and pushed through a steel door that read AUTHORIZED PERSONNEL ONLY. Before them was an arched corridor carpeted with mazelike geometric patterns. A few doors down, they stopped at door 7B: CONTROL BOOTH.

On the wooden door, Abbie rapped their secret rhythm.

Clem answered, wearing a black suit with a peak lapel jacket, a set of binoculars hanging around his neck, and a Glock held to an unseen person in the room. "You're late. What happened?"

"Had a minor hiccup along the way," Dylan explained.

"Well, I have a hiccup myself."

In the corner of the twelve-by-twelve room with a sliding glass window overlook, Kristine Mallory sat on the floor, arms wrapped around bent knees. She gave Abbie the once-over. "Well, Little Miss Flabby cleans up well. Almost makes your fling with Dylan conceivable." She turned to him. "Delicious, as usual."

Abbie's hair-trigger temperament activated, and as she stomped to Kristine, Clem ran interference and blocked Abbie's path. "Stay focused," he reminded her.

She took a deep breath, and when she relaxed, Clem moved to the side.

"*What* are you doing here, Kristine?" she demanded, seething.

When she refused to answer, Clem jumped in. "Apparently, she's Ben's personal assistant now, responsible for this evening's audiovisual presentation and lighting."

Abbie gave a derisive laugh at Kristine, a tragic joke. "The only reason he hired you is because you're as morally reprehensible as he is."

"Wait a minute," Uncle Jesse said. "Is this the miserable bitch who didn't give you the message about your mom being in the hospital?"

"In all her glory." When Kristine flipped her the bird, Abbie's eyes drifted to the ring on her finger—an exquisite gold-and-diamond infinity ring, exactly like the one she'd seen on Ben's desk the day she and Skyla had created the presentation. No way Hilda was privy to this entanglement between Kristine and Ben. If she knew, she would've sealed Kristine's fate, as she had Gia's—sentenced her to death on Terra Isle.

"Forget about her," Dylan said. "She's not worth your time."

"Hey, Abbie," Kristine said, smirking. "How's it feel being responsible for getting those retarded twins fired?"

Abbie lunged at her, and as she clenched her fingers around her throat, Kristine choked and sputtered, her fingernails frantically clawing at Abbie's hands.

"You're a complete waste of oxygen!" Abbie snarled and bore down tighter.

"Enough, Abbie!" Uncle Jesse said sharply and pulled her off. "She'll receive her due, trust me."

Focus. Unnerved and breathing hard, Abbie stepped to the glass overlook. Below, the theater hand was at the podium, adjusting the microphone. She took the "travel bag" from Uncle Jesse's shoulder, opened her laptop, and rushed to the audio-video control panel. Disconnecting the Wi-Fi from Ben's laptop that held the Envision Plus presentation, she then connected the Wi-Fi to her laptop, which held the presentation she and Dylan had created in the bunker earlier that day. All Clem needed to do was tap the play button at the designated time.

Right on schedule, the orchestra launched into grim music, similar in tone to the ASPCA commercials showing caged and starved animals.

Showtime, ten minutes.

Borrowing Clem's binoculars, she peered down at the crowd and watched a bevy of black tuxedos and evening gowns pour in from the lobby. *Mingling socialites, pasted-on smiles.*

She stopped cold. It was like they were standing right in front of her. "Hilda and Rex," she said through clenched teeth, with a thirst for revenge.

"Wait, Rex, the guy who helped Ben burn down our house?" Uncle Jesse asked. When Abbie nodded, he took the binoculars. "Where is he?"

"They're standing in the left corner of the orchestra pit," she said and pointed. "Look for the style icon wearing the only lavender tuxedo in the house."

He focused in. "Yep, that's him."

She took the binoculars back and scanned the perimeter of the theater. Four security guards, one at each exit. Soon, they'd find themselves in the bathroom, thanks to the laxative-laced delectables Clem had given them, at Abbie's suggestion, of course. She continued scanning until she focused on Hilda and Rex again. "What the—"

A flash of hollowed eye sockets, as evil as the backdrop of her nightmares. The binoculars crashed to the floor. She staggered backward and collapsed into a chair, the blood freezing in her veins.

As Dylan rushed to her side and took a knee, Uncle Jesse dug through her handbag, removed the Sour Patch Kids, and handed her a few pieces. Rubbing her trembling hand, he said, "Remember, the feeling will go away. Breathe. Count down from ten."

"It's not an anxiety attack," Dylan said. "What did you see, Abbie?"

It was Dr. Xavier. But tonight, he had styled his hair into a dorky bowl cut, not slicked back perfectly like he always wore it. Her mind flashed back to the Christmas Eve party, when she had met Dylan in Hilda's library.

The photo on the fireplace mantle.

Little Hilda was wearing a tutu and posing with Dylan's grandfather/father, Walter Rhodes, his hair combed forward into a bowl cut. Abbie hadn't been wrong in thinking his grandfather looked familiar—she had even asked Dylan if he was an actor or something. The reason she hadn't pieced it together then was because the man in the photo was young.

She peered at Dylan, the son of her mom's killer. "Dylan, Walter Rhodes is Dr. Xavier, our family doctor!"

As Dylan scoffed, not believing this outlandish claim, Uncle Jesse snatched the binoculars from the floor and pointed them at the orchestra pit.

"Holy Christ. That *is* him. That's Dr. Xavier!"

Annoyed, Dylan took the binoculars and looked for himself. "Wait, what the hell's he doing here? I haven't seen him in years! That's Walter Rhodes, my grandfather."

"I'm sorry"—Uncle Jesse looked at Dylan sympathetically, shaking his head—"but it looks like he's been living a double life, son."

"If you think about it, it makes sense," Clem piped in, his gun still pointed at Kristine, who for the first time in her miserable life kept silent.

"How do you figure?" Dylan said defensively, still spying through the binoculars.

"Your grandfather was a professor of medicine at Cornell, right?"

Dylan shrugged. "It's merely a coincidence."

"But medicine and drug testing are closely related, right? I remember you telling me he once headed the department of microbiology and immunology."

Lowering the binoculars, Dylan idly turned to Abbie, the shell shock stealing the air from his lungs. He was a victim of yet another deception, but how could she console him when she couldn't console herself?

"How could I be so goddamned blind?" he said to Abbie. "Your, your mom. What he did to her. And to all those people. My own flesh and blood." Unable to harness his emotions, he burst into the hallway and disappeared.

Chase after him, tell him bloodlines don't matter?

"It's a mind fuck for sure," Uncle Jesse said and guided her out the door.

CHAPTER TWENTY-SIX

Dark violin tones filled the theater, host to a century's worth of performances. Abbie and Uncle Jesse sat in the aisle seats closest to the lobby, which Clem had reserved for them. Dylan had already taken his seat beside Hilda, front row left, closest to the stairs leading to the stage.

"Sounds more like a funeral than a fundraising bash," Abbie observed.

"Might be ours by night's end."

His sarcasm wasn't helping. Something in the private loge directly under the control booth caught her attention—a lavender tuxedo. It was Rex, adjusting a camera on a tripod. She tugged at Uncle Jesse's arm and pointed.

He squinted. "Hope that bastard enjoys his last evening of freedom."

Rex waved to someone in the audience. When they turned to see who was on the receiving end, Abbie spotted Hilda waving back. Meanwhile, Dylan was looking for somebody himself. *The sperm donor/killer.* Abbie wagered he'd be watching the show somewhere away from the public eye.

The violins faded. Hilda stood, and the audience erupted into applause. She waved at them like a beauty queen who had won the diamond-studded crown. Anybody still standing sauntered to their seats. With a drumroll from the orchestra, Hilda daintily lifted her gown's hem and mounted the stage, the camera operator trailing her. At the podium, she lowered the mic.

"Good evening, ladies and gentlemen," she said as the rustle of collective human movement settled. "Thank you for being here tonight. I know many of you were expecting my husband, Ben, to present the show, but I'm afraid duty has called him away on urgent business."

"We love you, Mrs. De Young!" yelled a guy about Abbie's age sitting in front of her. To avoid attention, Abbie slid down in her seat, out of Hilda's sight.

"Oh, thank you, young man. I love you all too," Hilda said and blew him a kiss. She moved in closer to the mic. "Many of you know my husband and I have worked many years for women's and children's causes, that we've gladly given to Humboldt County and beyond, and how our foundation has helped feed and clothe children throughout the region. I implore you to reach out and give of yourself as well. As John F. Kennedy once said, 'Ask not what your country can do for you, ask what you can do for your country.'"

The audience stood and cheered, a sea of faux do-gooders rising in a united front.

Hilda gestured for them to sit. "We have a special show for you this fine evening. Live music, a comedy act, even a magic show. Anybody anxious to be the magician's victim, I mean, assistant"—she winked—"raise your hand later."

As laughter filled the theater, she unzipped her handbag and pulled out her cell phone. "It is my great pleasure to present our son, Dylan De Young, who has so graciously agreed to read his father's speech." She motioned him up to the stage.

"What's she doing?" Abbie hissed. "This isn't the plan."

"No shit," her uncle said.

Hilda motioned to Dylan again. "Come on, babycakes, don't be shy."

Dylan reluctantly stood and mounted the stage, looking like Hilda was summoning him to the slaughterhouse. At the podium, he shuffled his feet from side to side.

"Just look at my handsome son," Hilda remarked as she pinched his cheek, jiggled it, then gave it a pat. "He's blushing like a toddler caught telling a fib."

Does she know something?

The audience "awwed," like it was the most adorable thing they'd ever seen. Hilda handed him the cell phone, and there he stood, frozen. She jabbed his ribs with her elbow. As Dylan read out the first few sentences, the look on the viper's face showed she was enjoying every second.

For the next five minutes, he stumbled through the rest of the speech, and after the final word, Hilda waved a piece of paper at the audience.

"This is a check from my husband and me for five hundred thousand dollars," she boasted. "Who will match it or do better?"

Dozens of people in the audience stood and raised their hands. After much jubilation and millions in pledges, Hilda wrapped her claws around the mic. "Thank you, everyone. Now, please take your seat and enjoy the show."

Kristine, following Clem's orders at gunpoint, dimmed the wall sconces.

Here we go. As Abbie's heart raced with a mix of anticipation and dread, the presentation she and Dylan had created that afternoon lit up the screen.

The opening clip read HILDA AND BEN DE YOUNG: TRUE HUMANITARIANS. In the background, an upbeat instrumental played. What followed were artistically arranged photos Abbie and Dylan had found online of Ben serving meals at the Bayshore Homeless Shelter, and of Hilda bottle-feeding starving, fly-covered babies in Africa. It was entirely a photo op; the real reason for the trip, according to Skyla, had been ivory poaching.

As Hilda's face brimmed with delight, Uncle Jesse whispered, "The night's about to hit full throttle."

"Put on your helmet," she warned.

The presentation cut out, leaving a black screen… A glitch? She spun to the control booth, where shadows bounced off the walls.

A gasp from Uncle Jesse. He was staring at the screen, his pupils black and fully dilated like a wild animal's. When Abbie turned to see what he was looking at, her eyes opened wide with shock.

In fast-forward, Uncle Jesse was dragging her hope chest through their backyard, with Ty's corpse inside. Scrolling across the top of the screen: JESSE SPENCER & THE DECEASED, TY HAWKINS. REST IN PEACE.

"Please make it stop," she muttered, the shock boiling her brain.

Uncle Jesse leaned into her ear. "This is Kristine's doing. Clem's lost control! I'm heading up, you wait here. I mean it!" And he ducked away.

Next clip: Uncle Jesse and Abbie hoisting the chest onto his tailgate, and her losing her grip, causing it to plummet to the ground and burst open. Out rolled Ty's bloody and swollen corpse onto the gravel. A gasp from the audience. Then, a close-up of her face as she cried into the night sky. The screen was a giant mirror, a witness to her ghastly state of mind.

Through the clamor of shocked voices, Hilda was shouting, "It's her! It's *her!*"

Next clip—*Oh God, NO!*—Abbie grooming her private areas, the camera zooming in up close and personal.

Ben must have told Kristine everything!

Dylan had turned away from the screen, his mouth a slack, gaping hole. And the guy sitting in front of Abbie, Hilda's admirer, was recording the invasion with his cell phone. "This is going viral," he joked to his buddy next to him.

After the longest minute of Abbie's lifetime, the video stopped playing, thank God, and in its place was now her and Dylan's presentation. They were back on track, but what had happened up there?

Hilda flinched at the podium when Dylan held the dull side of his knife to her back, the audience oblivious. When he spoke into her ear, she gave him a hateful look and nodded tightly, like she promised not to disobey his command.

Now playing was the headline ILLEGAL HUMAN DRUG TESTING, and footage Dylan had pulled from the Terra Isle security cameras of naked people strapped to gurneys, struggling for their lives as the medical students injected them. At the bottom of the screen, Abbie had embedded photos of the architects and facilitators: Hilda Rhodes De Young, Ben De Young, Jayden Vaughn, Carter Waldron, and everyone involved in the surrounding region. Rex Clark, too. Why not?

Uncle Jesse was missing this glorious moment; was he okay? She peered up at the control booth, where shadows were still bouncing off the walls.

The sliding glass window opened, and…

What the fuck? It was Gia pointing a pistol into the audience!

The deafening sound of a gunshot echoed throughout the theater. Her target: Hilda, blood saturating her white gown as she collapsed behind the podium. The audience had already jumped from their seats screaming, and some were lying facedown on the floor, their arms covering their heads.

Dylan! He stood there paralyzed, too stunned to move. His bulging eyes shifted to the control booth, and Abbie's followed. More chaotic shadows. A brawl between Kristine and…

Is that Skyla? Most definitely!

When Kristine grabbed her by the hair, Skyla shoved her backward so hard that Kristine backflipped out the window and plummeted thirty feet headfirst to the floor. In the chaos, people stampeded over her body as they fled to the exits, the theater a war zone.

Ears buzzing, Abbie shoved her way through the stampede to the stage to find Dylan. Something whacked the back of her knees, and when she fell to the hardwood floor, people's fleeing feet stomped the air from her lungs. If she couldn't stand up, she was going to die. *Fight!*

She gave a hard chomp to somebody's calf, then another, and another. A hole spread big enough for her to stagger to her feet. Elbowing her way through the terrified crowd, she broke free and mounted the stage.

Dylan was now holding his knife to Dr. Xavier's neck, and Dr. Xavier was keeping pressure on Hilda's gunshot wound.

"She's dying!" Dr. Xavier shouted as Hilda stared blankly at Abbie. "Where's the goddamned ambulance?"

Marlon Langley, the event coordinator, yelled from the floor below, "They're on the way, along with the port guard enforcers!" He turned to help an injured woman whom the stampede had trampled to the floor.

"Dylan, it's not worth going to prison," Abbie said.

Dr. Xavier peered at her, his glimmer of recognition switching to indifference when he noticed it was her. He returned his attention to Hilda.

Moaning, she said to her father, "Kill the vermin!" Like a creepy plastic doll, her eyelids flipped closed, then open, then closed, and stayed closed. Her life force visibly drained out of her.

Dr. Xavier checked for a pulse, then bolted backstage, Dylan chasing after him. "Get to the car and get the hell out of here!" he shouted over his shoulder to Abbie.

As she turned wide-eyed toward the theater of empty seats, her thoughts tangled. She was alone with Hilda's corpse, a swamp-like red mercury pooling around them. Taking a step to move away, she slipped and fell on her butt, waves of pain rippling up her spine.

Gurgling sounds popped from Hilda's mouth. She was still alive!

As Abbie slid off the stage, there was a loud three-part whistle, a whistle she knew well. It was the hunting signal she and Uncle Jesse used to alert each other of their presence if they became separated in the woods. And now he was running down the aisle with the man-purse hanging on his shoulder. He stopped short at Kristine's split-open skull and checked for a pulse. A quick shake of his head, and he ran to Abbie as she met him halfway, where they collided into a hug.

"Kristine's dead," he announced.

"And the shooter was Gia, the girl Dylan and I saved."

"I figured that out."

"How did Kristine get control of the show?"

As they made their way quickly to the exit, he explained that when he kicked in the control booth door, Clem was lying on the floor, unconscious. Gia and Skyla had Kristine pinned to the floor, and that's when he unplugged Ben's computer, plugged hers back in, and hit the resume button. Kristine had fought her way to her feet, and when she attacked Skyla, Skyla shoved her backward out the window.

"Is Clem okay?" Abbie asked.

"Yeah, he woke up. He'll have one hell of a headache, I'd imagine."

"Where'd Gia and Skyla go?"

"No idea. And Dylan?"

"Took off after Dr. Xavier, telling me to take his car." She was confident Dylan would be okay, at least physically. But there was no time to waste; the fire exit doors boomed open, and in swarmed the enforcers, assault rifles drawn. Trailing them, the paramedics entered pushing a stretcher.

"Stay calm," Uncle Jesse said under his breath. "Innocent people don't run." Then, to a group of enforcers, he hollered country-western style, "The shooter's wearing a lavender tuxedo, silver hair, mid to late fifties." He pointed to the control booth. "He fired out that window."

Raising her brows, Abbie nearly choked.

The enforcers stormed away, except for one—a man large enough to play Hercules. In a deep voice, he barked into his two-way radio, "Perp has silver hair and is wearing a lavender tuxedo, repeat, a lavender tuxedo."

The radio crackled. "Ten-four. On it."

"Stick around," the enforcer said to Uncle Jesse. "We'll need your witness statement."

"Yes, sir. Won't go anywhere."

The enforcer disappeared into the lobby.

"They *will* realize Rex wasn't the shooter," Abbie said. "You know that, right? He won't have the gun."

He gave a wicked chuckle and pulled her toward the exit. "He was right in front of me when we pushed through the crowd. I dropped Gia's gun into his camera bag. Skyla said it's Ben's gun."

Abbie threw her head back and howled with laughter. "You little devil! But what about fingerprints?"

"Wiped 'em clean, darlin'. Oh, and I grabbed Ben's computer, too."

"Genius. But please tell me you didn't see the mortifying video of me in—"

He shivered. "Only briefly."

As they entered the service hall, cold air rushed their faces. The double steel doors leading outside were only thirty feet away, and someone had left them open, allowing the incoming wind to swirl leaves along the floor like a mini tornado.

Nearly home free. Sure, they had exposed the villains, but for them, nothing existed outside of that moment. The harsh reality was that she and Uncle Jesse were homeless and looking at a life on the run. And the only certainty was that the enforcers were now swarming Port Allegiance and both Ports of Entry.

She held his arm tightly. "Have I ever told you how much I love and appreciate you?"

"You've said it plenty. I love and appreciate you, too. You'll always be my—"

"Favoritest niece. I know, I know."

As they passed the massive clanking pipes, they came upon a five-tiered cart tipped on its side. Beside it were scattered platters of jumbo prawns and lobster tails that Piercy's Catering had abandoned for the safety of their truck, which was no longer backed up to the door.

Bending down, Abbie grabbed a fistful of prawns and stuffed them in her mouth. She considered swooping the seafood cache back onto the platters and bringing it to the Escalade. It was that last meal feeling, reminiscent of digging through the dumpster behind Clyde's Market, hungry and wondering if luck would put food on the table the next day.

Footsteps sounded behind them. They gave each other a side-glance.

Thump-thump-thump. Moving in more urgently.

Abbie swallowed the prawns before she had chewed them properly. Nonchalantly, she bent down and retrieved her pistol. "Make a run for it?" she whispered.

Uncle Jesse shook his head ever so slightly. "No. Stay calm."

Fifteen feet to freedom.

When they picked up the pace, the footsteps behind followed suit.

Ten feet.

"Daisy and Jeb West. Please stop. May I have a word with you?"

It was Marlon Langley, the event coordinator, in his tone a hint of accusation.

Uncle Jesse turned to him. Then Abbie, rotating the pistol behind her back, found herself staring at a gun. It was only a stun gun, but still.

"What's behind your back, Daisy?" Marlon asked and pointed his weapon at Uncle Jesse's heart. "Cardiac arrest, a most painful death. Whatever you're hiding, toss it to the ground."

Abbie readily complied.

With his other hand, Marlon showed them his cell phone. "Recognize this girl?"

It was the photo from Abbie's Bronze Access Card, the one where she looked like Ty's vomited leftovers.

Marlon said to her, "Thought I recognized you. You're the most wanted person in Port Allegiance. That half-million-dollar reward will keep me quite comfortable in my retirement. I must say, you clean up well, Abilene Spencer."

A stone's throw away behind Marlon, Clem appeared from the fire escape stairwell, a finger to his mouth.

Don't look, don't look, don't look.

With the stealth of an assassin, he swiftly maneuvered Marlon into a headlock, his arm squeezing tighter and tighter like a vise grip. As Marlon twitched and writhed, his face turning red, the stun gun fired and ricocheted off a pipe. Clem gritted his teeth and continued squeezing relentlessly. As Marlon collapsed, unconscious, Clem slowly eased him to the floor.

"Let's get the hell out of here!" Abbie exclaimed, and they darted outside to find two enforcers, one power-slamming Rex into the concrete and slapping cuffs on him, and the other digging through the camera bag and holding up the pistol like a trophy.

CHAPTER TWENTY-SEVEN

W HILE C LEM WAS UPSTAIRS SPEAKING WITH Ms. B, Abbie
set the man-purse on the bunker table. As she kicked off her
heels, her cell phone vibrated.

"Dylan?" Uncle Jesse asked, loosening his tie.

"No. A group text from Skyla."

*Hello, everybody, as you probably figured out by now, Gia
and I caught a later bus to San Diego. First, Clem and
Ms. B, we know our actions come as a huge disappointment to you both, and for that, we are deeply sorry. Your
guidance and love over the years will never be forgotten.
Thank you for scheduling Gia's doctor's appointment, and
for the financial help, but after what we've done, it would
be wrong to take your money. We will send it back. With
what we have in savings, after any medical treatment,
we're going to move east to heal the profound pain this
nightmare has caused. Abbie, without your balls and per-
sistence, Gia would undoubtedly be dead, along with so
many others. "Thank you" will never be enough to express*

our gratitude. I hope someday our paths cross again. When they do, you'll have that journalism degree and be traveling the world writing articles for your dream magazine. We'll be following you. Love always, Skyla and Gia xoxo

As Abbie handed the phone to her uncle, a profound sense of loss filled her. The opportunity to build a closer friendship with Skyla and Gia had ended. Could she and Dylan have undying love like theirs, when it had only been eight days since they'd reunited? Would looking into his eyes feel like looking into the eyes of Mom's killer? In the control booth, he'd needed her to pacify him, to tell him bloodlines didn't matter. Did they? The cognitive dissonance messed with her head.

"Wow," Uncle Jesse said faintly, setting the phone on the table. "I'm concerned for them."

"Me, too. For Gia's sake, I sure hope Hilda didn't survive. Gia needs a little peace."

"In time, she'll find it, darlin'. Have a little faith." He kissed her forehead, gathered his street clothes, and shut himself in the bathroom.

Faith. An odd choice of words, coming from him. The lack of it in herself had come from the belief she was powerless to spur change. But as a key player in busting open a drug-testing syndicate among the highest echelons of society, she had proven anything was possible, even for a little fish like her. Pleased with herself, she opened her laptop. In KnightScape, she typed, *port allegiance news.*

The top headline: GIRL ON VOYEUR CAM IS SAME GIRL AS ON GRISLY DRONE FOOTAGE.

About to lose the contents of her stomach, she read the two-minute "article," if you could call it that. In the comments section, she filtered by "best." The top result wasn't a comment but a link. Dare she click on it? Her finger twitched, making the decision for her.

Someone, Kristine, most likely, had uploaded Ben's voyeur videos to an adult website. The embedded counter widget was flipping past ten million likes, the number growing by the second. She watched herself walking nude out of the bathroom and climbing into bed, her favorite country song playing in the background, a moment she remembered well. She had secured the best job of her life. Cha-ching, cha-ching, her college savings account was about to flourish.

Good God. The humiliation of what came next.

"What's wrong?" Uncle Jesse asked, coming up behind her silently.

She slammed the laptop closed. "Kristine Mallory is what's wrong. That coal-eyed bitch got the final laugh." Ordering him not to open her computer, she snatched her clothes off the floor and locked herself in the bathroom.

At the sink, she rested her hands on the cool porcelain and dropped her head.

Have faith.

A torrent of self-abasing thoughts. "Faith" was a bullshit word, like she had always believed. Hands shaking, she adjusted the hot and cold handles until the water temperature suited her. She unloaded a dozen or more pumps of soap onto a wet hand towel and, with unfettered abandon, scrubbed her face raw. After rinsing and patting it dry, she wondered how she'd navigate the world moving forward. If a life existed outside the bunker, what would it look like? Something needed to change, something big. The cost of freedom wasn't an expense she'd spare anytime soon.

Hair clippers lay on the floor, already plugged in, waiting.

In Mom's letter, on her death bed, her last words: *I love you, my precious daughter. Be bold. Now go get 'em.*

It was only hair, and Ty was the only person who'd insisted she keep it long. When she plucked out the brooch and bobby pins, her hair draped over her shoulders. Shave it bald, or leave *some?* It was December, several more months of cold weather.

Screw it. She clicked the half-inch attachment onto the clippers. With a flick of the switch and the pounding of her heart, she ran the buzzing device through her hair and the remnants of her former life cascaded to the floor.

A new attitude, a new beginning. Thank you, hot shower! Abbie dressed in her own clothes, then using a hand towel, she buffed the steam from the mirror and peered at herself. No need for a comb anymore. A quick spike to what was left of her hair, and she looked like a badass warrior, a blank slate, waiting for her to chronicle life's events in her journal. Whether the events played out good or bad, to a major degree, would be down to her decisions from here on out.

She checked her cell, no text from Dylan yet. Where was he? Biting her bottom lip, she debated whether to reach out. No, she wouldn't do it. He needed his space. His life was as much in shambles as hers.

Clem's voice outside the door. "It's dark and musty down here," he complained to Uncle Jesse. "Patsy and I insist you and Abbie stay upstairs until you develop a game plan."

The bunker *was* feeling pretty oppressive by now.

"Thank you," Uncle Jesse said. "That's very kind. Abbie might want to stay, but I need to tend to my brother. I'm heading out soon."

Abbie pushed through the door. "I'll come with you," she said to her uncle, and his jaw hit the floor.

Grinning, she ran a hand over her head. "Whadda ya think?"

"J'aime bien ta nouvelle coiffure," Clem said in a way she interpreted as approval.

Uncle Jesse wore a mischievous grin. "Didn't realize you inherited my fivehead."

She smacked his arm playfully. "You turd."

He hugged her and, with one hand, cradled the back of her head. "Seriously, you've never looked more beautiful."

She melted at the warmth of him. "Thanks. I feel like any-thing's possible now."

"Be patient for them blue skies, darlin'. We're gonna take this slowly."

Clem, his eyes wet, looked on and gave Abbie a reassuring wink. Then he gave them an update on Hilda. She was still alive, unfortunately, but in a coma, the bullet having severed her spinal cord. A nurse had told Ms. B she'd likely never walk again. But in Abbie's opinion, life confined to a wheel-chair wasn't punishment enough.

On KnightScape, Abbie found the *Sacramento Times*, the most respected news source around. The headline took her breath away. She read it aloud: "'Pharmaceutical Testing Nightmare Exposed. World-Renowned Former Ballerina Shot. Shooter in Custody.'"

"Read the article," Uncle Jesse said.

"There isn't one," she said. "It's a video."

"Don't worry," Clem assured her. "They won't televise anything inappropriate."

"If you're sure…" When she tapped the play button, her apprehension turned to relief. It was the presentation she and Dylan had created. Scrolling across the bottom of the screen were the blurred-out faces of the victims. Dylan's voice narrated the scheme for the world to witness. Images of naked people strapped to gurneys, nurses injecting them, timing their responses to the experimental drugs surging through their veins, the utter disregard for human life, it was all there.

The widget counter showed only two hundred fifty thousand likes, way less than for the voyeur video of her. What did that say about humanity? It said they were screwed.

After the video finished, a group of reporters sitting in a semicircle discussed the front corporation, Genome Sphere. One bulldog of a reporter peered directly into the camera and declared to the audience, "This could very well be the biggest failure of government we've ever seen. You, my friends, have the power to change the trajectory of your future." He carried on for several more minutes, his words riveting.

Abbie shut the laptop, and they sat there stunned.

"Damn," Uncle Jesse said, tears flowing down his cheeks. He squeezed Abbie's hand. "Shit like this doesn't happen in real life."

"Only in movies," Clem agreed.

Abbie's phone rang, Dylan lighting up the screen. Her nervous stomach came on quick. Grabbing the phone, she hurried into the bathroom and closed the door. "Where are you?"

"You're safe?" His voice sounded low and strained.

"Yes. We're in the bunker. Clem's here, too."

A sigh flowed through the airwaves. "I'm at the Arcata airport."

"You going somewhere?"

"No. I stole a car from the valet and chased my grandfather, or whoever the hell he is." He choked up. "I…I needed an explanation, Abbie, ya know? But ultimately, I wanted to, I *needed* to, I dunno, take him down, maybe even kill him. But I missed him by a hair. His pilot was already waiting on the tarmac to whisk him away. The fucker."

"I can't imagine what you're going through."

"What matters is our plan worked. But who shot my mother? I heard on the radio she's in the ICU, and the enforcers have somebody in custody."

Abbie explained Gia had been the shooter, that she and Skyla had returned, that Uncle Jesse had slipped the gun into Rex's camera bag and pointed to him as the shooter. Dylan thought the move was brilliant, and he wasn't surprised by Gia's determination. He didn't fault her. They spoke for a few minutes, small talk mostly, as if they were avoiding discussing what truly mattered, which was them. If there was a "them."

"When are you coming home?" she asked.

Silence.

"Dylan?"

"I'm not, Abbie. I need time to sort this out."

"How much time are we talking?"

"A week, a month, I don't know. Just know I love you. I have since Lake Tahoe all those years ago."

The call ended.

Near the stroke of midnight, Abbie drove the Sprinter van, Uncle Jesse riding shotgun, to their hunting site to reunite with Dad. As she fought the wind, the rain eased, leaving way for a dense fog to creep in and entomb Eureka. And the driving conditions for the next fifteen miles to Blue Lake proved no better.

"Awful quiet, darlin'," Uncle Jesse noted, peering out the window. "What's on your mind?"

She sighed, her heart heavy. *Don't judge the broken,* he'd told her. "Dad. I was thinking back to Christmas night, when I rejected his hug. He was in so much pain over Mom's passing. He was trying to connect with me, but I didn't know if his affection was a manipulation, and if I forgave him, and then later he reverted to his old ways, it would send me into a tailspin."

"Aw, kiddo, I understand. Trust is earned; it's not a right. And if it helps, he hasn't drunk a drop since then."

Two days of sobriety was hardly a noteworthy feat, but then again, the fact he hadn't drunk himself to death showed his strength in the face of tragedy—multiple tragedies, in fact. It was time to dismantle her deep-seated, and misplaced, anger. Mom would have wanted that. She'd want the two of them to be close again, like they were before Sammie died.

"Dad not drinking is a good start," she said and turned right on Mill Creek Road. After a few minutes, she turned onto the obscure one-lane goat path that meandered up the hill to the clearing where their tent stood. As they exited the van, Uncle Jesse blew his three-syllable whistle to alert Brodie they were approaching. Dad whistled back.

They entered the musty ten-by-twelve canvas tent, furnished with three aluminum-frame cots with sleeping bags and a folding table and chairs, plus a week's worth of bottled water and canned food. Dad was lying down, his bloated bare ankle elevated and twenty shades of purple. On the floor next to him were bottled water, a piss jug, and his handgun. It was going to take a while to acclimate; Abbie's brain was still stuck in an alternate universe.

"You made it back safe," Dad said, sounding deeply relieved. "Well? How'd it go? And jeez, you both look so different!"

"Mission accomplished." Uncle Jesse set the man-purse on the table, then set two chairs next to his brother, his gaze locked on Abbie.

"Your hair. Damn, it looks great!"

She thanked him and tossed her jacket onto her cot. It felt good to retire her usual sarcasm. When she sat, he took her hand, his eyes reflecting years of regret. He appeared more sober than he had in years. His skin even looked less sallow. Their six-year war had finally ended.

"You pulled it off, huh?" he said with a sly grin.

"It was a team effort."

"I'm dying to hear about it, but I need to tell you first how disgusted I am with the monster I'd become. I was horrible to you and your mom. No more drinking. No more lying. Abbie, I've made so many—"

"Stop," she said firmly, holding up her other hand. "All we can do now is move forward and be kind, listen to each other more, right?"

He pulled her hand closer and kissed the top of it. "Deal. Now spill it. Tell me everything that happened."

It was the same sordid story she'd told Uncle Jesse after he'd accompanied her through the secret tunnel. But Dad needed to hear it from her.

She began with her relationship with Dylan and how he'd introduced her to the bunker. It made Dad happy she'd met a nice guy, and made her happier when he admitted Ty had been a douchebag. Then on to the QDAC game, where her employer, Ben De Young, had gifted her the drone footage of her and Uncle Jesse dumping Ty's body off the bluff as a form of blackmail to keep her from going public with his assault on her. (The embarrassing footage of her private moments she kept to herself; he'd likely find out soon enough.)

After answering an onslaught of questions, she went on to tell him that Ben and his butler, Rex, had burned down their house because she had failed to comply with Ben's demand to meet him in the sauna, and that Rex had caged her and Dylan in his car, and that Tony Wilkins had saved them as Rex escaped on foot.

Finally, and most importantly, she told him the unfathomable truth about Dr. Xavier using Mom as a guinea pig. "If she'd taken the antidote he'd left for her, she would've had a fifty percent chance of survival."

He shot her a questioning look. "Fifty percent of the victims survived?"

She nodded, feeling a pang of anger at her mom for not taking the pill. "Tell me about that terrible day. Start at the beginning."

"Well, she woke up feeling awful, nothing unusual, right?" he said, his voice low and apologetic. "I know, it sounds terrible, but that's how exhausted I felt. I chalked it up to her depression, and honestly, I was sick of her complaining, and I told her so. God, I'm a prick." He held back tears.

"You're doin' great, Brodie," Uncle Jesse said encouragingly. "Go on."

Her father took a deep breath. "Dr. Xavier rang the doorbell around, I dunno…" He looked to Uncle Jesse.

"Around ten, I think."

"That's right, ten. That's about when I crammed the turkey into the oven. I answered the door, and there he was, standing there with a big ol' jolly smile on his face, like he does, you know? He handed me a spiral ham and that prescription bottle. Said the pill would make her feel better, his Christmas gift to her."

"Sick SOB," Uncle Jesse said, looking repulsed.

"Can't get any more sadistic," Abbie added.

Dad continued, "Then he wished us a happy holiday and left. I went straight to our bedroom and read the instructions on the side of the bottle to her, told her Dr. Xavier said it would make her feel better. She peeked into the bottle and complained the pill was coated with a toxic artificial color. I got pissed, and when I ribbed her about being a wacky granola, she ordered me out of the bedroom and told me not to come back. Until I did. The rest is history."

"See, bro," Uncle Jesse said, "there was nothin' you coulda done."

Shame flushed Dad's face, and he sunk his head into his pillow, his arms crossed over his chest. "I know that now, but I feel like somehow I contributed to her death. Physically, I didn't kill her, sure, but emotionally, well, I nailed her coffin closed."

Abbie thought back to Mom's letter. "She loved you, Dad. She admitted to treating you terribly as well. She took responsibility for her share of our family's unraveling, and for Sammie's death." It was the first time she'd uttered Sammie's name to him since that fateful day at the pond.

He looked stunned, like her bringing him up was blasphemous, as if two hot wires had crossed and shorted out his brain.

"We can't avoid the conversation forever," she said and touched his arm.

His lip quivered; he was building up the courage to speak. "B-but, I'm the one who fell asleep. I should've been watching him."

"It was a perfect storm," she said. "It happened. It's in the past. Like I said, all we can do is move forward from here."

He closed his eyes to rest. "So much lost." Then he bolted upright and flinched when his foot fell off the pillow. From under his cot, he pulled out Mom's blue carry case and handed it to her. "I nearly forgot I grabbed this for you on the way out!"

A huge grin stretched across her face. Dad had considered someone other than himself. *Full redemption.* "I can't believe it! Thank you so much, Dad."

"It was the least I could do, after failing you as a father."

"We're beyond that, remember?"

"Abbie, honey, I don't deserve you."

"I *am* pretty badass, huh?" She shot him a playful grin.

"Just like your mom," Uncle Jesse said. "What are you waiting for? Open the damn thing."

She chuckled, then dug through the side zipper of her purse and found the key. It had been years since she and Mom had sorted through the treasures inside. Heart racing, she unlocked it.

On top of the pile were a few family keepsakes, but what Abbie wanted to see was Grandma Spencer's wedding ring. Digging a little deeper, she found the Oriental red silk pouch adorned with yellow cording. She unzipped it and emptied the contents into her hand. There it was; the ring looked exactly as she remembered, but way smaller. She held it up, the diamond catching the overhead light. When she was younger, seven or eight, she used to wear it and pretend she was Princess Fiona marrying Shrek.

"I think you should start wearing it," Dad said.

She wasn't sure.

Uncle Jesse added, "Your hands are small like hers. Go ahead, darlin', put it on."

Gnawing at her bottom lip, she slipped it over her right ring finger, then extended her arm and admired it.

"There you go," Dad said. "Your mom and grandma are smiling down at you."

"It looks pretty, doesn't it?" She couldn't take her eyes off it.

"Very," Uncle Jesse said.

From the case, she pulled out a few tiny ceramic cow keepsakes and set them on Dad's cot. At the bottom were two unmarked envelopes. She opened one, pulled out several folded papers, and read.

"What the—"

"What is it?" Dad asked.

She sat there stunned and read the first paragraph a few more times.

"Abbie?" Uncle Jesse prodded. When she didn't answer, he took the papers and read for himself. "Holy shit," he said to Dad. "Ana left her a life insurance policy! There's enough money here to send her to any school she wants!"

Blown away, Abbie ripped into the other envelope and read. "A policy for Dad, too!" She handed it to him.

Studying at John Cabot University in Rome was going to come to fruition after all! She imagined herself sitting in the Villa Borghese Gardens overlooking the temple dedicated to the god of healing. In a giddy daze, she tucked the papers back into the envelope.

"I don't deserve this," Dad said, clutching the papers in his hand. He turned to Uncle Jesse. "This money should be going to you. You were the one taking care of Abbie and Ana ever since we moved here."

"Just stop," Uncle Jesse said. "You were her husband, and she loved you. Buy yourself a house, get a decent rig, create a new life."

Dad dropped his head back. "But how? Where do we go from here? We're homeless."

"The Redwood Manor bunker?" Uncle Jesse suggested and shrugged. "We were offered room and board until we figured it out."

There's no way I'll enter that city again, Abbie thought as Uncle Jesse and Dad discussed various ideas. She had enough money in savings, if Hilda hadn't frozen her account, to skip town, go to another state, like Skyla and Gia had planned on doing. The only state that sounded acceptable was Idaho, North Idaho. Not Sandpoint, though, because the locals knew them all too well, Dad specifically. His brawling at The Tam, the oldest bar in town, had become legendary.

"I say we move to Coeur d'Alene," she interrupted.

"I'd love to," Dad said, "but our names are linked to Ty's death."

"Tell him, darlin'." Uncle Jesse pulled out his wallet.

"Dylan hacked into the Port Allegiance driver's license bureau through Hilda's computer and made us new identity cards the fifty states will recognize as legit."

Uncle Jesse handed his own ID card to his brother. "Meet Jameson Ross Kelley."

"Well, look at you. Cool-ass name to boot."

Digging around in her purse, she found Dad's card, shot Uncle Jesse a mischievous look, then gave it to her dad. As he peered at it, she held a hand over her mouth to keep from prematurely laughing.

"Linus Elmore Finch? What the fuck?"

Laughter filled the tent. The look on Dad's face was one of utter betrayal.

Abbie swore the names had come from an autogenerator, but Dad wasn't buying it. She kicked back and watched her men engage in jovial banter, like when life had sailed along peacefully, back when they'd lived in Sandpoint, their idyllic small town on the shore of Lake Pend Oreille.

CHAPTER TWENTY-EIGHT

February 14

Dear Mom,
Here I sit in my room at the Timber Crest Lodge in Lake Tahoe. I'm overlooking the ski slopes crowded with people as tiny as ants, all happily traversing the mountain, their behavior somehow composed like an orchestra.

My mug of Constant Comment tea tastes okay, but not as good as your custom blend. As you can see, I'm ready to write again—to you. My journal was a good ear, but it was yours I should've spoken into. I'm desperately sad we won't have more time together. Maybe we'll meet on the other side, if there is one. I hope so.

I'm a miserable excuse of a daughter for missing Christmas with you. In the end, you suffered alone, no one to take care of you. It's heartbreaking. No words can make it right. And thank you for the life insurance policies you left for Dad and me. They're going to change our lives. We've picked a few charities that represent causes close to your heart and have donated a portion of the money towards them. One is a fund for underprivileged children, who may not have access to basic necessities like food, clothing, or shelter. Another is a program focused on helping adults with disabilities find meaningful employment—something you've always advocated for.

Dad and Uncle Jesse have settled into a rental house near Coeur d'Alene, only an hour from our former house in Sandpoint. Liza's in hog heaven enjoying the deluxe pen they built for her. It's way nicer than the one in Eureka. They wanted me to stay, to move in with them, but I've decided to take an extended road trip in my new/old car. Where to, you ask? Anyplace the road takes me. Thanks to you, my possibilities are endless.

I think about Grandma a lot. It's taken me awhile to understand the wisdom behind her words: "Home is wherever you plant yourself." I realize now that it's not just some empty phrase, as I had thought before. For the first time in my life, I feel like I belong wherever I am.

I see Dylan has left his room and is walking toward the Blue Ridge Trail. Haven't spoken to him since that night in the bunker. I hope it's not a mistake showing up unannounced at his sacred meditation spot. I'll give him a half-hour head start. Wish me luck.

With love for you, Mom,
Erin Ensley Reid

AS THE EARLY-AFTERNOON AIR rushes over my face, I hike up the mountain, my feet following Dylan's snow-packed footsteps. The trail looks far different from what I remember.

Over the years, the ponderosa pine saplings lining the trail have grown to at least ten feet tall. I breathe in the aroma of burning oak, reminding me of Sandpoint and the bonfires my family and I huddled around when it was cold. I stop for a moment and take it all in. *The stillness of silence…*

I'm still unclear about my motives for seeing Dylan. We parted under extreme circumstances, things between us left unresolved. After saying he loved me, he hung up without waiting for my response. What if he hadn't hung up? How would I have responded? Would saying "I love you" back, which was the truth, renege on my promise never to let a guy tether me again?

My head fills with a million other clashing thoughts: Carter evading capture, and the fear of him stalking me. As for Hilda, last month the hospital transferred her to a high-security nursing facility on Alcatraz, an island in the San Francisco Bay, where she'll receive twenty-four-seven care for the rest of her miserable life.

Sometime later, breathless, I approach the summit and pause. Up ahead, Dylan sits sprawled out on a folding lounge chair. In the primitive stone firepit, embers pop and crackle, and the flames gently sway in the breeze.

Next to him, the moai, the giant rock from my memory. The flashback plays like it was yesterday: Dylan's dog had just died in a bear trap close to where I'm standing, and I consoled him as we sat at the base of the majestic rock. He was grieving the death of his beloved pet, and I was grieving the loss of Dad, Sammie, and the home I'd never regain.

As I move closer to Dylan, the crunching snow under my boots alerts him to my presence. He jumps to his feet, and his unease melts when our gazes collide. We had left so much unsaid.

His face lights up, and he inspects my short, now ash-blonde hair. "You remembered I came here. Happy Valentine's Day, Abbie."

"How could I forget?" As I saunter closer, Lake Tahoe, partially frozen over, unfolds before me, taking my breath away.

"After Clem told me you and your family moved to Idaho, I thought I'd never see you again. I've wanted to call you, but every time I pick up the phone, I lose my nerve."

"I could've called, too, but I wasn't sure if you were ready to talk. It's only been six weeks. And when you hung up on me—"

"Yeah, that. I'm a jerk for not being there for you in the end, for not helping you sort out the mess. I made it about me, about my drama."

"Stop. I never resented you for staying away. Learning the truth about your—"

"Call him Walter."

Fair enough. "It must've been beyond shocking and painful. I know you loved him. When you were a child, he was your everything. Anyone would've hidden under a rock after that night."

He smiles faintly, like he doesn't deserve my understanding. "You're too generous. Did you read about that person spotting him on their plane to Venezuela?"

I nod, imagining him lounging on a private beach, a fancy cocktail in hand. "He's smart. He knew the country was known for refusing extradition requests, even though they have a treaty with the US."

"Exactly," Dylan says, and guides me to his chair, where I sit. Then he rolls over a chunk of wood and sits beside me. "The thought of him hurting another person makes me ill. How can you look at me after what he did to your mother?"

"Listen to me, Dylan," I say firmly. "Biology, DNA, whatever you wanna call it, doesn't dictate who we're destined to be. We're not responsible for the evil acts of others."

His eyes dart back and forth between mine as if searching for his own clarity. He shakes his head, his eyelids relaxing a bit. "I appreciate it, thank you. I loved your mom. How are you coping?"

A sigh escapes my lips. "I'm in a good place. Before we left for Idaho, Clem picked up her ashes at the mortuary. We scattered them in the pond behind our old house in Sandpoint. A cathartic moment."

"Your little brother, Sammie, drowned there," he says with a pained look on his face.

I nod. "Without the sadness, the beauty of life would unfold in grayscale, nothing appreciated, nothing to be grateful for."

"Well said, Abbie."

"Thanks." I had thought long and hard about this radically different philosophy on life. "And get this: while my dad and uncle checked out our collapsed barn, I hiked to an old poplar tree on the hillside above the pond to get a better view of the property. I found a carving in the bark that read, 'Happy 9th birthday, son. Forgive me. Love, Dad.' He'd been there three months earlier. Mom and I thought he'd gone on a weeklong bender and died somewhere. I was so busy holding on to my anger, I couldn't see his pain."

"Are you two okay now?"

As I gaze down at the lake, a rush of peace tingles through me. "Very okay. He's in AA now, taking responsibility for his life. I'm proud of him, and he's proud of me."

"Glad to hear it." He tosses a few pieces of wood into the pit, the sparks catching the breeze and dissipating quickly. "Redwood Manor's like a ghost town anymore. Some big changes coming, though."

"Yeah? What sort of changes?"

His demeanor shifts, like a promising future has replaced the darkness of the past. "Next month, the state is demolishing the Ports of Entry. Anyone who wants to visit the city can. And with Clem's and Ms. B's help, we're turning the manor, which is mine now, into a museum, with them as curators. After operating expenses, the proceeds will go to the victims of Terra Isle. And the money I stole from my parents will help rebuild Eureka."

Tears of joy fill my eyes. He's an awesome human being, and I tell him so. I listen to his vision of Eureka's and Port Allegiance's future, and everything he's describing sounds incredible. I'm still in shock he owns the manor now. Hilda certainly didn't have a say in this. I imagine her plotting Dylan's demise once she awakens from the coma.

"Guess who's back at Redwood Manor as live-in employees?" he asks, giving me a warm grin.

Mystified, I shrug.

"Here, I'll show you a photo." He whips out his phone from his jacket pocket, swipes it until he finds the one he wants, then shows it to me.

"Devon and David, the twins!" Joy and pride radiate from their faces as they sit atop Hilda's two prized thoroughbred racing horses.

"Ms. B and Clem found them at the shelter and brought them home. They're taking riding lessons, something they've always dreamed of doing." Dylan scrolls through a few more photos.

My heart sings. "This is the fairy tale ending for them that Kristine viciously tried to take away. Not a day has passed where I haven't thought about them."

"Well, they're thriving," he says and drops the phone back in his pocket. "And so is the house without my parents' and Rex's dark energy staining the walls."

"Rex. What happened to him? Why isn't he in the news anymore?"

He gives a wicked grin. "Because the prosecutors are preserving evidence until his trial for the murder of Ben."

I jolt back. "Ben? I don't understand."

He explains that the Feds had found his body in Rex's storage unit where Clem had placed it after the fundraising gala—and Dylan called in the anonymous tip later. I laugh at this, although I shouldn't have. Later, while Dylan was auditing HR Enterprises' books, he discovered Rex had actually embezzled nearly half a million dollars. Dylan sent the evidence to the Feds along with a note saying Hilda and Ben had discovered Rex's crime—the only way for Rex to avoid prison was to kill them first.

"This entire ordeal is insane," I say, and we continue discussing it until we're spent.

"On a happier note," he says, "I talked to Skyla and Gia on the phone yesterday. They were getting ready to leave San Diego."

"So I heard. They called me after they hung up with you. What a relief that doctors finally gave Gia a clean bill of health."

"Man, that poor girl," he says. "I'm glad they took Clem up on his offer to stay at his time-share on Bainbridge Island. It'll be a good respite for them until they come up with a plan."

"I was so happy when I heard. They said you're having dinner with them in San Francisco in a few days. Why there?"

He turns cold at my question and walks ten feet to the ledge where the mountain drops off. "I didn't tell them the real reason why I suggested we meet there."

"Real reason?"

He looks back to me, tears building up, but he's fighting hard to stop them. "Last week, Hilda awoke from her coma. She called me from Alcatraz, said she needed to see me."

"What for?" bursts out of my mouth and startles him.

"I have no idea. Initially, I said absolutely not, then I got to thinking. Maybe I should see her one last time. All my pent up anger, Abbie. If I-I don't get it out, it'll consume me. So, there you have it—the day after tomorrow I'm catching the ferry to Alcatraz. Unfinished business, one might say."

I walk to him, lay my hand on his shoulder, and want to tell him he's insane. I want to tell him his mother will manipulate him, and then eat him alive. "Yes, of course, you need to see her. I'm sick you're living through this."

He's peering at me like he's building the courage to ask a sensitive question. Or maybe he wants to kiss me? My ears start fluttering right before he—

"Is there a 'we,' Abbie?"

Shit. Either I misread his body language, or he chickened out. I'm pretty sure it was the latter. My embarrassment is flushing my face, and I feel a bit foolish. Back to his question. I tell him straight up that I don't know if there's a 'we'. I tell him about Mom's life insurance policy, and how it allows me to attend college. To save money, I'll fulfill my prerequisites at a community college somewhere, then maybe on to John Cabot University in Italy.

"So, in September, you'll start classes?"

"Yep. That's the plan."

"That leaves over six months."

"For what?"

He leads me back to my seat and sits beside me. "For us to know each other better. Please hear me out before responding."

I nod, not sure where he's heading with this.

"Come with me to San Francisco tomorrow," he says sincerely, his eyes pleading. "You can stay at the hotel while I confront Hilda. Then you, me, Skyla, and Gia can have dinner together. Then after, you and I will ditch California and explore places you've always dreamed of. I'll drive so you can enjoy the scenery. As for your car, we'll store it somewhere."

His proposal is intoxicating, and I'd love to see Skyla and Gia, but, but, but.

"What do you say? It'll be fun," he reassures me.

Truth be told, the Smithsonian in DC crosses my mind, and there's nobody else I'd rather see it with. But what about my need to be independent? An epiphany hits hard and is so clear and simple in its meaning. Ty Hawkins hadn't tethered me down. I was the one who pounded the stake into the ground and tethered myself to it.

No more hesitancy in my feelings for Dylan. I accept his offer, the future unknown. San Francisco, here we come!

A LETTER FROM THE AUTHOR

Dear readers,

I hope you enjoyed reading *Tetherless,* my debut novel. I would be eternally grateful if you could write a review. They assist other readers pick books, and they help writers polish their craft. I look forward to reading your comments!

Regards,

C.K. O'Donnell

www.ingramcontent.com/pod-product-compliance
Lightning Source LLC
Chambersburg PA
CBHW061631190726
48289CB00006B/1556